Charlle

The making of a real True Love story

Charlle

The making of a real True Love story

Charleston Malkemus

www.charlle.com

CHARLLE: THE MAKING OF A REAL TRUE LOVE STORY.

Copyright © 2010 by Charleston Malkemus

ISBN 978-0-9829096-0-7

For additional copies or information of this publication, please contact:

Charlle Marketing & Media
1900 N Bayshore Dr. #1007
Miami FL 33132

Phone: (305) 747-1523
Email: info@charlle.com
Website: www.charlle.com

This publication is available online in digital format at www.charlle.com.

Talle Gilmore
I Love you…

Contents

Preface

The stories of our lives are bound together. We share everything. We feel each other's joy and sorrow. We feel the suffering and sacrifice that burdens, the happiness and joy embraced, the fear of worries and doubt. We are one species always connected, always alive.

Our stories are enormously powerful. They quake each person's soul, awaken our minds and move our hearts. They are emotional and energetic, filling our eyes with light. We pour out our shared feelings. Our heart squeezes in pain and joy to share the emotion.

A story is a human phenomenon. I don't even understand how it works. The shear power of relating a tale, an experience, and a life can cause people to have the most disrupting reactions or instill the greatest inspiration. We understand. We know the feeling and simply retelling it causes us to grow closer, live it again, and overcome together. We have God's ability to create. Our imagination empowers us to share experiences. Even the experiences we have not yet had or the feelings we have not yet felt, we can share through a simple story.

This is not an easy story. This story is not made from fairytales or fantasies. They wont have magical godmothers telling them it will be ok. They will have to listen to their hearts and have courage to follow their instincts. They will have to write this True Love story all on their own.

This story is of a young couple in love. The love is unique to its strength and magnetism. It is innocent and young navigating its way through the obstacles of life. Dealing with the challenges they are confronted with each day. Fear is ever present in life, separation, and war. They must rely on their faith to guide them. They must be willing to surrender to each other completely. They must make choices.

Love is one of many choices that we make in our lives. We choose to allow love into our hearts. We choose to love someone so much our heart and soul overflows. Many times love seems like it is not a choice at all, but at some point along your magical journey you will be confronted with some of the most challenging choices of your life.

Love, like any story, must be written. There are no backseat drivers in love and as such we must work to preserve it. If you wish to have the most memorable love story of all time, then you must create it. Some men climb mountains. Some men fight wars. Others love greatly and never ask for more. The choice is yours. My choice was Talle.

I met Talle Gilmore 5 years ago on a moonlight night in Southern California. We were instantly attracted to each other. Our initial eye contact from across the room quickly pulled us together like gravity. While we were physically separated not too long after our first encounter, our love has made us inseparable ever since.

True love is the story that two people write together. This is the making of a real True Love story. Two months after I met Talle I deployed to Iraq for the second time. Every moment I had we corresponded via emails, letters, or phone calls. We were in love, but it was new and fragile. Seven months is a long time for love to wait, especially when you have just met.

This is a collection of those emails and letters that we shared over seven months. Without even knowing it, we were writing our story with every word. We were strengthening our love with every keystroke. This is the legacy of the love we cultivated during some of the most challenging times in our generation.

Notebook

I met Talle on May 15, 2005. I always liked the numerology, 5, 15, and 25. Five seems propitious and powerful. I never bothered to research the significance, but I didn't have to. I knew regardless of what some book might tell me that this date and our encounter was going to be something magical. I had faith from the very first night that our connection was great.

I visibly remember staring into her face as if pondering the skies and time eternal. Like many new loves do, I was just observing all of her in wonderment. I stared into her hazel eyes and thought to myself. I think I just found the one. I remember feeling odd in the moment as if I just unexpectedly walked into Eden and realized this is what paradise feels like.

Looking back in my notebook I find my first entry after meeting Talle interesting. I had been working to define love for sometime. We as humans often talk about love. We use the term to characterize so much of our lives, but how would someone other than Webster's define love. How would you explain it to someone completely foreign to the concept? I don't find it odd that one week later the answer came to me.

We were quickly in love. Seeing her that night was enough to spark the flame. She inspired these thoughts. These excerpts from my notebook were written during my second deployment. The ones I have chosen are relevant to my love and struggle. They elucidate questions I was having about myself, and my love with Talle. I think they are characteristic of many questions people have starting out in a new relationship. Many people spite love and runaway from it. They fear giving in and losing themselves to its awesome power. They fear the pain that may come if they do. All this fear prevents people from actually loving, so they struggle. They fight, resist, evade and throw away the gift of love. Without ever even realizing, this struggle is with yourself not with whom you love.

This may sound all good on paper, but I am well aware that this is of very little use in the real lives of loves. Couples are so consumed that they don't have time for such notions. They don't have time for questions let alone answers. Though if they don't make time to answer their questions, then they risk too much. They risk their struggles ending in soul crushing defeat. They risk losing the flame. The spark and fight for love will be gone. The settling will begin.

**

LOVE = ACCEPTANCE + SACRIFICE
May 21, 2005

Love is defined with Acceptance and Sacrifice. Sacrifice transcends compassion and mere friendship. The idea of sacrificing is completely irrational, because it is not in our self-interest. The very nature of sacrifice forces us to hinder, endanger, or limit ourselves. Animals and humans are mostly self-interested, but we have the ability to love because we are capable of sacrificing our very selves for each other and that is what distinguishes love.

Acceptance is a precursor. You must be willing to accept people as they are, not as you would have them be. You must be content with accepting them without change or illusion. The roots of friendship begin with little bits of acceptance. You tolerate certain characteristics or traits that you may not have tolerated in others. Total acceptance requires a greater degree of tolerance, all the bad and all the good.

Jesus personified love and these principles. He accepted humanity through forgiveness despite our sins and sacrificed his life for us through crucifixion. He did not want to change us merely save us from sin, enabling us to reveal our inner beauty. He forgave us as we should forgive ourselves and asked us to love our neighbor, as we should accept each other. Jesus may have been preaching love, but he was living acceptance and sacrifice.

Our love on Earth is defined by how much we accept and sacrifice for each other. Allowing people to be who they are or do what they want is the beginning of acceptance and many friendships. Unfortunately you can't love people in parts. If you do not accept the whole person, then you cannot love all of them. You must accept them completely or you will be fighting them partially.

Bonds of love are formed once you are also able to sacrifice for them. This sacrifice must be genuine. You must ask yourself honestly if it is. Do you sacrifice for want or for love, which requires nothing in return and does not waste? Would you sacrifice your money, your time, your dreams, or your life? How much are you willing to sacrifice? What is truly valuable? Would you forsake it if you truly needed it?

ISABELLA
August 22, 2005

I met a German girl while in Darwin, Australia. This is what I learned. Temptation is a sugar coating. Attraction is only skin deep. It begins with the possibility of the unknown. The desire ends with the truth, reality. Temptation is foolish lies and deceptions making reality hidden and mysterious. True love stems from action.

Enjoy doing the same things.

Enjoy discussing and learning the same topics, helps you grow together.

Must have similar wants.

The world is full of possibilities and therefore temptation, but if you are honest with yourself then you will not be misled. My love for Talle is far more than fantasy. It is a truth grounded in reality. No lies or misperceptions can be in the relationship.

THE ROOT
August 30, 2005

The root of my love stems from trust. Could I trust someone to love me enough to prevent me from self-destruction? In my natural state, I would give everything away gladly. I would sacrifice and serve for someone or something that I love. In order to protect me from myself, I would require someone who could love me in return. Love me selflessly. Be willing to give up their idea of self for someone else. This true love requires faith and a release from your own limits. You can't really love unless you can see past the self. If you have experience with sacrifice or suffering then you realize your insignificance and can give your love and life purpose through giving it up instead of hoarding it. In my experience I have never loved someone, who genuinely loved me vice how I made them feel. This selfish form of love evolves into control. The desire to continually satiate the want of a feeling drives the love relationship. In love each must be willing to submit to the other. You must have faith in each other not to abuse your submission. You also must protect each other from submitting too much. You have to find someone that can love you more than his or her self. If they love you less than his or her self, they will constantly be trying to exert their will over you.

The root of love – Comes from loving someone more than yourself. If you can do that and receive it in return then nothing more is needed.

You must ask yourself if you are willing to sacrifice yourself for the other person? I am willing to sacrifice myself for someone who is willing to sacrifice in return.

You can't love God if you cannot love more than yourself.

You can't find true love if you are not willing to give up everything.

Someone who loves you will not allow you to give up yourself. You can put down your guard and relax because they will look out for your interests. You don't have to be on the defensive. I learned as an officer in the Marine Corps to rely on my Marines to look out for me. I learned that as long as I looked out for them they would accomplish the mission. I just had to have faith and care for them more than myself.

You must be fearless in love because fear will be an obstacle that will prevent you from submitting or letting go.

Love is a choice, but you should choose someone you can love more than yourself and will love you in return.

SHAME + SEPARATION
September 9, 2005

Shame has its' origins in Genesis. God calls to man after they have eaten the forbidden fruit. Both man and woman hide themselves for fear of God's wrath. God continues to call to them. When they came out their bodies were covered with clothes because they were ashamed. They were ashamed of their actions and attempted to hide. Clothing or covering was the symbol of their shame. Sexual acts are not shameful. The shame comes from your own personal guilt, which leads you to cover up afterwards. One could argue that God admonished them for their actions or for their deceit, covering up.

If you are covering up in your life this is a good indicator that you are ashamed about what you are doing. You have either been convinced that what you are doing is wrong or are acting against your true instincts. You should ask yourself which is true. If "society" has convinced you to "cover up," then you must be unafraid and reveal yourself. Do not hide these "faults" expose them to be accepted. Be willing to be held accountable. You are exactly as God created you and there is no shame in that. However, if you are acting against your true instincts, then you need to stop. You must have faith in the instincts God gave you and be willing to follow them.

FOLLOW YOUR HEART
September 29, 2005
You cannot be afraid to follow your heart. God is inside you and he speaks to you through your heart. You must have the courage to follow it. God has created everyone uniquely. Our passionate instincts are a major part of our individuality. You must not inhibit yourself because of thought, fear, or doubt. Clearly understand your feelings and follow them. The wild heart is the one that truly lives. If you do not follow your heart then you will become stagnant. Bypassed opportunities become obstacles. God has laid out his plan through your passions. Each time you limit your impulses you create hurdles that must eventually be overcome to move forward and you will be stuck until you follow through with your heart's desires. Your mind can misinterpret your passions, however the results of your actions will reveal the truth. The bottom line is that you would have never known without performing the action and now you will not wonder what could have been, a.k.a. be stuck in time. The truth is… An experience exists that must be had and your soul cannot advance until that experience is fulfilled. I cannot explain the reason why an experience must be had. Just as, I cannot explain God's reasons or everyone's unique instincts. Every time you follow your heart your life changes forever and a barrier is knocked down. Your heart is speaking when you have impulses that stir up emotions and feelings. Until you release your heart from all limitations you will not BE WHO YOU ARE or live YOUR life.

TRILOGY OF LIFE
September 29, 2005

A battle to be fought...

An adventure to be had...

A beauty to rescue...

These impulses drive the emotions of men. They stir up their imaginations and spark life into action. All men are pursuing these ends in some form or composition. Most great stories and movies are completed only when they incorporate all three elements. Just as most lives are fulfilled only when they have pursued all three ends. Men can be identified, as lovers, adventurers, and fighters, because of a stronger pull toward one. However, every man possesses elements of each one and you will only complete your life with all three.

CAPRICIOUS
September 30, 2005

My heart does not lie, but like many men I have my doubts and concerns. I do really love Talle. My love is not fraudulent. My questioning comes not from her but from me. I am not satisfied with myself. I have a strong desire to be in a position to provide for my loved ones, which requires a certain amount of financial stability and professional success. I do have some selfish desires for personal accomplishment. My passion is creating to help people, and I have not proven to myself yet that I am able to create something beneficial. Until I find professional success that does not corrupt or manipulate I will be unsettled; or accomplish personal goals, I will be unsatisfied. If I am unsatisfied with myself, then I cannot completely love another.

Love should bring peace and energy not chaos and worry. The idea of freedom may be a hoax. Our desire for liberation from ourselves our "responsibilities" is a false quest, misguided from a wrong perception. God has made us free to choose whatever responsibilities we want. We become confused with our wrong choices and as a result we desire to cast off the whole lot. Our responsibilities should be perceived as gifts because that is what they are. We have lost our love for the small activities. We have lost our labor of love to enjoy doing menial work. In this confused state we punish ourselves to rid the chains, but not until we are broken do we realize that all we had is all we wanted. Only in our mind do gifts bind or restrain our souls. Talle is a gift, not a worry. Stop predicting the future. Live the present.

ACTIONS
December 7, 2006

In life you are what you do. Your actions are what define you. What you feel, think, or believe does not matter if you do nothing with them. If you do not act on them, then they may as well not exist. However, your instincts are real and normal. They are part of who you are. They are genetic, animal, and natural. They are not good or evil. These ideas merely dramatize someone's opinions. To kill is not to kill if you are protecting yourself or others from harm. To steal is not to steal if you are taking what you need to survive. A person who claims ownership of the river cannot make a thief of the person who drinks from it. Owning property is a society driven concept. We are born and die with nothing. We own nothing. Therefore what could you steal? To cheat is only instinctual and base. We are animal. Our actions are nothing deeper or more sinister. Could you hate a cat for attacking a fish? It is expected. Smoke, drink, lie, gamble these vices of society are all part of our customs. They are our animal rituals and games. We are social creatures, who live to interact with others of our species. We are normal to want to do all these activities. They will come naturally to some. Giving in is not always giving in to the dark side. It is doing what would be expected of us nothing more. Would you change a cat and make it something else. We have taken humanity so far from what we are fundamentally. The concept of evil has corrupted the way we view our self, our action, and each other. We hold the grudge of evil against man, dehumanizing him and making him less than animal.

God's universal law is free will. He gave us the ability to pursue our own passions and make our own choices. The only feasible violation of this law is the obstruction of someone else's free will. Therefore, we have the ability to live our lives freely under that one constraint. While we must have the courage to follow our instincts with so much freedom we must be cautious of indulgence. Desire and temptation wait for us at every corner. There is no shame in making those choices, but one day your passions will naturally lead you toward sacrifice. People will not understand. Sacrifice is an unnatural restriction on our free will, but will seem natural, instinctive, even desired because you are pursuing love. This is where sacrifice doesn't become sacrifice at all. Where you will see love and passion others will see sacrifice.

You are what you do. Love in any form can lead us TO DO great things. If love leads you to live an idea then compose that idea and live it truly. You have the ability to choose your own principles and give your self-definition. If purity is an idea that you want to live by then ask what constitutes purity and live by it. Because it makes me a better or certain type of person is not a reason. What purpose or gain do you achieve for doing it? Ultimately it can only be your choice.

Letters

The ideas captured from my notebook shaped the conversations we had over the course of our separation. Many of the issues presented you will see underlining the letters and emails to come. I had questions. While not uncommon this is ultimately a wrestling with faith. Faith requires you to submit completely. No halfway exists. You cannot bargain, negotiate, or compromise with faith. I can relate with the struggle many people have. We live in a world that we are constantly trying to prove and you must have faith to prove faith.

There is no absolute way of knowing that Talle is my one and only true love, and yet I believe she is. I choose to believe she is. I know myself well enough to know what I want. I know that I need to love someone, who will love me in return. No matter how madly in love I am with someone I believe it would not be true love or healthy without reciprocation.

I will note here that these are my beliefs and that I am addressing a specific type of love. True love forms a self-sustaining bond between mates. Loving people has its limits, but true love is limitless because it is mutually reassuring, each feeding from and providing to the other. The physics of true love demand a self-sustaining dynamic to complete the bond; hence, it cannot be real if you don't receive as much as you give.

If you give completely without receiving anything in return you would find yourself wasted. The light will be smothered and you will have very little of your true self left. The physical relationship becomes unsustainable. I was willing to submit myself completely to love, but I was also aware of the dangers of losing myself completely.

I don't want to confuse people. Receiving as much as you give is not quantifiable or linear. You must be willing to give without expectation of return. What you receive is always a gift. An accepting relationship requires receiving gifts on their terms and giving on yours. I will give a crude example. If you give a pen and receive a letter, do not waste time wondering what happened to the pen. Many people will continue to look for the pen not recognizing the gift they already have and try to quantify the benefit of a pen with a letter. Only you can decide whether you are fulfilled with what you receive and answer whether the letter is enough.

I wrote these letters hoping that they would be enough. We were physically separated. I didn't want our separation to estrange the enormously powerful connection I felt. I wrote to her, these letters in ink. They were letters of love, but not necessarily about love. I felt closer to her when I wrote to her, so I wrote about anything, how I felt, what I was going through, and many of my questions. I took the opportunity to work them out writing and communicating with Talle. I knew giving into my love was the only way to find out if it was True Love.

**

August 25, 2005
Talle,

The vilest of creatures springs from suffocation. In this confined environment one must find comfort in the deformity of life. Sewer rats' relish in the hot stank of steam pipes. They glisten in moisture that hugs their depravation. I cannot help, but conceal myself. I become a former friend angry and violent. I do not know how strong the transformation will become but I will not be the same when I return. I know that it will take time. I will be made cruel for that is the sort of person who survives fighting. I will not be cruel in nature, but empty in heart. No pulse of life will exist only death. Death is fearless and love fears loss, so I will say I love you in case I can't take you with me.

I want you to know how much I think of you. I may need a road map back to love, because like waking from a dream my return home may not be so clear.

I remember now that depression comes from inhibition, feeling trapped…

I must have been looking for you. When I saw you that night and held your hand. We fit so perfectly. I remember that your hand squeezed mine as if to reassure a mutual feeling. I remember feeling so delightfully surprised and relieved. Relieved was the feeling that caught my attention. This relief carried so much certainty and comfort, like old friends who had just found each other. That first night I felt I knew you. Is it possible to have two of the same energy separated from the beginning raised differently and still recognize each other after so many years? Is it possible that I've known what you would look like my whole life? I've been a blind man searching for you my whole life. Can you even believe I knew when your birthday would be? Does that make horoscopes real!? Is there anyway that I can be certain that this is true or just a projection of my imagination? Does God only know? Or, do I have the power to choose to believe it. You have asked me so many times how I could be with you. Would you believe that I am supposed to be? Would you believe that you are the direct reflection of myself only exposed to and brought up in a different environment? Is it possible that having had the same experiences we would be the exact same person, or do you think that we are so completely different? If I listened to my mind, then it might be a different story, hazy and unclear. This however is what my spirit knows and my heart feels. My mind has tried to exhibit restraint, but my soul has loved you from the first day. I have faith in you, but I fear that you will not know me as I know you. If you do not break free from your constraints, then your mind will cloud your soul. It will dampen and depress your spirit. Whatever restrictions you think you have you must break, so that your soul may restore itself to life. I believe that your depression was a sign that your soul is already aware of its chains. Most people are imprisoned without knowing. Your soul has been struggling to be free, crying to let go. A passion exists so greatly in you. I saw it the last night we were together. You have so much beauty, compassion, and light to shine on all those around you. I swear this is true. I know it as I know myself. You have a storm of energy never released. If you search inside yourself honestly, then you cannot tell me that you do not feel it! You are a gift of heaven, perfect at your core. I carry you in my dreams.

My love is your gift! Till we are truly together...Love, Charleston

September 3, 2005
Talle,

I don't really have a reason to write you a letter. This is solely an emotional initiative. I love you so much. I am happy just to write it, to say it, even think it. I love you... I loved coming home and having you there. I love how you can sneak up on me while I am at my desk or in the kitchen. I swear you are the only one, who can do that. I love how you curl up in bed and fit so perfectly. I love that my arms don't miraculously go numb. I love singing "Edelweiss" to you and listening to you sing "Rain Drops on Roses." I love looking at you. You are beautiful. I love making you happy, like cooking chocolate & strawberry pancakes. I love how physically attracted I am to you and how sexy you are. I love how mischievous and exciting you are. I love that you are such a good person, so pure of heart and soul. I love touching you and holding your hand. I love that you stood up on your surfboard and suffered through the cold and bruises. I love that you read books that I give you and are willing to try different things. I love that you are a lady in every way. You are always composed, elegant, courteous, graceful, hospitable, and calming. I love that you took me to the gym and church. I love that even though you were going to pass out you still did those exercises. You really are tenacious. I love that you were enthusiastic my last night and not sad. I love that you are strong emotionally, which is very uncommon. I love that you came into my life unexpectedly. I don't think that I ever suspected finding you, certainly not in California. I love that you love Disney. You are a woman of my heart and soul. I am in danger of being seriously addicted to you. I love talking with you and hearing your thoughts, ideas, even if strange. I love how you walk as if every step is on air. I love you and will think on how much I love you often. Love, Charleston

September 29, 2005
Talle,

What a dream you have become. My heart is smoldering with love. You were in my dreams in Egypt. You are always there when I need you.

Egypt was awful. All the plans for our arrival had been misleading. As a battalion we attempted to execute training in Egypt that was not feasible. Ranges for live-fire training were limited and the Egyptians were very inflexible. They were quick to exert their power over the Americans. After ample training preparations were made, the Egyptians would venture out and cut your time in half or simply kick you off the range. No reason was needed or given. The maneuver and non-live fire training areas were literally flat desert. The training value from this type of terrain is little. Most companies had nothing but free time, which is terrible for morale in the middle of a hot desert, especially when the living conditions deteriorate. We lived in tents where Egyptian workers took the liberty of defecating in them. Most of the sanitation was horribly kept, which resulted in very bitter and negative Marines. Fortunately this is not why Egypt was awful.

My Marines actually had a great time. I kept them away from the negativity. As far as they knew everything was as it was planned and conditions could always be worse. I feel that a lot of my job is to absorb all the bad and never let them see it. I guess in a way I deceive them as much as I can without lying to them, so they stay focused on the mission. I am blessed with an exceptional second in command. My platoon sergeant and I see completely eye to eye when it comes to leadership. He is a great leader and example for our men.

A positive mental attitude really makes a difference and never once did we let the situation become negative, but it was tiring. I got to the point where I couldn't stand being around anyone. I couldn't listen to any more complaints or negative comments. Watching my Marines helped me through it. They are amazing. These men are so close. Where most platoons are fractured, they are a true band of brothers. They do everything together and for each other. They are disciplined, respectful, intelligent, energetic, and fit. The best day that I had was waiting 4 hours on a Range. We were kicked off early and had to arrange for transportation that could not make it earlier. Instead of being miserable waiting in the hot sun we began to play games. I haven't laughed that hard in a long time. We did square pushups. Four men lie feet on each other's backs forming a square and have to pushup in synchronization. We did 3 man squats, upside down pushups, fireman carry relay races. We had a great time and they enjoyed each other, which matters the most. After that day nothing could bring me down until…

We did cross training with snipers from the Netherlands and Germany. They always wanted to post-train with beer. We had a fantastic time with the Germans. Ziggy Ziggy Hoy Hoy Ziggy…!! Unfortunately one night ended in disaster. A Marine from another platoon came after my platoon sergeant and he may be at fault. Every time we go to the desert something bad happens. I care for him very much. I have probably learned more from him then taught him, but it is my job to protect him just like everyone else. I am struggling to find a way to protect him, because I think even trying to sacrifice myself will not save him. I have to find a way and I know one exists. The Marine Corps is an idea, a standard, which is admirable to all but upheld by few. My platoon sergeant is one of the few who always protects the honor of the Marine Corps even to his own detriment. Now I must wait until the investigation is concluded. Waiting will be worse than the resolution.

I spent many nights thinking of you. I dreamt that I was searching for someone. I dreamt that I had been searching for you for a long time. I passed you in my dreams and your picture was so clear. The feeling was the same relief as I described before. Your image was one that was fuzzy until then, but once completed it was so clear and obvious. As if I were standing in front of a picture but couldn't quite make it out until I put on my glasses. I really do love you, but I do have fear. I do fear that I might hurt you and that worries me more than anything. I could not stand to bring you heartache or pain. I presume this comes from not being able to fully interpret and trust my feelings. I still have a lot to clear up. My heart is unpredictable to even me at times. I don't think the Marine Corps gives me any help in this department it only fuels my fire. I know that I may have a lot to do to correct myself and I am worried how it may affect you. If I become too attached then I may not have the courage to fix the turmoil in my heart. If I try to fix it I may hurt you in the process. I am ashamed to ask but if I could ask, then I would ask you to give me up without letting me go. In time you will know all of my heart. Sometimes I can love too greatly. I almost fear doing it. My heart can get so worked up I can overwhelm just about anyone. I am like a phoenix. I fly straight toward the sun and in a blink am gone to ashes. My love never goes, but it can be overwhelming. It can hurt people and myself in the process. Oddly if you tortured me I might love you forever burning till every ounce of passion had been sacrificed for you. But you love me dearly and I will overwhelm you with all that I have to give. Can you control someone who will destroy himself for love? For that exuberant rush of pure energy that comes from sincere thoughtless desire makes you an adrenaline junky. This only exists in pure, natural, innocent, qualities. I think that I have gotten to the point of writing nonsense. When you are unafraid I will love you without restriction. When you love me without restriction I will fear no more. Love, Charleston

September 30, 2005
Talle,
I received a package from your grandmother, Grace George. You have
embraced me into your family. All of them have been so kind. You
have a beautiful family. They are magical. Each one of them is their
own romantic story. You have a family of fables. I am inspired to have
met them. Every person dreams to have such easy love that seems to
come so naturally to your family. Grace met here husband the day
before her 16th birthday and have not been separated since. They have
been married for 56 years in a blink. I am almost ashamed with their
story. Did I grow up in such a different environment or have times
really changed? I have never experienced such purity of love till now.
Grace is an amazing lady. Her treats mean far more to me. I would
love to meet here one day. Her story must tell like a fantasy. You do
me such a great honor by taking me into your family. I will love each
and every one of them. I wish that I could have met you at 16. You
were adorable that I am sure. Vitality is a precious gift in life, which
goes only if we give it up. If Grace has any incriminating photos of
you, I want them! I would bribe her to see them. Above anything else
I wish that I had more pictures of you. Oddly I never have seen any
from your past. We didn't have much time before I left did we?
Everything moved so fast. You hardly know me. If I could see you
right now I would just sit looking contently into your eyes, observing
and admiring every detail. I would try to learn every detail about you,
so that I could love you more. You captivate me, and so I would sit
silently observing in order not to miss a thing. Tell me how you were
when a child? What did you love to do? Tell me everything that
touches your spirit and brings a smile to your face. I love you,
Charleston

October 1, 2005
Talle,
        I just received your package. I sincerely appreciate that you
took the effort to send it to me. I would never take your love for
granted or expect gratitude for mine. I do admit that I am not entirely
certain about the purpose of the Jimmy Choo sales receipt. Unless, you

were coyly hinting something: a time more memorable shared, a gift to be replicated, a note to acknowledge appreciation, or nothing at all?

Writing love letters infuriates me. The word love does no justice to the surge of passion and emotions felt. Only thought and ideas can be translated with any sense of paper. You must act to communicate feelings. If they are genuine then only action brings satisfaction. What words can replace an enchanted embrace, a sweet kiss, or a tender touch. What creative words can say I love you more than a morning smile, with strawberry chocolate pancakes, a surprise visit at work with flowers, or a massage before bed. Love written cannot impart the agony of separation. Where even minor details like remembering whether coffee is latte with two sugars or one is unbearable because I can't ask. I can't dress up love or make it smell better. Given the expanse of written love letters I can't even make it unique. Turn on a favorite song. Watch a beautiful sunset. Sip a delicious wine. Do a good deed and I will be with you. This is the extent of my love to be with you in moments of peace. When the sands have stopped and the hurry has slowed I am right in your heart where you are with me. This is my act of love to share my life with you. I fight with you, suffer, struggle, laugh, stare at the moon, wonder, and inspire with you. I am grateful to you, but please do not believe my words. Have faith only in my actions. With those in mind I write I love you.

We are heading to Iraq. Admittedly I am afraid for my Marines. I have no reason to be. I wish that I could blame you for giving me reason, but I know that I cannot. You are more than enough reason to live, but I have unfinished business. You have given me this and I can't really make much of it yet. I know this is wrong to have going to war. I know what is unfinished between us. I only hope that I will be able to conclude this matter. Iraq is not my only obstacle. I have more when I return. I must find some good from this worry. I believe it might be that I worry about being with you. The importance of being with you has shaken me. The only doubt of which I may have is the doubts you have. I am certain of you. May I love you forever...Charleston

October 10, 2005
Talle,

I enclosed some books. Could you please put these in my house? I started ripping out articles from ocean drive and then realized too many existed. The magazine has some really good articles on clothing designers new and old. Also discusses some popular boutiques. I think this might be some good information to gather research for a boutique. I thought Cavalli's idea of integrating a café with a store was brilliant. This is a simple concept that makes shopping more of an experience. I also included a magazine from wilderness travel. Please save this magazine. It has really good pictures of the world. I am curious, which locations inspire you! I want to be a part of your dreams. I want to do what you are interested. I want to have your input and know your mind. I love you and that means I love all of you.

We have already passed the halfway point. I miss you and can't wait to see you again. If I take off when I return then I really want you to come with me. Would you be able to do that? Honestly…I dream of you often. Thank you, Charleston

October 21, 2005
Talle,

My sister sent me this postcard. I thought was pretty funny. I can't write you and not immediately think I love you so much. I feel awfully redundant. I am really going to have to be creative with how I express my love for you.

Currently I am sitting in a sandy tent freezing in the desert. The weather has dropped suddenly. Patience in war can be excruciating, but we must sit and wait while they figure out what they need my battalion to do. I can always occupy my time thinking of you. I love you. I'll see you soon. Love, Charleston

November 12, 2005
Talle,

Hello my love, I only have time for a quick note. I know that you do not watch the news, but we have been pushing through Al

Qaim for the last week. The fighting is making the time go by quickly. However, I can only clear so many minefields. All in all this has been a very successful operation, STEEL CURTAIN. My platoon has done some pretty intense missions, but they have all been good for my men and the battalion. I don't take too many risks, but I am less afraid then most when it comes to danger. Most people's true colors are revealed when rounds begin shooting overhead. Some of my best people have turned out to be my weakest. Even though they are all strong and capable. I am lucky to have a great platoon. I love you very much, but don't have time to write now. Your prayers are helping I am sure because I always feel God with me and the shadow of fear never comes. The Military has taught me so much mostly about the differences between men. Men only differ in their abilities to control their fear. Some control it better than others; otherwise very little in life separates us. I have forgotten some things, but I have not forgotten you. My letter with the books had meaning. Don't let me forget. I love you, but you have to be willing to die here and in order to die you have to be willing to give up everything. God has blessed me and watches over me. I know that your love protects me, but I will be all right no matter what happens. Do me a favor please. The past few nights have been cold. Wrap yourself in some blankets and pour yourself a hot cup of tea. As you sip the tea and inhale the steam think of me, so that I can share your warmth. I love you. Sleep soundly. With love, Charleston

November 26, 2005
Talle,

First things first I love you. Believe it or not I have even grown more enamored with you since we last spoke. Your letters are brilliantly written. Everything was addressed so well. Any concerns, worries, questions have been effectively neutralized. I really think that you must be my identical half. Your reactions are too perfect. I've never felt more complete. I do have a problem with pushing people away and I commend you for recognizing it. I pray that I don't as well, but sometimes I feel like I don't have a choice. I feel like I have to sacrifice that I am not worthy of the happiness or someone else deserves it. I will innately punish myself to make someone happy for which I care. This is a force that I work hard to control, but it is there. I also don't think that I have ever had anyone tell me not to be afraid and I like it! This tells me you are generally paying attention, which is rare in everyone. I honestly believe that you care about what is happening over here, but more importantly you have the strength to handle it and not make it a bigger deal than it is. This makes me want to share everything with you. I want to tell you everything, but just like me you have to keep me in check. You have to not let me get too intense, overwhelming, crazy, which is why I love your "afraid" comment. You really are incredible. I want to share and explain so many things that I have learned. When you wanted to be a teacher what did you want to teach?

Sometimes I wish oddly enough that you would put up a fight, but only because I want to fight for you. I want to show you how far I would be willing to go to what ends and pain I would endure. I know this must be awful, but I do. I care for you so much that I would enjoy the misery. I would be satisfied with every agony, because you are worth it. Your letters have taken on your scent and every smell carries a warm wave of comfort that pervades my whole soul. Men can be shallow with cheap words and short distances. I want to fight for you like no one has before. I want to do things for you that would shake the world. I just don't know if you want that. I know you don't require it, but I may need to do it. The pain or misery would be a gift. They should never be shunned, because only on Earth can you experience them and they make everything else sweeter. Can you imagine and eternity where you could never experience pain? Pain can be beautiful. I love you. I just can't wait to see you. You have changed so much since I first met you. I love you so much. Love, Charleston – Ps. The Mongols believed that your soul was carried in a persons scent. I think that I do to. Love you…

November 27, 2005
Talle,

If only I could hug you till we gasped. Kiss you till I needed air. Hold you till the sun came up. Watch you till my eyes dropped and love you till my heart stopped. Do I know that I could love you forever…only if? Nothing. I do know. I love you. When you look at the moon blow it a kiss, so I can see it, smile, and know that I am missed. Love, Charleston

November 28, 2005
Talle,

Strange finding you when I did. I wonder what it will be like to get to know you. You seem so strangely similar. I think it is something in your eyes. A spark of soul that often appears to be asleep exists inside of you. I recognize it as I recognize my reflection. Now even your broken pinkie on the same hand symbolizes a very absurd similarity. I think you were supposed to go to Paris that summer. I think that on your path you strayed when you didn't go. I think that magic in your soul must have been surprised that day you chose not to pursue it. Can you remember that day? Can you remember the day when you were told Paris was cancelled? Did you think however brief, "well I'll just go it alone," or did you immediately concede? I think that day your heart must have roared, but for some reason your mind said it was impractical without even knowing. I think Paris might be a good idea. In life we must fulfill every instinct.

Mine will be fulfilled when I see you again. Hold you and feel you. Place your head on my chest and kiss you again. Touch your hand and caress your face. Look in your eyes and know you are there.

I can visualize every part of your body, but I miss the sound when you breathe. I know the contours of your shape, but I miss the texture of your skin.

I have forgotten so much and will feel like I am seeing you for the first time. I can't quite remember how we kissed or how you taste, where you were ticklish or how you were aroused. So much seems lost, but at least I get to find it again. I can't wait to hold you and …

I love you so much. Will think of you often. If you need me I will be in the rolling tide when the moon shines sending you a wink so that you know I will be there in a blink.

I love you. Love, Charleston

Ps. Sing to me often and I'll never let you go. All my love.

December 12, 2005
Talle,

I love you, but since I can't show you let me describe the feeling. The feeling begins with a thought, a picture, or a memory. I can see your beauty. You are incredibly gorgeous, enchanting, and dazzling. After spending hours looking at hundreds of people in Maxim magazine or through whatever other trash is sitting around. I honestly think there are no comparisons. You are perfect in every detail. Your eyes the way they look illuminate brilliance. They carry sincerity and a hidden sensuality. Your facial features are meticulous, cheeks, nose and lips. Your neck and collarbone exudes grace and sophistication. I am stopping. This is far too much temptation. I'll get all worked up. I fantasize more about you then I think I have about anyone. Your figure is outrageously sexy. I love every part of you and it doesn't stop with your body. Have you ever sat in a bathtub when the water has gone cold? You turn the hot water back on and as it runs into the water you feel the warmth begin to blanket your body. This is how I feel when my thoughts turn to you, a heart pumping warmth flowing over a cold body. You turn on the heat!

As I sit here writing you I only want to hold and speak to you more. The writing almost hurts better not to think on it too much yet. I love you. Light a candle for me on Christmas and blow me a kiss on New Year. I'll be coming home soon, but only to fall madly in love with you. For my birthday this is my wish. I want you to plan a trip to anywhere you want to go in the world. I want you to choose everything with no time limit. You choose the place, the time limit, and the activity. This is the gift I want from you, your choice. I'll take care of the meaningless stuff. One more time, I love you. God bless you with the passion of life forever. Love, Charleston

December 30, 2005
Talle,

How much can I give you? Love, I mean. I received your package. You are beyond incredible. I can't believe how well you selected everything. I loved the buckeyes. You have panache for sweets. The real estate portfolio blew me away. You out did yourself.

Can I keep you... You do great work! The snowman card made me laugh out loud. I am completely enchanted with you. You are such an exceptional, beautiful, gifted person. Writing is not enough; I can't wait to spend time with you. This doesn't do the emotion justice. I know that we have some obstacles to overcome, but I am really excited to face them with you. Honestly I have a lot of personal obstacles, but I think you understand that very well. I have so many ideas, moments, experiences that I want to share with you if you will let me. I can be awfully pushy and I don't want to be. I just have a lot of trouble when people see limitations, because I don't. The limitless imagination spawned when we were born is the most important part of my personality. This makes me impulsive, stubborn, and bold. I know that God lives in each of us. His strength and power are ours to use. We can do anything if we have faith. I truly believe anything can be accomplished with it. I have so many thoughts that I would like to ask you when I return. I expect that it will be very difficult for you at times. I will not take that lightly. I care for and love you. Nothing will change my feelings, but you have to make your own choices. I don't want you to ever feel like I am making them for you. A time may come when you might not like what I say. In the end love requires faith. Faith doesn't come easily.

You are far more remarkable than I wager you think. I want to show you if you will let me. I think given the opportunity you will find and discover revelations about yourself. You will also find how deep my love goes. I am sending home your book "The Purpose Driven Life" because I would like to read it with you. I already signed it, but I am hoping you will be my partner and we can read it together. I know you have already read it, but I think we could learn from each other. I can't stop loving you.

Love, Charleston

December 31, 2005
Talle,

My love, I have been thinking about you. Yearning to know what it will be like when I return is excruciating. I am constantly envisioning you and how you've changed. What you have learned and experienced. I would like to share everything with you, but of course not all at once. I want to dance with you. I remember when we first met we danced. I remember thinking how well you moved, smooth, rhythmic, and sensually. You were a turn on, subtle and sexy. I remember kissing you on my bed for the first time touching you, looking into your eyes. Your body has been driving me crazy for months. Your neck inspires warmth, grace, and elegance. Your chest and waist draw lines so perfect that they leave nothing to waste. Your hips down to your feet connect two notes of a song. My mind plays music when I think over you for very long. If you listen you will hear my heart beating with every touch, every caress of the hand, smile, and wave of your hair. I crave your body, your being to touch, taste, and hold you here. I am waiting for those first embraces that kiss. With nothing but time I am becoming crazy for you. Goodbye, my darling.

Email

The emotion written in my letters was very hard to control. I loved Talle greatly in those first months that it made my writing very messy. I couldn't prevent my feelings from overflowing on paper. I wanted to be with her and share every moment with her. People have compared love to a drug for its addicting affects. I think the love I was receiving from Talle was very addicting, but that wasn't what drove my emotions. The love I had, made me want to give not take. I wanted to write songs and symphonies. I wanted to build monuments and skyscrapers. Just the thought of her moved me to moments of sheer bliss and inspiration. In a large part this record and our story are a continuation of my overwhelming love for her.

Love moves me to create and I don't think that can be said about any drug. Creation can be spawned from many avenues: pride, greed, boredom, and love. I would like to wager that love's creations are eternal, but I have no historical evidence to support this. I only have glimpses of artists, who passionately painted, sculpted, and erected their love, or whispers of poets, musicians, and writers who wrote odes to their muses. I know that love creates honorably. It is selfless in its pursuit. I know it does not create for money, entertainment, or fame. Love creates only for love.

When the bonds of love are formed a spark ignites a flame that produces vice consumes. I was compelled to create for Talle. I wrote those letters with little thought. They were an uncontrollable reaction to the love we shared. At the time I didn't even know that I was writing our story. I didn't realize that every word was for love. I didn't realize that every word was making our love grow.

While fire and love are almost opposites, one consumes and the other produces. Like fire, love feeds on itself. The more wood you feed a fire the greater it grows. The more you create, the more acts of love you make, the greater your love will become. I didn't realize this at first. I was feeding the flames of love. Every email we wrote was fanning those flames. Every keystroke begets more love. We loved each other with words. Sharing our lives created a greater bond between us.

True love has to be written, maybe not in words, but in moments, looks, or acts. In the beginning my subconscious was compulsively doing the writing, making it very sloppy and clumsy as new loves are. When I became more aware of what I was doing, I realized that I could choose. I could choose what and how to create. I could choose to be more artful and wield my impulses more precisely. I could suffer not sharing to surprise or entice. I could form words to inspire emotions or tell stories to spawn laughter. We had the power to write our story. We also had the power not to write our story.

I am delighted each time I read over these emails, but I also think what if we had not written. What if we chose not to write? Seven months is a long time to wait for someone you just met. We might have not survived the deployment. Our love might have become like many others that faded over time. This is why I am also grateful each time I read over these emails. They are a record of those questions and emotions, but mostly of our love. They serve as a reminder to us that love is a story we write with each other. This story is not fictional, but it can be whatever you make it. It can be as magical and wonderful as you create it. This power comes with only one responsibility. Like all stories, it must be written.

**

Part One

A lot of loving someone is about knowing your self and each other. In these first few months this is exactly what we were doing. We were communicating thoughts and opinions, so we could better manage expectations. We were learning each other's likes and dislikes, determining whether we were a good fit. We were discussing the social conventions of relationships, proposals, and marriages, so we would be more aware of external influences.

While this active learning and sharing helped us set boundaries, it was also subject to limitations. Like traveling, this process exposed us to vulnerabilities, insecurities, and unresolved issues that we had to work out. These internal struggles could have clouded issues or created hypersensitivities, but we overcame them. We may have felt like we were testing our love with so many questions, but everyone has questions. If we were uncertain or needed answers, we only had to ask. We may have felt like sharing too much would be a burden, but it never is. If we were going to give all in to love, we couldn't let personal issues tear us apart. We had to follow our instincts and take risks. We had to know what we want and say it openly. We had to expose our ideas and share our inner secrets.

Fear might have prevented us from taking these steps. Fear might have limited the love we shared, but our love was overpowering. Ultimately we held faith in each other, not horoscopes. We had faith in our choices and we chose to love each other despite our circumstances.

"DEPLOYED JULY 15 2005"

HI!

July 16, 2005 – Hi Charleston!

I hope everything is going well! I love you and miss you already! I hope you are able to get some sleep. You must be exhausted. I know I am! Today was a long day but it went fine.

Your Mother called me at work. It was sweet! She said a lot of nice things about you and me and us! I am going to get together with her on Monday. I should only have to work a half-day. I'm looking forward to spending time with her and getting to know each other.

I am so thankful that you came into my life Charleston! As much as I am going to miss you, I am truly excited about the things I will have time to do and learn. I know this time will pass quickly for both of us.

Please be safe and take care of yourself! I'll be praying for you everyday.

I love you so much! Talle

LOVE YOU

July 18, 2005 – Hi Charleston,

I hope everything is going well. I miss you very much!

I spoke to your mother again today. We didn't end up doing anything because they were pretty tired from the Ocean Festival yesterday. It sounded like they had a great time. We made plans for Wednesday, so I am looking forward to that.

I only worked a half day today, which was great! The new gym across the street opened over the weekend. I am really excited because it is so convenient! I went and rode the bike today. I would rather run, but until my toe heels the bike will work.

I love you and I'm thinking of you. Take care of yourself!

Love, Talle

ZEPHYR

July 20, 2005 – My Love,

I have to first explain the e-mail situation is not exactly what I had expected it to be, so I am e-mailing you on this account, which is easier for me to check. I miss you too, but I am excited and looking forward to my return, which is a new experience for me. Typically I don't really mind being away. Thank you for spending so much time with my mother. This means a lot to me, because I would like her to know you. This e-mail will be a little erratic, because I didn't expect to be able to send you a message.

You were an exceptionally rare and beautiful person before you met me. My love is simply reassurance of that fact. I am the one who is thankful to have met you, because the heart decays without love and in my world, love has very little presence. You are much stronger than you believe, but you will see that for yourself. Don't be afraid to follow your instincts. They will not lead you astray. I love your enthusiasm.

I am so excited to hear about the biking. Let me know when your toe finally heals. My father wrote me. He rode 60 miles, but is still having trouble losing weight. I think that I might need to look into that. However, It would be great if we could all go biking. I'll send you my address soon. I will keep writing as much as I can.

Love, Charleston

July 21, 2005 - Hi Charleston!

It is so good to hear from you! Thank you for all of your kind words! They truly made my day!

It has been nice spending time with your mother. I went to the house yesterday. She picked up Sonny's for dinner. We ate and watched part of a movie. It was ironic because she told me earlier in the evening she thought I looked like Audrey Hepburn (which is a huge complement!) and one of her movies came on! We had a nice time. We talked a lot about you. She also was very complimentary of me. I believe everything went well and I could not be happier about it!

I think my toe is just about healed. I went to the gym again yesterday morning and did the elliptical and my toe was fine! I would love to go biking! Hopefully I will be in good enough shape to keep up with your dad! He is amazing!

My brother went back to Ohio yesterday. He and I both were so busy I hardly was able to see him. I spent some time with him on Tuesday night. We had dinner at the Cheesecake factory. We both got strawberry lemonades and I thought of you! A few of his friends were going to the fair, so Camilla and I went too. It was nice for the three us to hang out together it doesn't happen very often.

I am having a hard time at work. My business is horrendous! It is beyond the point of saving for the month. Everyone has been very supportive; luckily they see I am doing my best. I am going to focus on planning some things for August so I can potentially pick up some volume.

I cannot wait to hear from you! I miss and love you very much! Take care of yourself!

Love Talle

July 22, 2005 – Audrey,

I am riotous over the loss of business. I don't think that the evaluation is just. Your merchandise must have been the culprit; thus, the only proper conclusion Janet could make is that you must be a buyer so that you can prevent further losses for her store's petit department. Obviously the current buyer is not on top of the trends that are affecting your store. Well enough of that I can't speak of it anymore or I will have to go to the gym again.

Elliptical is a killer burn on the buns, which now that I think about it reminds me. Either all the men on the ship are having separation anxiety or are getting entirely too close for comfort. I have had an unusual number of smacks on the bottom today, which might seem perfectly appropriate in team sports. Strangely we haven't played any team sports on ship and very few of them are close enough friends to get away with an unwarranted "good game" pat.

The toe is certainly a happy tiding. Actually now that I think about it this is terrible. Without a broken toe you will be able to pursue all your fancies, which means that I will be in a state of nail biting paranoia about what possible devious acts you could do. I however have a brilliant solution. You should break your other toe or maybe something bigger, so that it takes a little longer to heal like maybe six months. I am only slightly joking. No seriously. I am joking.

Second thought you do look like Audrey Hepburn except incredibly more beautiful. I was thinking about you for hours today, but I must have been a little sleepy because I could only think. I love you. I love you. I love you. I love you. I love you etc...

I knew my mother would like you.

How did Madeline get along?

Today we had these lectures on Iraq from a student studying for his PhD at the US Naval Post-Graduate School. He was an Iraqi, who fought in the Shiite uprisings in Iraq in 1991 against Saddam Hussein. Being a bit invasive I asked a couple of questions about his personal background. Most of his family still lives in Najaf, which is like Rome for the Shiite religion. Najaf is a very controversial city in its own right, which we invaded last summer as the first of a series of campaigns against the insurrection. Muqtadar al Sadr led most of the fighting against Americans in the city. His story is interesting.

Muqtadar is the son of a very well respected religious intellectual in the Shiite world. His father, who is considered a martyr, was murdered during Sadaam Hussein's regime. At the time the Grand Ayatollah, similar to our Pope, was grooming him and one other as his successor a very prestigious and powerful position. Not long after his father's death did his fellow scholar became the current Grand Ayatollah al Sistani.

Needless to say Muqtadar holds some resentment. After we invaded Iraq he saw his opportunity to regain some of his family's power. With the Grand Ayatollah al Sistani firmly in his position as the religious representative for Iraqi Shiites. Muqtadar reached out to the Iranians and Syrians, who were willing to support someone that would give them access to influence Iraq. Within Iraq he spent his time working to sway over the Badr Corps and militarize the Shiite people. He used his father's memory to garner influence with the Badr Corps, which is a militarized organization that works for the political body known as SCIRI - Supreme Council for Islamic Revolution of Iran. It was this quasi-militia that Marines fought against in Najaf. Americans have been very suspicious of his direct involvement with the insurgency; nevertheless, we maintain a relationship with him. Many people often ask why we maintain relationships with such people and the response, which is typical for Middle Eastern politics, is "it's complicated."

The bottom line is that most likely this student teaching our class, who is now an American, has a direct relationship through his family with the people we fought in Najaf. The surprising fact is that in America it doesn't matter. Just so your not lost none of this was discussed in his class. I think he spoke on something irrelevant like cultural awareness. Do you know Iraqi's consider it rude to show them the bottom of your feet?

For my Marines, I am having them write a paper on Bushido. Bushido is a discipline of study for Samurai's in Japan that was written over 400 years ago. Their culture developed a warrior philosophy, whose principles are explained in this book. Their base tenet is to *keep death in mind at all times*. With careful thought the idea reveals a tremendous sense of urgency to shed useless living in pursuit of life's love. While more provocative amongst warriors and in combat the idea is common throughout many eastern and now more recent western philosophers. If every breath were your last would you do things differently? How?

Just wanted to give you a snapshot of ship life, probably too much. I love you sweet dreams. Oh and strawberry lemonade without me that means war!!!
July 22, 2005 – Hi Charleston,

I think your ideas about my business are right on! I wish it worked that way.
About those smacks on the bottom, that is my bottom and they have no right to be smacking it! I am very upset!!!

You just called me!!! It was so wonderful to hear your voice! I miss you so much!

Madeline did great! She keeps herself very busy playing with her car and cleaning it with Windex! She is adorable and has so much personality! Whenever she gets something out she puts it right back where it belongs as soon as she is done. She even gave me a cookie! Your mother found a shuttle service that took her to the airport today. She kept telling me that she did not want me to take her because she was picturing me getting into an accident on the way home. How odd is that?!

I like the idea of Bushido. It makes sense and is something I've actually been thinking about. For me it is a matter of figuring out what I want to do and how I'm going to do it. Which, I am working on. I have realized a lot of things and am excited to start on them. Unfortunately I keep having minor setbacks, but there are other things I can do in the meantime.

I would stop caring about what other people think. You know I feel this way and even though I cannot seem to just let it go, I have noticed a difference.

I have felt differently than I expected with your departure. I knew that I would be able to be strong and do what I needed to do. I also knew I would have moments filled with emotion.

I have those moments but they are not sad, they are happy! I think about the things we've done and conversations we've had and I feel so lucky to have you in my life! It is such an overwhelming feeling of happiness and it is very new for me.

Take care of yourself!

I love you! Talle

July 27, 2005 – Talle,

I restricted access to the bottom and have had to clamp down on the team play on ship, so that should take care of it for now. Monday was not too good; however, I did see *Wedding Crashers* and that was probably the funniest movie I have seen in a while. I went with John, the Newly Wed. John went out skanking with everyone else. I was literally laughing so hard that I was hitting John in the movie. I was surprised at how unpredictable it was, which definitely added to its humor. Monday I lost a Marine in Hawaii. He just decided not to come back to the ship, which was bad. Since I was taking so much criticism for it, I had to tell everyone the truth that he ran away with the circus. Unfortunately he showed up a day later just in time to make it on board one of the other ships. Our ship had already pulled out of port. Bastard foiled my cover story. Well now he is going to be slammed by the command, so he might have been better off running away with the circus.

Since were sharing medical diagnosis, one of the doc's yesterday told me that I have a fungus!!! Yea Fungi are FUN. I guess whatever caused my skin to discolor is some kind of fungus. Luckily it is not contagious. Although sharing a fungus would be a new level in the relationship. They gave me some crazy shampoo that I have to lather my body with once a week. I'll be thinking of you during the lathering. I love you, but got to go. Being kicked off the computer again.

Love, Charleston

July 27, 2005 – Charleston,

I cannot believe one of your Marines did not come back! That is ridiculous! I liked your cover though.

I'm glad you liked wedding crashers. I will have to put that on my list of things to do.

I'm sorry to hear about your fungus!!! At least now you know what it is and you can cure it!

I am going to rest some more. I love you! Take care of yourself!

Love, Talle

TWO WEEKS NOTICE

July 25, 2005 – Hi Charleston,

I went to the orthopedic this morning. They took more x-rays and decided I need to have surgery. So, tomorrow at 3:00 I am going in for surgery. They need to put pins in my right pinkie. I guess I will be able to move my finger right away, which is important. They are making me take two weeks off work. I am not happy about it but I don't really have a choice. Janet was great! She even gave me money because I will not get paid my full salary while I am out. I was really impressed. I took pain medication and I am really tired so I am going to go to sleep.

I'll probably be out of it all day tomorrow but I will let you know how everything goes as soon as possible. I love you very much! I hope your sunburn is feeling better!

Love, Talle

July 26, 2005 – Talle,

I love you. I love you. I love you. I have no idea why every time I think about writing you these are the only three words that come to mind. I feel like I am a little kid when I write you. I sit high in my seat with a big grin on my face trying to think of charming words to write. The surgery is not going to restrict the movement in your finger is it over the long term? I am excited for your two weeks off work. I think that is exactly what you need. Oh wait selfish thought, can you delay your surgery for when I return, because I could think of some really exciting places for you to spend that time. Well I am sure that you could use the time to rest, think and do some much-desired activities.

Being over concerned about what people think is a problem if it leads you to second guess your instincts. I feel like women have this problem more than men. Nonetheless, I think traveling is a good exercise for anyone with this problem. Traveling exposes you to so many different worlds and cultures. Every culture has its own opinions, standards, and realities. You quickly learn that the only truth is your own. There are so many opinions in the world and most if not all are inappropriate for you. People's opinions are a reflection of how they feel about a circumstance, which is totally different than how you may feel. I think a ruthless; however truthful opinion a politician once said was I don't care for people who don't share my opinions, because I can always find someone who does. The most that can be asked is to respect people's opinions and use them to help develop your own, but truly only your own will be of any use. This is reinforced when challenges present themselves. Travelers tend to encounter many challenges that only they can solve. No one else is there to help them and as a result they have to use their own judgment to overcome the situation. This builds a lot of confidence and self-reliance. It opens many people's eyes to how capable they are if they just follow their instincts.

Travelers tend to congregate and find each other, especially when needed. As you travel people have a habit of joining your journey then fading away. Your bonds are still very strong, because you make friends through activities, which is the nature of traveling. When you are at home you rarely go to a museum, ride a jet ski, or walk through a park. This opens many people's eyes to a world community, where friends are easily made and lost, but your shared experiences linger on. We learn that people will come when we need someone. We are all travelers through life and many of our friends will only play small roles in it. Moving, new jobs, life changes drive people apart. While they are not necessarily forgotten they are not near. You can still value them for those shared experiences and leave it at that. Ultimately we can't take anyone with us, so attachments are imprudent. I think travelers know their time is short; therefore, they have no illusions.

Lifetime friends are very special and exceptional. These relationships develop through shared experiences, which evolve two people along parallel paths through each stage of life. It goes without saying that this is extremely rare even for married couples; however, for married couples this is the goal and the challenge growing together.

I am being kicked off the computer, so I will write again later. Love you...Charleston

July 27, 2005 – Hi Charleston,

I am glad to know you feel the same way I do! I get so excited when I get e-mails from you that I cannot stop smiling! I love you so much!

I guess the surgery went well. The only thing I remember is the tremendous burning that occurred when they gave me the anesthetic. I was not expecting it. Basically all I've done is sleep. I am really dizzy even sitting here. I hope that goes away soon. My hand is in a cast-like contraption on the pinky side. I can only use two fingers and my thumb. Tomorrow the cast will come off and they will put a different contraption on that is removable. I should be able to move it tomorrow.

Hopefully I will be able to get up and do things soon. I tried reading a little bit today but my eyes could not focus. I will try again later. At least I am getting some rest.

Mindy came up to help yesterday, which was sweet. She and Camilla were so helpful! Camilla has been my personal nurse today as well. She has been great!

I received a package from you before I left for my surgery yesterday. I didn't open it but you did not need to do anything else for my birthday. You have already done too much!

I love you Charleston! I cannot stop thinking about you and how wonderful you are!

Love, Talle

July 27, 2005

A package? I would certainly like to claim credit for this wonderful surprise, but that just wouldn't be my style. However, I am imagining that the handwriting might look awfully familiar to my mothers, just a hunch. This smells like something she might do. Let me know how it goes though. I'd really like to know what I sent you. I'm glad you are getting rest and I think that is the most important thing you can do. Just sleeping sounds good. Everybody loves a fungus...

Love, Charleston

July 28, 2005 – Hi,

I went to see the doctor today. They took off the cast and gave me a removable one made of plastic and pretty pink Velcro! I'm supposed to do exercises with it throughout the day. I have had a hard time with it so far. I'm hoping it will get easier. Thanks to pain meds I slept most of the day again. I'm not going to take them anymore. The pain is nothing Advil cannot cure and I could do without the spins.

Camilla and I are supposed to go to Mindy's tomorrow for my birthday. I hope I will be up to it.

I hope all is well with you! I love you!

Love, Talle

*

HAPPY BIRTHDAY!!

July 29, 2005 – Talle,

My love for you is exhausting every creative capacity I have. Nothing I do seems to satisfy this invigorating feeling I have when I think of you. I must use every sense of discipline to prevent me from falling too deep. This was all written for you on your birthday. Enjoy...

Our First Night
A light in the crowd
you'll only see once.
was my heart beating loud
with every blood pumping ounce?

Real was this lady, so fare.
I hardly had time to stare.

She was dazzling, God's gift, a miracle.
Not good enough, how foolish was she?

She was magical and mystical
I wasn't even physical.

I'll love whatever may be whether she's free or with me.
I loved her on day one and we've only just begun.
Her smile is so sweet and sincere.
I wouldn't even dare.

For, she's in my heart; I have no doubt.
Even if I wanted to I couldn't keep her out.

Music to my Heart
She is music to my heart dressed in melody. Her skirt has rhythm
smooth silky with taste. Her hair hints and hides covering her face.
Coy smiles lurk from within. She is blushing. Oh no! Her comes her
grin. I can't stop glancing. Look at those eyes so full of love. Great
God thank you for this gift from above. How perfectly she fits hand
held in hand like the missing player for my band. She is my muse and
lyre sweet sounding trance. My eyes dance over her body. Shit! Where
are my pants? Hot footed I flee after stealing images of her sensuality.
The harmony's too hot between the two of us I am the one who's
shot. Just rocking along I hold her tight as I sing our song I love you
goodnight.

Love is a choice
I would love you forever

But forever never comes
And I can't choose you in the future
I can choose you today and smile tonight
Knowing that tomorrow I get to choose you all over again.
Happy 26th! I Love You, Charleston
July 29, 2005 – Charleston,

I truly do not have words to describe they way you have touched my heart. I really don't know what to say. I love you Charleston, I wish I could explain that to you in as beautiful a way as you just did to me. I am so overcome with thoughts and emotion right now that I cannot think straight. It just means so much to me that you wrote out your thoughts like this and shared them with me. It is beautiful!

I have to start thinking about something else or I am going to lose my mind!
Thank you so much for the beautiful necklace. I love it! I got a call today from a flower shop asking if I was home because they had a delivery for me. Unfortunately, I was in Carlsbad at Barry and Lauren's. She wouldn't leave it because it was too hot outside! They are going to deliver it tomorrow. (She told me it was from you!) You are too much!

I hate that I have to write all of this to you! I just want to jump on you and give you a huge hug and lots of kisses!!! You're in for it when you get back!

I spent the day in Carlsbad with Camilla and Mindy. I was in a fog most of the day. We had a nice lunch and then went back to Barry and Lauren's. Later on everyone came home from work and we had dinner and cake. Brian sang happy birthday. It was adorable. He was very interactive! I got an iPod from my parents. I'm excited to start using it! That will keep me busy tomorrow.

Thank you so much for everything Charleston. I am so blessed to have you in my life! Love, Talle

THANK YOU
July 30, 2005 – Charleston,

I have never seen such a beautiful flower arrangement in all of my life! It is gorgeous! I could stare at it for hours. Not to mention the candy! I had to try one right away. They are delicious! You've done way too much and all of it so perfectly. Thank You! You made my birthday so special! I can't wait to thank you in person!!!

I hope things are going well. I love and miss you very much! Take care of yourself. Love, Talle

August 1, 2005 - Hi Charleston,

I hope everything is going well! I miss you!

I've been trying to get everything in order the past couple of days. There are so many things to keep track of for this accident. I found out today that my car is totaled. I don't know how much they are going to give me for it but I have to start looking for a new car. I had wanted a new car for a long time. It's funny because I was thinking on the way to the airport that day that I didn't want to get a new car. That car was in pretty good shape and I wanted to work on saving money. So much for that idea! I don't know what I want to get but I'll have to come up with something soon.

I finished *Papillion*. What a great book! I am sad to be finished with it. He was an incredible man! It's amazing to think how people live through such horrible circumstances. It makes me think about my life and how good I have it! I have to admit these past few days have been very trying. I guess it is common to go through some sort of depression after surgery, which I hadn't realized. It has taken a lot of effort, which I don't think that I was ever willing to do in the past. I guess that is what is making the difference. I have had to come up with things that I want to do and can do to occupy my time. I went to the beach, in San Clemente, yesterday and today for a couple of hours. It helps to be outside and in a place that holds a lot of happiness for me. I also went to church and have taken some long walks. I caught up on some movies. Hitch was really cute. I liked it a lot! *Hide and Seek* with Robert De Nero and Dakota fanning was awful! *The Aviator* was interesting but long. I started reading *the Devil Wears Prada*. It is quick and witty. I've also been thinking about taking the train to Santa Barbara for a couple of days. I've never been there but I've heard it's beautiful. It would be nice to get away for a little bit. I'm not sure if I will be able to work it out or not. If I don't do it now I am going to sometime soon.

I think about you so much Charleston; you inspire me in so many ways. I am overcome with love for you. I'm going to be fine and I know that. I've been tested in a number of ways but this time I will not fail. I love You! Love, Talle

GETTING CAUGHT UP!!
August 2, 2005
I can't wait for you to thank me too when I return, but I don't know why... My favorite line was "I just want to jump on you and give you a huge hug and lots of kisses!!! You're in for it when you get back!" Just picturing this is exciting. Oh, and its like a surprise or a present I can't open yet because I don't really know what I'm in for when I get back. I mean it could be anything. I love this line whoever wrote this line is perfect. So what's all this about depression because if I got to look in the mirror everyday and see you I would be like damn everybody look out!! I was talking about you with another friend of mine, who has not met you. He asked to see a picture and he thought you looked like some Eastern European supermodel with the really high cheekbones and perfect facial features. He said I looked like your draped mannequin just filling in. I was like please. I had to bribe her to take the picture with me. *(Photo 2)*

Ooh an iPod you should go to my house because then you can load songs from my play list. This is really a good gift, but now that's one less thing that I get to buy for you which sucks. My mother should have left you with the keys to my house and if not you should still be able to get in through the garage door. This is very exciting. Let me know if you go.

When I read *Papillion* I immediately wanted to read it again. The book left me with a feeling of wanting to take advantage of my life. The Journey is so inspirational, how someone in the midst of such dire circumstances can be so hopeful as to never give up. Never become depressed. Always keep a positive pro-active mindset. He really must be an incredible man. I know for certain that you can choose your emotions, which would make me think that there must be something that you want to be depressed about. Well, I don't know what that would be, but I do know that whatever test you are talking about doesn't exist. I love you and that is all there is too it. I choose you and no one else. Although I can't say that is very difficult given I am floating in the middle of the ocean with mostly men.

"I've been tested in a number of ways but this time I will not fail." I am curious as to how you have been tested previously, but certainly please don't think there is any possibility of failing me. You do whatever you want for you and if you want my opinion on something I am more than happy to give it. I don't need you to do anything for me, well except dance. I need you to dance with me. Ok one thing, but I don't even need you to dance well, just with me.

I would say that I miss you a lot, but I don't think that is the right description. I feel like I have you inside me. The more I think about you the more I love you and the more you take over my heart. Every day we had together only got better. I think the last night we were at Sonny's was my favorite. You were so alive. I just can't wait to spend more time with you. I finally got my address.

1st Lt C.G. Thompson, USMC
2/1 Wpns Co SSP
Unit 40210
FPO AP 96610-0210

I love you my sweetheart, so say we won't part. I'll see you tomorrow, so please no more sorrow.

Goodnight, Charleston

August 2, 2005 – Charleston,

I'm really excited about loading songs from your play lists! I hadn't thought of that. I love your play lists – Yeah, I'm excited! I have your room and house keys so if you need me to do anything just let me know.

I guess what I mean by tests, are things that challenge me to stay focused and keep a positive outlook. In the past I have not dealt with problems in a proactive way. I was easily depressed and was given medication to get myself out of it. During the past two years I have been learning a lot about myself. I decided I wasn't going to allow myself to react to problems the way I had in the past. I also built up a lot of strength, but with your departure, stress from work, my toe, the car accident, and the surgery my strength has been tested. At first I was really proud of the way it was going. The past couple of days however have been harder because I have had so much time to think. I did pull myself out of it quickly and things have been better since. I learned what I have to do to stop it. I won't let myself go down that path again. It was just scary because those feelings were very strong.

My favorite day was our shopping day. I loved your enthusiasm and dedication to finding exactly the right pair of shoes! Even though we did not have time for it you still made it a priority. I was so impressed! Not to mention, excited about future shopping trips!

Oh, Charleston, I love you! Every time I think of you I am filled with so much love! I also choose you, but I am not floating in the ocean!

I love you!

Love, Talle

August 3, 2005

I wanna kiss you all over. All over again...

My Medication
My pictured dreams
how much I've seen
of you in spirit.

I long and cherish
to be foolish and garish
with you forever.

You are sweeter than sin
and temptation will win
every time you test me.

I can not resist
with you I'm in bliss
hot tempered and sweaty.

Your delicious energy
is going my way
to nourish this longing.

I feel parched and thirsty
waiting for this end at sea
to satiate this need

I want to drink you up
straight from a cup
and feel sparkling light
in this heavenly night.

Shoe shopping 2006 I'll be there.
Love, Charleston
August 4, 2005 – Charleston,

Thank you for another beautiful poem! I love it! I read the others all the time. They mean so much to me! I love you!!!

I hope you don't mind but I let Camilla borrow Kelly's wetsuit yesterday. I went to Oceanside with Camilla, Hunter, and their friend Justin. They went surfing and Camilla tried it again. She had a hard time because of the type of board and because there was not enough wax. She tried though, and I did see her stand up a couple of times. I would have liked to try it again but I still had stitches, so I couldn't get my hand wet. My finger is getting better. I got the stitches out today. I still don't have full use of it but it is getting closer. I am going back to work on Monday, hopefully it will be in good shape!

My friend Michelle and her husband are taking me out to dinner tonight for my birthday. We are going to Downtown Disney. I'm sure being there will bring back some exciting memories!!! Oh, I saw *Wedding Crashers*. It was hysterical!

How is your fungus? Has it gone away yet?

I hope everything is going well. Take care of yourself. I love you very much! Love, Talle

HAP HAP HAPPY BIRTHDAY! IS IT BELATED NOW?
August 5, 2005 – Talle,

Unfortunately my fungus appears to be hiding, but I don't doubt that it will show itself when I least expect it. I'll get checked out again next week. We've had a pretty fun week. My Marines did fast rope training, which is a technique we use to deploy troops from helicopters where they can't land. We had to start with sliding down ropes on the stern of the ship about 60ft. After that, we practiced out of helicopters hovering above the ships flight deck. Fear factor rises when the helo drifts off the flight deck and your looking at a 140-foot drop into the water. My marines don't tend to have a problem. I think they were competing to see who could injure themselves the fastest. The next day we did a helo shoot out of Huey's, which is not the safest helicopter. One of our forward air controllers (they are pilots attached to the battalion to coordinate close air support) told me that during his last deployment a Huey took off and the tail just fell off crashing the bird killing 4 Marines. We flew about 10-20 nautical miles in front of the ship. When we were in Hawaii we bought all these beach balls to shoot. We blew them up and then threw them in the ocean. The Huey would circle around, so we could have target practice. This was hard as hell. I couldn't even see the beach ball let alone shoot it, too many moving parts. When I actually saw it the plane was already flying by. The flight was really cool though just blue everywhere you look and there is nowhere to land except the ship. The weather is very erratic as well with patches of rain clouds and white squalls everywhere. The views are powerful.

I am jealous that you and your sister went surfing. Did she take as bad of a beating? Oceanside is more for short borders than long. She should really go to Oldman's in San Onofre and work the white water. Once she masters the white water move out. If it was a foam board and not a fiberglass or wood that would make a big difference. If she is renting than she should rent a good used one with lots of wax. Surfers are all pretty friendly, so best way to learn is to ask someone to teach you. I don't think Camilla would have a problem with people accepting. I hope that you can hit the waves soon. No worries about the wetsuit. I am glad that you have been to my house. Did you download any songs? Is my car all right? Steve Mitchell was going to check in on it. If you need to borrow it go ahead. Speaking of cars, I don't know if this would help you, but we have GM and Ford dealers on ship that sell vehicles at a discount to the military. I think you buy it without tax or something since we are on a boat in the middle of the ocean. I haven't really looked into it. I think the catch is that it takes a while to deliver, because it comes straight from the manufacturer; however, with some cars you can save like $9,000. Did you decide what type of car you want to purchase yet?

Ooh how is my cross? Now, you know that if you wear it you can't be sad. I've had that cross since I was sixteen years old. My mother gave it to protect me from evil. With the exception of my time in the Marine Corps I have worn it everyday of my life. I entrusted it to you, so I would know you were safe.

I read an article about Australian Riesling Wines. If you can find them you should try Jacobs Creek "Reserve" 2003 and I'll have to find the other one. Ok I'm writing too much. I'll save it for later. Love you have a fun night. Charleston

August 5, 2005 – Charleston,

I'm glad you had a fun week. It was nice hearing about what you are doing. I'm not too excited about the problems with the helicopter though.

Maybe Camilla and I will go surfing again and rent boards. Hunter and his friends all have short boards. I would like to do it again and I know Camilla does too. She didn't get any bruises; she's not as klutzy as her big sister!

Your house is great. I don't know if that guy came to look at your car or not. He didn't while your mother was there I know that much. If you want me to do anything with it let me know. I went back today and downloaded some music. Thank you for that idea I'm really excited about it! Your cross is doing well. It gives me strength when I wear it. It means a lot that you entrusted it to me. Your mother has talked about it a couple of times. She knows you took care of it but she doesn't know what that means. I wasn't sure if I should tell her I have it, so I didn't say anything.

Thank you for the wine suggestion. I will look for it. As for the car situation, I still don't know what I'm going to get. I'm concerned because I don't want to get taken advantage of. I don't really know what I'm doing. The military discount sounds great but how would it work? Also, I have to buy the car as soon as I get the check. I need to get out of my rental as soon as possible.

We didn't end up going to Downtown Disney last night. We

went to The Chart House in Newport Beach instead. It was really nice. They bought me a season pass for Disneyland. They have them as well, so we will be able to go together. Or I should say, Michelle and I will go when Mike doesn't want to.

I called Janet today to let her know I was coming back to work on Monday. I asked how Nordstrom was doing. She said, "The store is fine. I am really excited for your return though." I'm not quite sure what that means but it didn't sound good. We have inventory next week and my team is probably not ready at all. This sucks because inventory preparation is tedious and boring! Betty got paid extra to manage my department while I was gone. I really hope she did something to get started on the preparation. Starting back at work is never fun!

My mom called while I was writing this. She sends her best. She says she thinks of you all the time and prays for you everyday.

I'm glad to hear things are going well. I'm going to take a walk. It is a good one. There is a big, long hill at the end. It really works my ass!

I love you! Love, Talle

*

INTRIGUE
August 6, 2005 –

A heated debate ensued over wedding proposals. Unfortunately I live with a lot of married or soon to be married pansies. Remember the proposal at the Eiffel Tower while I was in Ireland. We couldn't agree on how best to execute a romantic proposition. Proposals are tricky. Should the female have a say in the moment or should the whole proposition be a surprise? If she does have a say in the scripting of the moment does it somehow diminish its' spontaneity? Should spontaneity even be a goal, if it leads to an impulsive expression of love? What if the result is a contrived "proposal type" event: hot air balloon, Eiffel Tower, fancy dinner, etc...? While this act may be spontaneous, without detailed thought it lacks personalization. Yet, you can't personalize without a woman's input, which would then also make the moment contrived.

How do we balance spontaneity with creativity and personalization with excitement? A proposition is a profession of love. We are articulating our love and commitment in a single gesture. Each man's expression of love should be as unique as the love itself; therefore, prepackaged gestures are not preferable. He must take a risk, creating a personalized moment not from her input but with his insight. He is gambling his knowledge of his love and risking disappointment if she visualized it differently.

Do most women fantasize about their proposals as much as their marriages and have them perfectly scripted? We assumed that most women had a location or locations in mind. Where would those be, obvious places of romance, or constructed moments from imagination? Second, Would they rather have their vision fulfilled or be completely surprised with an artistic gesture from their suitor? Your opinions are welcome. Whose moment is it anyway the proposer or the proposee?

Enough of that, I have many more things to discuss and poetry to share. So take a seat while I prepare a treat. I can't stop rhyming! I feel like it's "the wave of the future" in my head.

No Victims Here
Aah the satisfaction of sweet torture
ignites a burning pleasure of conflagration.
Souls are soldered in fires of rapture
giving great strength for our salvation.

This spawns the smile that lurks with delight
yearning to be battered bruised and beaten.
For your love is the hammer and sword that smites
and I can't wait for that wonderful feeling.

Desecrate my heart for I will grow stronger
Make your love be my instrument to provoke
I desire to share deeper and endure longer
become a force hardened without revoke.

I have no confusion or mystery
about what is done and doing
you are my own definition clearly
a choice I make without feeling.

Be your worst and never stop.
For victims we are not!!

I love you, Charleston
Ps. the second wine was "Leeuwin Estate Riesling Art Series
2003."
August 6, 2005 –
Why is it so unfortunate that you live with these married or soon to be married people? And why are they pansies? I think it is very nice that you live with married men! First of all, I don't feel that women need to have a say in the location. I think the person proposing should decide. They should decide how and where to propose. You ask whose moment it is and I have to say it is the woman's. Isn't the proposer trying to come up with something that will create a magical and memorable moment for her? The objective seems to be to make her happy and obviously say yes.

Second, yes, most women fantasize as much about the proposal as the wedding. Many probably do have it visualized. As an adult, I have not done this. I can however remember what I thought about as a child. It's funny, but I'll tell you anyway. I always pictured myself standing on top of a hill surrounded by rolling green hills. My "prince" would come riding up on his horse and ask me to marry him, and we'd live happily ever after. Since then I haven't given much thought to the how or where, I just hope it will be from the heart.

To answer your other question, I think most women would rather be pleasantly surprised. I think it means more that way.

I am amazed with the way you create poetry. Does it take you a long time, or do you just sit down and start writing? This one is more complicated, and honestly I'm not sure I completely understand it.

I learned how the wonderful car business works today. My first experience almost became my last. The man was so condescending I didn't know what to say. He wasn't that interested in dealing with me anyway so I just left. Luckily, the second guy was great and I got my confidence back. I wore your cross to give me strength! I went to a few other dealerships and got some ideas. I'm still not sure what I'm going to get but I'll know by the time I have the money.

I love you!

Love, Talle

August 6, 2005 –

I did not intend to upset you. However, married or not they are pansies because I don't know how much choice they had in the matter. I fear that most of them caved or will cave to convention, which brings up another point. This is true from my personal experiences. Women demand timeliness when it comes to such matters. The considerable planning of marital events concludes that certain deadlines must be met. Many women believe in a specific time: a time for a career, a time for marriage, and a time for children. They have broken their life down into these discrete blocks, which not only set unrealistic demands on themselves but also the people around them; thereby creating convention. The effect is really no different than a goal oriented individual, who doesn't meander through life. They are focused and certain, which is understandable but adds unnecessary pressure. This was a contentious discussion. Most of my roommates feel that they must satisfy these demands before their time is up. Many had to commit because the clock ran out. I don't think this diminishes their love just elucidates the pressures of social convention.

Would you agree that such demands exist? Do you think that the deadlines are relative to the individual or are uniformly accepted as some cultural norm? What would those times be and how do you think it affects people of our age?

I also have a lingering question about the previous topic. I agree that the moment is about the proposee given that she is the focus of attention. Wouldn't this indicate then that instead of the proposer masterminding some vivid moment he visualized in his head, he should construct the moment she has in hers? If the purpose is for her to say yes then would she not be entirely more agreeable toward something she expects. Expectation gives her that comforting and reassuring feeling of familiarity. The conclusion determines the creator. Under these circumstances wouldn't she serve better to be the creator and he just the executor of this proposition?

Please excuse this outpour. I hope this is not hostile, more playfully curious. You are an honest and unbiased source for these questions. I wouldn't dare nor want to ask some other source on these topics, so I hope that you will not be upset with me asking. Obviously my mind carries downstream when not gainfully employed. On another note...

All inventions require purpose. They must have a reason to be created. Without that purpose life cannot swell into them. Even poetry must have a purpose or muse, for albeit modest it is an inventive use of words, a creative manner of conveying emotion. Since my poetry is emotion, ideas of feelings, my mind tends to mess it up. I don't spend much time thinking about it. It is instinctive to a degree like when you feel compelled to hug, but I absolutely can't force it. I have to have a reason to write. I have to have you. You are my reason. The greater and deeper my feelings are for that reason the more lucid those emotions and feelings become. Once I can clearly see what I am feeling then I simply have to bring pencil to paper. The hard part is that sometimes the emotions are overwhelming and I begin to write without clearly seeing first. This happens quite often and although heartfelt the results are messy. Nonetheless, I could not write at all without you...

I would recommend against buying a car from a dealership, especially if they treat you poorly. If I can help, let me know.

Love,

Charleston

August 7, 2005 –

I agree that those demands exist. Honestly, I feel them myself. Growing up I had a timeline depicting my adult life. It wasn't all that long ago I realized it was not going to work out that way. You are right about the blocks that people put their lives into. I think the pressure comes from our culture. I came up with my timeline based on what I witnessed growing up. How old my family members or friends were when they started their first job, got married and had children. Things I saw in movies or read in books. There is definitely pressure to get married by a certain age. I understand what you mean about people caving into convention. People are so consumed by this that they rush into marriages with the wrong person just so they can have the comfort and security of the marriage. I think it may stem from cultural pressure more than individual preference. My Iranian friend Niki is 28 and has been married for 5 years. People ask her all the time why she hasn't started having children. She wants to have children but she is not ready. No one can understand. She's been married long enough and she is not getting any younger. "It's only going to get more difficult the longer you wait" most people say. She has this constant pressure because she was brought up differently. She still feels like she is too young to have a baby. Even getting married at such a young age was very controversial, but she truly stands her ground despite conformity. I'm proud of her, because even her husband pressures her. There is an enormous amount of pressure to do things in a certain order, in a certain amount of time, and if these are not accomplished a lot of people feel inadequate.

About proposals: Since a lot of women have it planned out in their heads they may want it to happen that way. However, I have two points: One, how is the man going to find out what her fantasy is? If he openly asks her and then does exactly what she envisioned, there will be no creativity on his part. He won't put any thought into it. Two, I think women have a vision, but they secretly hope it will be exceeded. Their vision will be fulfilled, but something more will be special or unique to the proposer. Oh, and I am certainly not upset with you for asking me these questions!

There was a really good sermon today at church. It was about fear and taking risks. It made me think of you. He spoke about the things fear makes us do such as: be sarcastic, stubborn, and shortsighted. He said, "When you're afraid you cannot imagine a better life than the one you have." I thought that was a good point. He also talked about how to take wise risks.

It was all relative to my life. It goes along with many of the things you and I have discussed.

Well, back to work for me! I'll let you know how it turns out.

I love you!
Talle

*

BACK TO WORK
August 9, 2005 – Charleston,

The transition back to work went smoothly. Although, the night before I felt like I was preparing myself for my first day back to school. I wasn't crazy about the way my floor was set, but that was inevitable. Merchandising is my favorite part so it will be easy to fix. Betty did a great job getting ready for inventory. I have to say I was pleasantly surprised. Nordstrom promoted some people while I was gone. Marianne was promoted to Studio/ Facconable, which means we share a cash wrap and her desk is next to mine. It will be fun having her around. The TBD manager left the company. Her desk was also in the same stockroom. Julianne took her position. She is the girl that I was friendly with until she met her boyfriend. This will be interesting! Other than that I'm trying to catch up on e-mails and paperwork. Business is still suffering. However, I'm optimistic about this month. I think we can make it!

I'm going to see *Charlie and the Chocolate Factory* with Michelle right now. I love you!!!

Love, Talle

August 12, 2005 –

My sister sent me a picture of us. You look so beautiful. I think of you everyday. I love you too much. *(Photo 5)*

Love,

Charleston

August 12, 2005

I love you too much too!

I'm going to a wedding tomorrow. It's for my friend Houri. I was her assistant a couple of years ago. It's all the way up in Glendale but it should be fun. I wish you could come!

My grandmother, Granny, and husband, Al, are coming into town on Sunday. Aunt Mindy is having a gathering at her house, so

Camilla and I are heading down for the day.

I have been doing my finger exercises and have gotten excellent at bending. I think all of the bending left it in a permanent bent position. Now I have to wear this contraption that clamps onto my finger keeping it straight. I have to wear it for a couple of hours each day. It is awful! It hurts the entire time it's on.

My mom has been listening to her Les Miserables CD. She wanted me to thank you for making it and tell you that she loves the music.

Work has been keeping me busy. Inventory is on Monday. It will be a relief when that's finished.

I hope you are doing well. I think about you all the time and wonder what you are doing. It's been a month, but feels like one of the longest months of my life. I think it will go faster now that my life is back to normal. I just can't wait to spend more time with you! Take care of yourself!

I love you!

Talle

DANCING

August 14, 2005 –

You would have been proud of me last night! I attempted to dance! The wedding was interesting. Houri is Armenian and Ari is Mexican. The ceremony was in an Armenian church so the service was given in Armenian. It was interesting to watch. It was actually easy to understand what was going on without understanding the words. The reception was beautiful. They served so much food! The tables were already set with different appetizers, a bottle of wine, and a bottle of whiskey. The servers continue to bring different appetizers until the bride and groom arrive. I tried a few of the dishes. I had hummus and some potatoes with chicken and beef. I could not bring myself to try all of if it, especially the raw beef!   In between each course everyone dances. They played both Armenian and Mexican music. I have no idea how to dance to Armenian music, but Houri's brothers were trying to get everyone on the dance floor. I decided I would try. I didn't know any of the other guests very well so I didn't care if I made a fool of myself. Houri's brothers and her best friend tried to teach me some moves but I am hopeless! I started to get it towards the end but it was tough! It's a good thing I am starting dancing lessons soon! I had a really good time. I'm glad I went even though my date, Michelle, bailed on me.

Camilla, Hunter, and I are about to leave for Aunt Mindy's. Granny is very excited to see pictures of you! She has heard so many good things about you from my family. I'm sure she will have tons of questions. I'll be happy to answer because I love talking about you! I could talk for hours about the amazing man that I love!

I love you! Talle

August 14, 2005 – Talle,

Wow! I am so excited to hear that you were dancing. You are amazing!! Bad dancing doesn't exist; as long as your heart is in it and you are having fun, then you are doing it right. You'll have to show me some of the moves that you learned. I love different cultural dances. I am very proud of you, but for more than this. I love you so much. The bottle of whiskey sounds enticing. What a festive wedding! Armenian and Mexican is a good mix. I am sure their life will be filled with a lot of energy. We are disembarking in Australia today. I will be training for the next couple days, but will call you as soon as I get a moment. I love you very much. Enjoy every minute with Granny.

God bless, Charleston

August 16, 2005 – Charleston,

I am so glad to know you are in Australia! I can't wait to hear from you!

I had a very nice conversation with Granny. I showed her some pictures of us and she was very impressed. She's happy because she can see that I am happy.

Brian was so much fun! He was so much more interactive than ever before. He bonded with Camilla and wouldn't leave her alone. It was very cute! I could watch him for hours. He is so entertaining.

Inventory is over which is a huge relief! Now I can concentrate on my business. I'm still optimistic about this month. I know we can pick it up!

I hope your training is going well. I hope to talk to you soon.

Take care of yourself!
    I love you! Talle

PHOTOS
(Photo 1) Picture of my platoon as we were pulling into port in Hawaii
(Photo 7) Picture of training area on fire just south of Darwin, Australia

August 20, 2005 – Charleston,
    Thank you for the pictures. You look really hot in the picture of us!!! I love it!
    I'm so happy you were able to call. It was wonderful to hear your voice. Whenever I talk to you or read an email from you I am filled with so much positive energy. It is such an intense feeling unlike anything I've ever felt. It makes me cry but at the same time I have a huge smile on my face. The tears come from the overwhelming sense of happiness that you are a part of my life. I thank God every day for bringing us together. YOU are perfect! I love you with all of my heart!
    I need some time to think about the things I have to have in my life. While I'm thinking you need to do the same. It's just as important to me that you get everything you need.
    Take care of yourself and be careful. I love you!
    Love, Talle

BACK UNDERWAY
August 20, 2005 – Talle,
    Did you get the photos I sent you? I love you so much. Please excuse the abrupt phone calls. I know that they were frustrating. This is the information my sister sent to me all very interesting. Tell me what you think. I am so excited for your classes. Let me know how everything goes. Don't forget what I asked you. I have a couple of favors that I need, but I feel horrible asking. If you think that you will have time then please let me know.

The Relationship Book – July 29th & February 18th:
"Palpable Magnetism"
    Together these two know how to charm the pants off people.

Part of the reason their relationship is so magnetic is its deep understanding of what others want. But, people are also just plain attracted to them because of the chemistry between them, which is magnetic itself and palpable. Can sense coming trends & even create them. This pair can be successful at anything they do. Leo I - Aquarius-Pisces love affairs can be deeply passionate but the couple also risks becoming dependent on each other or even falling into sex & love addictions. They could extend to drug use and become deadly. Both partners must be careful to stay somewhat objective and guard against excessive behavior due to such magnetic desire. Marriages & working relationships are especially favored here. Leo I offer THE emotional, financial, & moral support for Aquarius - Pisces to find success. Aquarius-Pisces can help Leo I mates discover their inner sensitivity and express their feelings more easily,

Strengths: supportive, charming, perceptive

Weakness: Excessive, addictive, cool

Best: marriage

Worst: love

Advice: You know what others want, but do you know what you need? Don't be afraid to show your feelings. Beware all addictive drugs.

The Birthday Book – July 29th:

"The Date of Cultural Assessment"

Strengths; observant, loyal, concept-oriented

Weakness: opinionated, clannish, restricted

Highly adept at sizing up the characteristics, potential, morality, & accomplishments of those around them. They are usually able to make very impressive predictions about the outcome of dynamic processing within their family, society or organization. They may contribute to stereotyping or prejudiced thinking due to the observations they make. They function well as organizers and event planners. They take great pride in their children, their mates, & relatives and place importance on social functions that involve the whole family. They tend to be particularly protective of their own conjugal unit and defend it against any threats. They are excellent arbiters in disputes. Due to exceptional group loyalty they may forget they are individuals of free will who need to be decisive in their personal lives.

Tarot - is Priestess – a spiritual woman who reveals hidden forces, and secrets empowering us with that knowledge. Health - over concerned with hereditary illnesses – usually convinced they are bound to a similar fate. They usually subscribe to the wisdom of a particular diet, sleep pattern and generally have a sound idea of health care. August 21, 2005 – Charleston,

Please do not ever hesitate to ask me for a favor. It would make me very happy to help you with anything. Just let me know!

This is interesting information. I've never seen the comparison by actual dates. It starts off really good. I like that it says we can be successful in anything we do and that we have chemistry that is magnetic and palpable! The addiction part is a little scary. I don't understand how the best is marriage and the worst is love. Shouldn't love be the reason for marriage? If we are a bad match for love, then how could we be good for marriage? I really don't get it.

I was surprised when I read the description for my birthday. I don't fit into the typical Leo molds but this was pretty accurate.

The small business management class starts tomorrow and I am going to petition to be let in. Hopefully it will work.

Let me know what I can do to help. I love you so much!

Love, Talle

HOROSCOPE
August 23, 2005 – Talle,

I don't know why, but I laughed after reading your reaction. I don't really understand either, about Marriage and Love. I would say that I am just as confused. I would have to see how they define both of them. Either way I love the description. You should really have faith that comes from yourself rather than a horoscope, but I don't think I could create a better description for the two of us. I even like the addiction part. I wouldn't mind being addicted to you. I think maybe that they simply prioritize four different types of relationships because they weigh Marriage, Love, Friendship, and Work. All of them are related and you can't really have one with out the other. I would presume that love alone with no commitment would be the worst because of the addiction factor. If we took addiction to be a great dependency, then I could imagine a love so magnetic that it would cause people to be insanely jealous. Like many addictions an element of control would develop because of the lack of security causing mistrust and fear. In other words the love alone would be too great to sustain the relationship and weaker people would quickly destroy themselves with the addiction; however, marriage provides insurance. It allows the couple to have the comfort and security without the fear of loss. Work and Friendship has a different element of dependency one that would probably have the possibility for flare-ups, but still without the craziness that love can cause. I would agree with your description. I think your misperception about not being a Leo is not entirely true. Leo's have a perception of being vocal or spot lighters, but I would say it more or less comes from their strength and grounding, which you have. I have always said that you have immense strength and a deep awareness, which is very Leo. I think you just channel your attributes differently. Question how do you interpret the "outcome of dynamic processing..." I don't think that I fully understand what this means.

I have two requests. One I have already asked in part. After some thought, please write three lists: Must Haves, Important Things To Do, and Topics To Learn. Then, write how someone could betray your trust and lose your respect. These last two are important because they set boundaries. You must be brutally honest with this information. I actually took the time this morning. I couldn't sleep and I woke up at 4 am, so I wrote them out. I divided the must haves in life and in relationships. You must really be honest with yourself, so please be as open hearted and as truthful as you can be. They are all very important. Must Haves should not conflict. Things to Do should overlap, because eventually that is all you have. Topics to Learn should match or be interesting to the other person, because then you can grow and learn from each other. I want to give you time to do this before I send you mine.

The second favor is shut down my cell phone. I have tried to send my deployment letter to Cingular Wireless, but the email given does not work. I was supposed to send it to Albra Askins (800) 444-

0500. I am enclosing a copy with this e-mail. If this is too much trouble then don't worry about it.

I am really excited about your class. I will pray that they let you in. You can always tell them I'll come for them if they don't. Jump off any piers lately...

I love you too much, Charleston

August 23, 2005 – Charleston,

The class situation has changed. I found a better class. It is a seminar that meets on five Mondays for three hours each. Each session focuses on a different aspect of small business management. It starts at the end of September. I am really excited about it! I went to the other class but it is not what I wanted.

I will take care of your cell phone tomorrow. I have your deployment letter.

I don't understand the part about dynamic processes either.

I started thinking last night about my list of must-haves. I'll need some more time to think about the others. This is sort of hard for me. These are important questions that I've never sat and thought about. To be honest it makes me nervous. I communicate better in person. Writing this to you is going to be difficult. I know it is important to you and it is probably a good exercise for me, so I will do it.

I had a very interesting day today. I was MIC for the night at work. My first call was amazing! A customer called because she was in the store last night shopping in lingerie and got involved in a situation. There was another customer being fitted for prosthesis. This is a very time consuming and sensitive experience. There is a lot of paperwork that has to be filled out for the insurance companies because they typically pay for the prosthesis. A credit card is required but the customer did not want to have her number on the form for security reasons. The customer that called me overheard the other customer at the register.

The prosthesis customer ended up leaving and not purchasing the forms. The customer called me today because she was upset that the other customer was unable to get her prosthesis and wanted to pay for it herself. I was blown away! It is not often that people offer to do such generous and selfless acts. Anyway, I was unable to let the customer pay for it because of privacy issues, but we took care of the situation and the customer got her prosthesis. I was just amazed at the kindness of this woman! I also got another good call complementing a salesperson. It is so nice to hear good things. In between all of this I was getting called non- stop because of bad people trying to make bad returns. It was a crazy day!

Camilla needs the computer so I will write to you tomorrow. I love you very much!

Love, Talle

*

MANAGEMENT
August 23, 2005 – Talle,

My e-mail did not go through yesterday, so I re-sent it today. I was disappointed because I wanted to hear from you. You should have received three e-mails in all, a letter, a platoon picture, and a deployment letter. Let me know if you didn't receive one of the three. I read an article in Men's Fitness today about depression. The recommendation made was to increase your intake of Fish Oil typically found in fatty fish, i.e. Salmon, and Tuna. I thought that was interesting because you don't really eat fish, so you probably have low levels of it. I would recommend trying some fish steaks because the texture is rougher and heartier or finding substitutes in vegetables, nuts or vitamins. If you wanted to it might be worth adding them to your diet. I also finished that book by Michael Gerber *E-Myth*. The book is about entrepreneurship, but it has a focus on small business management. I made a PowerPoint slide summary of the books main points. They might help you for your class. Did you get in? I will send you the slide show. I love you very much. God bless and good night.

Charleston
August 24, 2005 – Charleston,

I faxed your info to Cingular today. Everything should be taken care of.

Thank you for sending the PowerPoint. I couldn't get it to

open here so I sent it to work. I should be able to pull it up on that computer.

I kind of bought a car today. They didn't have the color I wanted so they are doing a dealer trade, but I did all the negotiating. It was a learning experience to say the least. I really do not like how the car business works. At least the salesman was knowledgeable. He was the first person I've worked with that seemed to know what he was talking about. I should get the car tomorrow. It is a Honda Accord. It's really nice! I'm excited!

Have you ever heard of K Adorable? I read about it today in W. These two guys started making their own t-shirts, which somehow became very popular. They distribute their t-shirts through a subscription. They make a limited edition shirt every month. You pay for the subscription for 5 months and every month you get the shirt. You never know what it will be and they are not available for sale. They also make tees that you can buy individually. They make both girls and guys t-shirts. I thought this was a really cool idea!

I hope you are taking good care of yourself. I love you!

Love, Talle

MUST HAVES

August 28, 2005 – Charleston,

Here are my lists.

Must-haves in life
Love
Companionship
Encouragement
Accomplishment
Family
Sunshine
Fun

Must-haves in relationships
Love
Trust
Honesty

Respect
Friendship
Affection
Attraction

Important things to do
Travel
Get married
Have children
Open a boutique
Help people
Try new things

Topics to learn
Skills to be a buyer
How to be a great leader
How to successfully manage my finances
The Bible
Politics
Dance
Yoga

How someone could betray my trust and lose my respect
Breaking promises
Cheating

> I love you very, very much!
> Love, Talle

August 28, 2005 – Talle,

I love you too much. For you I will do anything. Ask it and I will give it. You make my heart smile from reading this. Although I was a little curious about the "politics." I can't help, but think that maybe that one was influenced. However, the thought of it being influenced does bring a mischievous smile. Don't take this to be condescending, but I must complement you on your choices. You made me re-evaluate mine. We responded to the categories a little differently. These were the most unexpected; therefore, the most loved sunshine, fun, friendship, affection, help people, try new things, leader, the bible, politics and dance. Sunshine is so simple, but honestly very important to me too and can change the experience of a whole lifetime. Friendship, most people think is all you need in a relationship. I don't know if you need it to have a good relationship, but I know that I want it. I think the idea of having an equal is appealing to most people until they realize they are not in charge and that their mystery is taken away. A good friendship will last forever, but requires exposure which most people fear ruins attraction. I think it strengthens it. Helping people is at the root of my soul. Trying new things gives a great sense of adventure. Adventures are really invigorating, but more often than not they have to be sought out. A leader will always think independently and be principled. Personal principles are always admirable. The bible is never a bad choice and often well intended. Do you read any of it now? Politics is a way to help people. Dance is just as good as it gets. I once told my sister that I just wanted someone to dance with for the rest of my life. Now I just want you. I wonder if you hope as much as I do, because I hope that I match your choices.

Must have in Life
Exercise
Water
Sunshine
Freedom
Peace
Music
Books
Love
Innovation

Must have in Relationship
Choice – Particularly with regards to where I live, and Children: how they are raised.
Truth – Absolutely no secrets, requires thick skin and an open heart
Trust – Don't gamble or risk, should be complete
Respect
Partner – I imagine like your friendship, a partner in action, to share life's burdens, and social responsibility.
Affection – Intimate and open, passionate and animate.

Sacrifice
Acceptance - (Laughter) These two are how I define love. Sacrifice is how you communicate it.
Learn – From each other

Important to Do: I interpreted as a list of activities on a regular basis.
Surfing
Exercise
Sailing
Snowboarding
Horseback Riding
Traveling
Create
Cultural Arts
   Classical = Museums, Theater, Opera, Symphony
   Pop = Movies, Festivals, Dances, Concerts
Dance

Important to Learn
How to do...
Politics - History - Social Issues
    A way of helping
International Relations
Economics - Finance
Art: Paint, Music, and Fashion
Cultures - Lifestyles
Literature - Life

Thank you for responding. This took a lot of trust and courage, because I know it takes a lot of trust for me. I have now shared more with you about me than any person including family. I love you terribly. If you have comments or questions don't ever be afraid to ask me. If you need something tangible or emotional I will always give.

    Love, Charleston
August 29, 2005 – Charleston,

    I love you so much! Thank you for asking me to do this. It was very difficult for me but worthwhile. Thank you also for sending me your lists. It is so important to me that you trust me enough. I hope more than anything that I match your choices. You are absolutely perfect for me and I just hope you feel the same. I am so blessed to have you in my life. Thinking of you makes me feel so alive and you're not even here. I can only imagine what it will be like when we are together again. I dream of that day.

I love your list of important things to do. I thought about doing it that way. I definitely would have put snowboarding. I have always wanted to go sailing and I really want to go horseback riding. Everything on your list is very appealing. Choice is important in relationships. I hadn't thought of that. For must haves in life books and music are important. I would add them to mine. You didn't tell me a way someone could betray your trust or lose your respect.

I'm so in love with you. My feelings for you are very powerful; it is unlike anything I've ever felt before. I just think of you and smile. I can be having the worst day and I'll look at your picture or remember something you said and it all gets put into perspective. I hope that everything is going well on ship. Do you get enough sleep? What is the food like? Do you have much free time? I try to imagine what it would be like. I have so much respect for you.

Love, Talle

*

A LOT TO WRITE

August 30, 2005 – Talle,

Before I forget thank you for handling my cell phone. I really appreciate the help. I also wanted to comment on K Adorable. I think that it is a very innovative idea. I would definitely investigate its current success. From a business standpoint it is a very efficient model, because it limits and minimizes your costs. You don't hold an inventory because everything is made on demand and with a subscription they already have a clientele to service. I would be curious to find out how people have reacted to the idea, because I would presume that most people require seeing something tangible before they purchase it or they purchase it on faith, which works with name brands. Magazines are a great source of information. I love that you emailed me about this. I think that the same concept could be incorporated into other ventures with a specific type of clientele.

Have you ever considered studying fashion in France? Do you think that would help you in the end? Have you ever heard of the Sorbonne? Something to investigate if interested.

Besides my Marines, your words and emails are the only sense of happiness that I have on ship. My Marines are the only ones I care for anymore. I have seen enough of the Marine Corps and I will be forever ashamed of the officers. I have spent three years observing officers in action, and I have concluded that the enlisted Marines are the noble ones. They carry the true spirit and ethos of the Marine Corps, where most officers have only disguised themselves with it. I came into the Marine Corps for the principle, education, and discipline. In this world words have substance. They have meaning through their practical application. The principles have never met my expectations. I have rarely observed officers uphold the principles, which we are taught. This has been the greatest cause for my frustration since I have been in the Marine Corps. The truth is many officers are frauds. Marines are the ones who are held to the fire and expected to represent what is good and right. For the past 6 weeks I have witnessed nothing but cruelty, bickering, and a general lack of consideration. For the past three years I have witnessed gross displays of leadership and abuses of power. I am beginning to have a difficult time avoiding the negativity. I find that I am talking less, avoiding people, and generally keeping to myself. Everyone appears to be choking on his or her own bitterness. Except for those who have it the worst, the Marines reside beneath us when they should be above us. I could not bring myself to complain about my life on ship when it could be worse. The food, my bed, my lifestyle are good enough.

Before I continue I want to explain that this is difficult for me to explain to you. On the one hand I want you to know and be apart of what goes on, because it means so much to me that you are apart of everything that is me. On the other hand I don't want to share anything with you, because I have a martyr complex that will always compel me to miser my suffering. I couldn't ever bear that I added to the frustration or worry in your life. Even worse my pride would worry that you may interpret my desire for you to share in my life as whining or weakness. This would be unbearable. I love you too much.

Continuing, I will tell you a recent story. One of the great naval traditions (I am stressing the sarcasm when I write great) occurs when you cross the equator for the first time. Supposedly the ceremony dates back to the Vikings; however I have no validation of that fact. WOGs are people who are crossing for the first time and shellbacks have already crossed and run the event. I think it is rooted in pirate tradition because all the shellbacks dressed in pirate outfits. The experience at one point obviously used to be much worse, but now it has become a rather silly hazing event. Since it is a command approved hazing event (legally does not exist) they have to make it voluntary. I personally don't have a problem being exposed to humiliating or hazing activities. The event begins at 0400 shellbacks come barging into your room and drag you to the showers. They crammed about thirty of us in the bathroom wet us down and smeared all sorts of condiments on us: mustard, shaving cream, honey, ketchup, etc... Threw shredded paper to finish the feathering and had us sing a bunch of old pirate songs. It was rather funny. Next we elephant walked all throughout the ship singing swing low sweet chariot and ventured down stairs to the mess decks where we are served a delicious green bacon and black egg breakfast that of course we eat without hands. After I got Tabasco and Worcester sauce in my eyes and mustard in my ear canal. Oh come on not the ear canal!!! Up there it goes... I realize that Worcester burns worse than pepper spray and picked up my tray with my teeth and threw it at them. Everyone at my table followed suit. This only provoked the shellbacks to retaliate. Next we duck walked flapping wings up to the flight deck where we had a round robin of hazing events including getting dropped on my chin. I asked for it though. Continuing with the duck walking now with a guarded apple in your mouth we had a series of physical events constantly cycling through getting smeared with shaving cream and then hosed down with salt water. Finally the fattest man in the navy (pretty fucking fat!!) decides whether your day of sorority pledging ends. In truth I would do it again, but that is just my sense of punishment. I thought it was hysterical. Others didn't have the same opinion. They choose not to partake in the humiliation, which they were fully entitled. What bothered me though was that they were persecuted for it. Not in the bravado way of "Oh you chickened out," but in the completely disgusting way that it is a reflection of you as an officer for not participating (Bullshit!!). In any event what was a brief period of some senseless fun and amusement, officers turned into a regrettable event. Choosing not to partake quickly became an excuse to personally attack people.

Enough I can't write anymore on this subject to you. I love you very much and just taking this time writing you has made me feel much better.

I will continue on another e-mail.

Love, Charleston

*

A CONFESSION
August 30, 2005 – Talle,

There is something else that I want to share. I am confessing and this is the whole truth. Because of what you have written I don't want to misperceive you. I confide in no one, but you are an incredible person. I love you painfully and trust you. I must caution you, because I am not an easy person. If you are serious about what you say then I must warn you. A life with me would be full of passion without convention or attachment. While on the surface may sound appealing would be very difficult. My heart is too full and it tends to eventually overflow. The dangerous part is that I enjoy the overflow. I take in as much suffering as I can but I reach limits and then I have to let it go. I won't allow myself to have attachments and I have a tendency to revolt against convention. I will never just accept life. I have to create each day as much as I can. I think this would be very difficult for anyone to accept. I demand a lot from life.

You asked what would betray my trust. This is difficult and you may not like the response. In my natural state I will give everything and I do mean everything, but eventually I do have a limit. So, I would say someone who takes advantage or someone who allows me to give myself away. If I am not cautious I would sacrifice myself for someone I loved. If I let down my guard completely I would destroy myself for their happiness and be pleased to do so. Without thinking my love for you would only be bounded physically. For me to love truthfully I would have to have someone willing to sacrifice everything in return. I am almost afraid writing worried what you might think. In love I can only protect myself by having someone who is the same. This is the reason behind everything and probably would explain from where the "addiction" would come. I have never met someone who is capable of really loving selflessly, or at least loving me selflessly. I have had many people who have loved me greatly, but in the end they didn't love me. They loved how I made them feel. They loved the way I impacted their life or uplifted them. They loved how I absorbed their suffering and stripped them of it. But when I reached a limit they were never reliable. I could never trust them to return the love. In the end, I was alone walking down a one-way street. No matter how much I tried, no matter how much faith I had in them, they could never see it that way. They could never give up what they loved most, the idea of themselves. Now I have lost my innocence and am more guarded. I know their is a limit to people's love. They are capable of sacrificing only so much, so I don't expect much and I don't give much. I really wish to be able to give everything to you, but I don't know if you could say with certainty that you would not betray my trust. Knowing now what you "have to have" could you just throw it away? This is asking a lot. Isn't it? I don't intend to test you but I almost have to ask. I have to see how far I can go before I get burned out? Only one other time have I dived in without worrying and I almost drowned. I don't really expect as much as I desire a response, because I understand this is a lot to take in. I also don't know if you could even give a response. If you've never really given into yourself, then how could you know if you are willing to give it up? I would never have shared this, but you have never been anything but honest with me, more than anyone else. I could write more, but this is where I will stop. I hope that you do not take offense to the truth. I wanted you to know, who you were choosing to love. I can't expose myself anymore than this.

Love, Charleston

August 30, 2005 – Charleston,

This is definitely a lot to take in. There are some things I don't understand so I'm going to ask you. When you say you do not allow yourself to have attachments, do you mean to people? When you choose to be with someone isn't that an attachment? If you never make attachments how will you ever get married or have children? I've asked you before if this is something you wanted in your life and you said it was. Am I taking this the wrong way?

You are saying you would be willing to sacrifice yourself completely for someone you loved and that you need to be with someone who would do the same. I have two questions, one, have you done this before? I'm not asking for any other reason then to understand why you feel this way. And two, are you saying that both people have to be willing to sacrifice themselves for each other but neither one would ever let the other do it? Or that they really do sacrifice themselves.

You talk about limits. How are you getting to these limits? People pushing you to do things? People always taking and never giving? You say they were never reliable? In what way? I'm not really looking for specific examples I just want to understand how you were betrayed.

I guess what I really need clarified is that you say someone would betray your trust by allowing you to give yourself away. But you want to be able to give everything and have the other person do the same. How do you decide what is too much and what is not enough?

You are asking me if I could throw away everything I "have to have" to be with you. I feel like if I answer this question you won't take me seriously. I know how I feel. I know how I've loved in the past and how I received it. You are unlike anyone I've ever met and I know you know you are very unique. Maybe because of this you think I will end up the same as everyone else. Well, there are no guarantees in life, but I don't see it happening that way. I choose to love you no matter how hard it may be. I would risk everything to be with you. To me you are worth it. I appreciate your honesty. I'm sure that was not easy.

Love, Talle

Part Two

Communication is an imperfect medium. No matter how much we explain; our words are subject to misinterpretation. Even if we articulated perfect English, the biases we have color our understanding. We were beginning to feel the impacts of these imperfections and we wanted answers. We knew that we were in love, but we didn't know how we individually defined that love. Was it a selfless love serving each other or one of attachment and jealousies? Were we capable of selfless love?

Being selfless is an unnatural act. It is very difficult to exercise. We are often consumed with our own feelings, such as unhappiness, frustration, or uncertainty. These personal emotions can discolor the love shared. It can smother the magic and love inside us, yearning to come out. It can knock us off course. If we navigate with our instincts, then we can distinguish between what is real. We can do what is right for us; submit to the traditions, conventions, and principles that are ours; and be true to ourselves, so we can be true to love.

Love is like gravity. We are naturally pulled toward it. If we wish to love completely then we must totally surrender. We must face our fears and never hold back. We risk more by holding on then letting go. Our spirit knows the way, because God is always with us whispering. We merely have to act. Obstacles will always exist, but we must be bold. If we focus on the solutions, then we will find a way.

CONFESSION

August 31, 2005 – Talle,

First thank you for asking. I had hoped that you would ask if I
didn't explain thoroughly. I have no reason to hold back anything at
this point. I will explain each part as best I can. This is complicated,
but if your heart is open it will recognize the truth.

Attachment is the cause of most suffering and in relationships
tends to cause jealousy. I began my life as you did with loss. From that
loss I have learned to appreciate the burden that was stripped from
me. In many philosophies mostly eastern, I have learned many times
over the wrongs of attachment. I have learned the crippling affect
attachment can have over a person from living a liberated life. I have
experienced it in love and in life. Attachment at its root stems from
fear, mostly of loss. Just as you should not be attached to your life you
should not be attached to your love. I don't believe that you have to be
attached to a person to love them and I wouldn't confuse with
commitment. You can appreciate someone for all they are without
wishing control, or ownership. I would not allow myself to get
attached. I'm not saying that it has never happened, but I will naturally
attempt to remove myself from attachments. They are incidentals that
occur without awareness, but the ready mind will intercept them.
Attachments happen by accident. Love could only be an attachment if
you make it so. Love is a conscious decision, a choice. Marriage and
children are no different than any other choice, for which I will gladly
bear full responsibility. Why would I ever hold an attachment to
people that I could not nor would not control? Only God has
influence over their life and with that I would set myself up for pain
and anguish. No matter how sweet, this would not be wise. I can
love. Real love is selfless. This is the defining feature that I was
confessing. Most people do not comprehend the concept of selfless
love. Loving someone more than him or her is not inherent.
Attachments produce selfish love. The kind I tried to describe. It is a
result of loving how someone makes you feel or impacts your life.
People grow accustomed or attached to the feeling of love they have
been given. To give love means to hold no attachment, because there
is nothing to hold. Attached love serves its' self. It is not a love that

serves and sacrifices for someone, or something else. If you cannot see past yourself then you will not see past attachment.

In love you should chose to love someone that you can love greater than yourself and you should commit to someone who can love you more than themselves. This is true love, because a truly selfless bond is eternal. Selfish bonds only last as long as it serves their interests.

Please feel free to ask me any question.

I could and have sacrificed myself for someone I loved more than myself. I once thought that my love alone would be strong enough for them to reciprocate. I tried and lost myself. They did love me terribly, but in the end they could not comprehend what it meant to love someone else more, too much pride. Instead of breaking up with them, I could have continued, but what I realized recently was that I have never wanted that. I have always wanted someone on equal terms. For me and especially now I am only willing to love someone who can love me in return. This is my choice. Someone could choose differently, but I want both people to be willing to sacrifice themselves for the other. There is a catch though, because a selfless love could never let them do it. By letting them fully sacrifice themselves you would be sacrificing your love. Do you see the catch? This is why it is so important for me to know you and why I ask so many questions. To know what you like, what you think, what you feel allows me to protect you, safeguard you and love you.

A few people have pushed me to my limits. They asked for things that I could not help to give and maybe they knew that and took advantage. These people tend to be the cruelest. Most often it is people who take and never give, which is why I caution myself and question people. I try to prevent myself from giving too much before they take advantage. I rarely ask for anything in return, but if I do the truth is revealed. Typically I can see it coming in their mannerisms and words. Only to be reinforced with their actions later. I have had people who if they described how they felt you would think that they must be madly in love, but it was not with me. I am good in the mind and heart, but their love did not come from the soul. Only they can influence their soul and how it loves. Most people don't believe that they have control or maybe know how. They never even understood that they didn't love me. They couldn't fathom it, but they also couldn't fathom how to love.

Do you love God? Can you love God? Loving god is no different than loving a person. Love your neighbor as you would love yourself. Could you really be so full of love and yet eliminate the pride that comes with it? The selfish feeling is what traps people. They cannot control it. If you cannot love more than yourself than you can never love God and in truth you can never love? Love in his image. He gave everything without anything in return. He sacrificed all hoping that we would not betray him. People lack faith. They cannot let go and it all begins with attachment. The attachment is what leads to the betrayal.

I would have been betrayed far more times if I trusted everyone for what they represented. I have learned to understand and read people as best I can. I had faith in a few that I believed might eventually understand. They committed their hearts and minds, but could not commit their soul. I trusted them with myself to support my faith, but in the end they betrayed their commitment and proved my faith wrong. I must admit that it is not really me they betray. Do you think that you will not betray yourself? Are you so sure of your conviction? Do you recognize what you lose and willingly give it up? Can you even control it? When it comes down to it, people act no differently than animals. As if they were being cornered, a fight for survival ensues and their instincts kick in.

How much you are willing to love decides what is enough. For some people they are happy with small commitments and sacrifices. This is enough. They run into problems, which causes the work in a relationship. The "work" comes from the struggle of the individual. Each is not willing to submit to the other. If you are willing to submit completely then there is no struggle. If I am willing to give it all, then I want it all. If you want me to only give a little then I will only choose a little in return.

"I would risk everything to be with you," because I error with faith. Though, I will ask you to look at your list and think about this statement. Tell me what images pop in your mind. Those are your doubts. Tell me what you would be sacrificing. If you can do this and have a clear mind then you have more conviction and faith then anyone I have ever loved.

I hope that this does not upset you, because these ideas could be disturbing. Honestly most people would be deaf to them. I hope that you know I do take you very seriously. I have never shared this much before. Typically I try to filter my thoughts. With you I am sharing all because I take our love seriously.

I have faith in you.

Love, Charleston

August 31, 2005 – Charleston,

You say that you love me. Do you love me selflessly? Is that something that takes time or occurs naturally when you love someone? You have to test me and ask me questions to find out different things. You want to know if I can love you selflessly. I wonder how you can love me if you don't know if I can love you in the same way. I know that in your heart you doubt my love for you. I've always felt this way. I try to explain it but the words never describe how I truly feel. I know you have faith in me but you remember how much faith you had in others and they let you down. This is justified but how are you going to get past it? Can you? You will have to risk everything.

You ask me to look at my list and think about risking everything for you. The one thing that comes into mind is my family. I guess I don't know what you consider sacrifice in regards to them. I do not have attachments to them in this way. As much as I love them and want to be near them I have learned to live my life on my own and away from them. As for Camilla we both know that the other could leave at anytime. So, I will never be tied to any one place because of them. If you consider this a sacrifice I have already made it.

I cannot tell you what will happen in the future. I can tell you the way I feel right now. I have strong convictions about my love for you. I love you for who you are and I love everything about you. I love the way you think, even when it is difficult for me to understand. I respect and admire the things you do. I am an honest and forthright person. I don't have any hidden agendas. You can take my words as truth or as a hope of truth. I can't promise I wont let you down.

However, I never want that to happen. I've given it a lot of thought and I truly believe that if I were loved selflessly I could only love selflessly in return.

Love, Talle

August 31, 2005 –

Oooh in the wise words of a very sexy charismatic woman... You're in for it when I get back. Now, I have no other choice but to love you forever. I do love you selflessly and it is a choice so it takes no time at all. I had to explain all this to you. I hope that it did not trouble you. I couldn't afford for you to have any misperceptions about what loving means to me. I need you to understand. Free will is your ability to choose, but most people have trouble making a choice. I choose to love you consciously despite the risks. I never doubted that you love me. However, I was unsure how you defined love. I didn't know if you had the capability to love someone more than yourself. I am aware this isn't an easy task, but the result is that I will live my life for you and with you. Rest assured I know the sacrifice is great, so I could never request it. To let you down would be to commit a sin against myself. I just needed to know you were capable and willing. Now that I know you are willing, I will give my soul to you and no other. I have never been more excited than today. I wish that I could hug and kiss you.

You are a blessing, Charleston

September 1, 2005 – Charleston,

Thank you for explaining this to me. I know I had a lot of questions but I needed to truly understand. I appreciate your honesty. It helped to open my heart. I had to be honest with you and myself. It has not been the easiest couple of days. You gave me a lot of important information. A lot of it was new to me and took some time to process. I love you for doing it. It was incredibly brave.

You say that you will risk everything for me. When you look at your list of must haves do you have any doubts?

To see these words written in front of me fills me with so much hope and love. Know that I give my soul to you and no other. I will always love you. I wish I could hug and kiss you back!

Love, Talle

September 1, 2005

Not anymore... I really love you. I wish that I could have done this in person, but maybe it was easier this way, giving you space. I just want to state up front though that in regards to the division of responsibility in this relationship you have to be the talker during conversations.

Did you ever finish *the Devil Wears Prada*? What did you think? I've never read it, but I thought you might like it? I always have random questions for you that pop in my head then I forget to write. The repetition and drudgery of the ship makes you shut off your brain, so I am constantly forgetting things.

Love, Charleston

September 2, 2005

What do you mean I have to be the talker during conversations?

Yes, I finished *The Devil Wears Prada*. It was good. The boss was truly awful. The way she treated people was disgusting. It was well written and funny. I enjoyed it.

Love, Talle

*

HUMOR

August 31, 2005 – Talle,

I thought you would find this funny or sexist (*Article 1*). This is definitely Marine Corps humor. Another Marine sent me this. Tell me what you think. The funniest part about it is the contradiction, because all Marines are puppy dogs with their women.

Did you conclude whether you ever wanted to study fashion abroad, France? Would that help you? Have you ever heard of the Sorbonne? When does your class begin this September?

If it is not too much trouble I need you to open the door from the garage into my house. I have a good friend his name is Steve Mitchell. He may be staying at my house until Tim comes home. I told him that if he needed my keys he could borrow them. I gave him

your number to call you. Do you know if the utilities are still activated in the house? Thank you so much. I love you - Charleston
September 1, 2005 – Charleston,

This is a very funny article. It made me laugh. It was unbelievably sexist but I guess that was normal then. My favorite parts are: "Remember his topics of conversation are more important than yours." and "Don't ask him questions- you have no right to question him." Unbelievable!

I have always wanted to go to Paris. I never really considered studying there. I have heard of the Sorbonne. It would be an amazing experience. I'll look further into it. My class starts Sept. 26.

I will open the door from the garage today. I will find out about the utilities and let you know.

I wanted to comment on a prior e-mail. I understand where you are coming from in regards to not wanting to tell me negative things that you are going through. I tend to feel the same way. However, I truly want to know what is going on with you. I don't ask much because I don't want you to feel like you have to tell me anything. I know sometimes you are not able to. Good or bad I want to know. As much as you don't want to add worry to my life I don't want you to suffer. Nothing you say would ever be perceived as whining or complaining. Please don't hold anything back. I feel so much closer to you when I know what you are going through.

I have to say that was quite an experience you went through as a WOG! Who came up with such an idea?

I had a very unfortunate month in August, which following the fiscal calendar ended on Saturday. We were getting so close to pulling out of the hole. After Monday we were only down $70 for the month. The next three days killed us and we dropped to $3000 down. When we closed on Saturday night we had missed the month by $319! I was so disappointed, as was Janet! Honestly though, my girls tried so hard. I am really proud of them. Even though Janet wants me to coach them that this is unacceptable, and all they had to do was sell an extra $100 a person, I'm not going to. They worked so hard and I know they tried their hardest.

I love you so much!!! Talle

September 2, 2005 – Talle,

I can't believe that happened after three days!! You go through such misery constantly trying to reach these markers. I agree with you and I think that your decision not to scold your employees is very prudent. Whatever attitude you take they will take. As always I consider this a very difficult problem they put you in because they don't give you the liberty and free reign to fully correct it. Inherently Nordstrom's system appears to be inefficient. Don't you think the buyers should really take the responsibility? What is your plan? I think you should throw a party, because at least you'll have fun for the both of us.

A sexist article it is. I laugh every time that I read it. Please don't ever hesitate to ask me questions. I think that would torture me. My father once told me never to discuss personal business and I have to agree completely. I think naturally I am a private person, but if I care and trust someone then I will be open. I think that you've already experienced my compulsion to share everything with you. Sharing and learning from each other are really important to me. I love hearing about your day, work, things you read, etc... To be honest, I really want you to be involved in all aspects of my life, but I certainly would not want to push you into my life.

Only the Navy could come up with such a day of humiliation. Though it seems strangely similar to my knowledge of sorority pledging. This is a picture of "Triton and the men you have to bow down and worship to graduate." *(Photo 8)*

My sister studied at the Sorbonne. I am pretty sure that they just teach French and culture, but it is considered an exceptional school. They have programs that last for 3 months to a year. When our Internet actually worked I downloaded this information on schools in France for studying fashion. I am sure that a lot more information exists, but I thought that you might have an interest in doing something like this. I guess that I got bored. I am excited for your class in September. I wish that I could be there to participate with you.

I have another very serious question to ask you. What am I gonna do with you when I return? God, I love you. Charleston

Are you a design or fashion student? Do you dream of studying in one of the most fashionable cities in Europe? If so France is the place to go. You can take classes while experiencing firsthand the splendor of Paris. Visit the museums, admire the ancient architecture, see a fashion show, go shopping or just sit in a park and watch what may walk by, every aspect of your life in France will be a learning experience and helpful for your career in the field of fashion. There are many schools in Paris and around France that offer this experience to American students. Here is a list of a few and their links for further information.

CREAPOLE - www.creapole.fr

ESCOLES DE CONDE - www.ecoles-de-conde.fr

ESMOD INTERNATIONAL - www.esmod.com

PARSON'S PARIS SCHOOL OF DESIGN - www.parsons-paris.pair.com

September 2, 2005 – Charleston,

I don't like how the system works either. The buyers do take some responsibility however. My dress buyers are in trouble because their portion of the business is what's bringing everyone down. I had the number one increase in Orange County for Sportswear but my dresses were so bad that I couldn't even make my month. This is very frustrating! This is my plan for September. Everyday a new collection comes in I will print out a list of all the customers who have bought something from that line in the past three months. I can separate it by salesperson so each girl will call their customers to let them know a new group has just arrived. Next, I will have a contest for the girls from Tahari. Tahari is mostly suits, but classified as dresses. I will have a focus day and bring in additional styles from other stores for a trunk show with Classiques Entier, which is a higher end Nordstrom label. The trunk show will feature clothing samples coming out in the next three months. The customer will have the opportunity to pre-sell. Which means they can buy them before they come out in the stores. Hopefully all of this will help me this month. So far so good, but I probably just jinxed myself.

I love you for looking into the Sorbonne. I looked into it a little bit and your right about the language. It seems amazing. I'll look into it more when I have some extra time.

My cousin Jessica is in San Diego for the week. She is coming to stay with me tonight. It will be nice to catch up. I haven't spoken with her much since she moved to Chicago.

I love you so much! Talle

September 3, 2005 -

Oh! Isn't Jessica the protective one? Do you still have that bruise from Surfing? Have fun and make sure you do something wild and crazy!!

I can only say that I am blown away with your plan for September. You really must be Janet's best manager. This is a really good plan. I can only imagine what you could do with more liberty. Your employees must love you. I don't think that you could do anything to Jinx yourself.

Oh and yes you have to be the conversationalist in the relationship, so I can just sit there and keep my mouth shut...Look pretty you know the drill.

Love you, Charleston

September 3, 2005 – Charleston,

My visit with Jessica was uneventful. We had a lot to catch up on, so we talked for a couple of hours. We were planning on going out, but decided not to at the last minute. Going out is an everyday occurrence for her so I think it was nice just to relax. I made something to eat and she fell asleep so that was the end of our night. She was skeptical of you and a little bit condescending. She even compared our relationship to a troubling one she had a few years ago. I just let her talk because I didn't know what to say. I have Sunday and Monday off so I am going down to San Diego tomorrow. Jessica is staying with Heather and Kevin and the babies. I haven't seen the babies since Brian's birthday party. We are going to spend the day at the beach. It will be good to see them.

Today is Michelle's birthday. We are going to dinner and see *The 40 Year Old Virgin*. I've heard it is hilarious. Tomorrow night we are going to Laguna. I'm excited because she never wants to go out.

Oh, and I'm not sure about you just looking pretty, although you do, I don't think it's going to happen that way!

I love you! Talle

September 4, 2005 –

Hmmm. Skeptical and condescending doesn't sound good. I am sure Jessica is genuinely wonderful, but it is a pity not to believe in love. Magic exists inside everyone and you must treasure it. Guard it with your life, because the world will tear it away from you ravenously. Love is the source of that magic and without it we quickly become hollow. When the light goes out I don't know if you can get it back.

I know some people, who are unhappy with themselves have trouble believing. They thrive on misery and certify their reality with pain. Some even pride themselves on suffering and justify their feelings with ideas of worldliness or experience. They glorify their troubles, so that they never really experience personal pain. This over developed defensive position protects a person from pain, but also won't allow anything to be sweet. If they just let go of their world and realize that life is sweet, then they may have to confront the fact that they had a hand in their suffering. Most people find it very difficult to be held accountable for their actions. Most people don't want the responsibility. They would rather leave it to fate, destiny, or magic, but the only magic that exists is the magic we create.

Her reaction is unfortunate, but I believe deep down everyone recognizes the love inside them yearning to get out. Love is like gravity. We cannot help but be pulled in its' direction. No matter how much we fight it, we will always move towards love. If she is related to you, then I am sure she has a reservoir of love.

You cooked!! I can't believe it. What did you cook? Have fun with the children. *The 40 Year Old Virgin* sounds dangerously exciting. I hope that you two don't get into trouble. Save the trouble for Laguna. I'm glad that you are getting out.

What do you mean it's not going to happen that way? You are too late. I claimed it first...

I received your card yesterday. Thank you I was surprised and certainly not expecting a card. I was so happy to receive it. I was also told that we are done with 27% of the deployment. Some people have these deployment trackers, which is a countdown program that tells you by the second how much time you have left. I couldn't have one, but I get regular updates. I can't wait to see you. I wanted to tell you.

San Clemente has a really good Yoga class. I believe it is on Victoria Street. They do predominantly Bikram's Yoga, which is the hot one. I don't know if your heart would have problems, but it is good.

I love you, Charleston
September 4, 2005 – Charleston,

Don't get too excited. I only cooked macaroni and cheese! It was good though! The movie was funny but some of it was just ridiculous. Mike ended up coming with us. She considered that good enough of a celebration and decided not to go out tonight. This is not surprising but a let down nonetheless. It gave me more time to spend with my family. The babies are sweet! Chloe is not going to have the brain surgery that they were considering. However, they found that she has Brown's Syndrome. She cannot control her right eye and she sees double. She may have to have surgery to fix it. It is scary when it happens. Her eye goes way down in the corner. Heather did get out of the Navy and she is going to school for nursing. She is very happy that she made the decision to get out.

27%. That's pretty good! I miss you so much! I cannot wait for you to get back!

Niki and I went to a yoga class last week at the gym. We are going to go to this Introductory Yoga class this week at a place in San Clemente. I found a flyer for it right before you left at the Coffee Bean. I haven't been able to go because of my injuries. We don't really know anything about yoga so it was difficult to keep up with the class. We are going to go to this other class because they explain each move and make sure you are doing it correctly. I'm not sure about the hot yoga. It makes me nervous.

I hope everything is going well. I love you!
Love, Talle

*

HOUSE KEYS
September 1, 2005 – Charleston,

Has your friend already been to your house? Does anyone else have keys? Everything is fine, I'm just wondering. I unlocked the door to the garage and the utilities are still on. I hope this helps. I love you!

Love, Talle

September 1, 2005 – Talle,

I believe Kelly has keys, but she should be it. He has already been to the house. Can you believe that he said he found a dead mouse? Bloody rodents!! We didn't even have mice when I was living there. I will let him know about the utilities. Thank you. You are the sweetest moment of the day.

Love, Charleston

NAME

September 4, 2005 – Talle,

I need some unbiased advice. I'm having trouble deciding on whether I should change my name. In the last eight years, I have grown accustomed to using my current name. I graduated college, served in the Marine Corps, have bank accounts, credit cards, and own a house under Thompson. Despite this my last name has played a limited role in my life. Most people know me as Charleston. Superficially I guess that I don't want to deal with the hassle of changing it, but I don't want that to dictate my decision. For all the reasons my dad would want me to change my name I agree with him. I believe in lineage, tradition, roots, and family, so I can understand what it means. Ultimately, I identify with my father's name. This is my dilemma. I may not want to go through the process of changing my name, because I've had it for so long, but I feel compelled to do it. I know the process of changing it will be a massive headache, but my principles tell me I should. Does the headache of changing everything out weigh my principles? I feel that regardless of my desire changing my name is right. Of course part of me would like to avoid the situation all together. Keep my name, but pass on my father's to my children. I know this is not right either. I need an objective opinion.

Love, Charleston

September 4, 2005 – Charleston,

This is definitely a difficult decision. First of all I do not think you should keep your name and pass on your father's to your children. It is confusing and I feel a family should all share the same name. Has your father been pressuring you since you've been gone? Is there anyone who is going to carry on Thompson? Is that a concern? I don't blame you for not wanting to change your name. You've spent your entire adult life as Charleston Thompson. You made the choice to take that name. However you say that changing it back is the right thing to do. Do you think you will regret it if you don't? Not considering tradition, how important is it to you that you pass on his name? When you changed your name you must have thought about this. What were your thoughts at the time?

I love you so much!!! Talle

September 6, 2005 – Talle,

I am so excited. I received three exclamations with your enclosing!!!

No my father has not been pressuring me. He wouldn't do that. He has said his piece and left it at that. He will leave it up to me to make a choice. Honestly, I was thrilled and amazed that he said something, because I had been thinking about it for some time.

I care strongly about lineage even though growing up I never knew my father's father or even my mother's father. I hold a special place in my heart for a man that was a dear friend of both my parents. Holly Kiefler was my Godfather. I only knew him when I was very little. I can't even picture him in my mind, but some how I regard him with such love and respect. I feel it without remembering him. The stories that I have heard tell of a boy who followed him everywhere, dressed like him, and mimicked him. He represents everything that I admire. I only have my Godmother, who I adore like a grandmother, and pictures to remember him. Most of all, I feel like he gave me the opportunity to know glimmers of my grandfathers. How they would have been? How we may have interacted? I know that I would have loved them just as much. I know what they might have said if I asked them this question, and I know that this wouldn't even be a question if they were still here.

I believe in the idea of passing on a name from father to son. This is part of your placement in history without it you only exist in the present. My father and his father would die with me. Their history would end. Immortality would be lost. I could never let that happen. They are too important to me.

My thoughts at the time were very little. Charleston, as a name, almost stood on its' own and I hadn't spoken to my father in a couple of years. I was living with my mother at the time, so it basically became convenience. The Marine Corps was the first time my last name became meaningful. We rarely use first names. Everyone knows me as Lt Thompson, but Thompson is my mother's maiden name. I know in some cultures men carry on both the father and mother's name, but that is not my culture. My grandmother has 8 children. Three are boys. They will pass on Thompson, so it does not risk being lost. Even though I love my mother's family, Thompson doesn't hold special meaning to me. I value traditions and unfortunately or fortunately carrying on my mother's maiden name is not part of my traditions. I don't think that I would regret it, because it is not in my nature to doubt the decisions that I make once I make them. I love my mother and father. I don't want to hurt either one of them, but I have to do what is right for me.

I had to re-write this all because I lost it. I hate that. I have lost memory of what I wrote. If you can make anything from this I would appreciate it. I love you so much. Thank you for being so wonderful. I hope you don't mind. The only way that I can send home all my books are by sending them to you. Would you mind terribly unpacking them and putting them in my room? In a day or two, we will be offloading for a while to conduct training, so I will be out of touch. I love you. God bless.

Love, Charleston

September 6, 2005 – Charleston,

Do you think it might affect the future of your relationship with either parent? I don't think you should make a decision based on that but it would be hard not to consider. I know you don't want to go through the hassle of changing your name but you feel like you should. You should do what you truly want. I can understand your dilemma. I think it would be terrible that your father's name would not be passed on, but even if you take it there are no guarantees. What if you don't have a son? That is a possibility and it would have the same end result. Ultimately you are his son and that is far more important than a name. Of course I will support whatever you choose to do these are just my thoughts.

Send your books to me. I don't mind putting them back in your room. Is your friend living there? Does he have a key? He never called me.

I went to that yoga class tonight. It was so different from the gym class. It was extremely relaxing. While that was very nice it wasn't much of a workout. The class at the gym really was. I think I'm going to stick with that one. I'll get a book or a video and spend some time learning it so I can keep up with the class.

I'm really going to miss hearing from you. I hope it won't be for too long. I love you so much!!!

Love, Talle

September 7, 2005 – Talle,

Ultimately I know my parents will love me despite my decision. Thank you for the advice and support. I appreciate the help. I love you immensely.

He is not living there, but I think that he is going to borrow my car. He said that he would call you if he needs the keys. The Bikram's in San Clemente is definitely not exercise. The routine is good for relaxing though. I am glad to hear that you found one that you like. We were told the tentative plan for Christmas today. They are expecting to be in Hong Kong for 6 days. This could be interesting. I haven't been to Hong Kong since I was 8 years old.

We will be training in Egypt for three weeks, but at least this will give you time to you? I love you and will take you with me when I go.

Love, Charleston

September 7, 2005 – Charleston,

Three weeks. I will miss you very much! It will probably be nice to be off the ship for a while. I hope everything goes well. Take care of yourself and be safe. I'll be thinking of you but that's nothing new.

Is there anything you need? Please let me know if I can send you anything. I want you to have everything you need. Don't ever hesitate to ask.

Good luck with training. I love you with all of my heart.

Love, Talle

*

RESEARCH?

September 8, 2005 – Talle,

Thank you so much for the support. I can't tell you how much I appreciate your offer. Our Internet is horrible and I can't get done any of things that I had hoped to look into while away. I have some questions to research, if you have time. I am looking for a distinguished music school or program. My location preferences are San Diego, LA, or San Francisco. I would prefer a program length of 3 -6 months, but I would consider longer. The program has to offer classes on instrumental and composition for beginners. I would prefer a creative versus a traditional environment, but the quality of the teachers is paramount. The goal is to learn how to write and make music not theorize and contemplate. The last lead that I had was a school titled SAE? I didn't get to research any specifics or whether the school was even reputable. If you find one, I need to know what time of year their program or class dates begin and roughly how much they are charging. If you don't have time don't worry about it, but this would really help.

I was battling with my friends over another female topic. They didn't believe me and I am almost certain that it is true for some people. Have you ever heard that when females break up with their boyfriends they go on a rampage? I was told that for every month they were dating they would sleep with that many guys to get over their boyfriend. Maybe I heard it in a movie. I can't remember. I will miss you while in Egypt, but I still have a day or two. I love you so much.

Love, Charleston

September 8, 2005 – Charleston,

I will see what I can find for you. I hope you always know you can ask me for help. I am happy to do whatever I can.

I've heard that girls will sleep with as many guys as the months they dated their ex. I, however, have never actually known someone to do that. I've definitely seen girls go a little crazy afterward but never to that extreme. I've always been somewhat naive so it is possible that it was happening and I just didn't know. It doesn't sound like a very good idea.

I made arrangements to go home in October. I'm really looking forward to it. I haven't been back in a year. I'm most excited about the weather. I absolutely love the fall. I love the smell, the trees, and the temperature. Everything about it is so comforting. I also really miss my dogs. They are so cute! It will be great to spend time with my parents as well. I wish I could take you with me!

I love you! Talle

EGYPT
September 10, 2005 – Talle,

We will be offloading in Egypt shortly. I love you!!!

Love,
Charleston

HAVANA NIGHTS
September 10, 2005 – Talle,

Ok I am sending one last e-mail. I can't resist. I am watching *Dirty Dancing Havana Nights* while I wait to be called away. A little cheesy girl flick, but I can't resist. The music is really good. I don't care if you can't dance. I am definitely taking you dancing when I return. Beware we are going Salsa. I love you. I'll see you soon...

Love, Charleston

September 10, 2005 – Charleston,

I don't know if you'll get this before you go. I love you so much. Be careful and take care of yourself. I'll make sure I learn Salsa. I love you!!!

Love, Talle

*

GOOD DAY

September 17, 2005 – Charleston,

I just have to tell you about my day today. I had the trunk show I told you about it. I was really nervous because I already had a big day. Last year the department did $6300. I wanted to try to do $7500 but to be honest I would have been happy making last year. That is a ton more volume than I typically do on a Saturday. I ended up doing over $9000! I could not believe it! The trunk show wasn't that successful. I only got one pre-order. At least we got the customers in the store and they bought what we had in stock. I can't take all the credit. There was a cosmetic trend show that brought about 200 women into the store at 8am. I'm just so excited that the event went well!

I also have to tell you that I went to a dance class last night. They teach a different dance every week. I learned the nightclub two-step. It was so much fun! I went with my friend Mary from work. It was only the two of us and one other girl in the class. The instructor was a girl as well so it was funny dancing with each other. You are not going to believe what the instructor said to me. She asked me if I have ever done any dancing. I told her I had not and she said she was impressed! Can you believe it? I was amazed! We are going to go next week. I'm excited!

I hope you are well. I really miss you! I cannot wait to be able to talk to you again!

I love you so much!!! Talle

MEMORIES

September 21, 2005 –

I was just walking upstairs and I heard the song "I like the way you move" coming from Camilla's room. I was thinking that song sounded familiar and then I remembered why. It is used in a Coke commercial. I thought it was funny. It made me smile and think of you.

I love you so much! I really miss you! I hope you are doing well. I can't wait to talk to you!

Love, Talle

HAPPY

September 28, 2005 – Charleston,

It was so good to hear from you the other night. I love you so much!!! It was amazing to hear your voice! I got a letter from you the next day. It made me so happy! Thank you, it was so wonderful, I can't even explain the way it made me feel. I called your mother and she was so happy that I heard from you. She asked me to tell you that she loves you.

I went to my class on Monday. We spent most of it introducing ourselves, but I think it will be beneficial. We also talked about what it takes to be successful, and some of the advantages and disadvantages of owning your own business. I'm excited about it!

Work has been really frustrating lately. It's such a negative environment. The most influential people have such bad attitudes. It's impossible to get anything done that involves them. My business is so up and down and this is the last week of the month. If I don't make it I'm going to scream! I had a good increase and it completely dwindled away. It seems no matter what I do it never works. I'm sorry to complain to you. I go through this every once in awhile, I'm sure it will get better.

I hope everything is going well. You sounded great on the phone. I really wish you did not have to go to Iraq. Will you need anything? Let me know, I will send you anything you think you'll need. I love you so much! Be safe and take care of yourself. I cannot wait to hear from you again!

All my love, Talle

September 30, 2005 – Talle,

I just returned to the ship. I really love you and am so happy to hear that you are finding exciting activities. I was so happy to talk with you too. I really wanted to speak with you before I left, but I did not get the opportunity. I had such a great conversation even though you were initially confused curiously enough. I am glad that you finally received my letter, but I must admit that you would be intelligent to not listen to me sometimes. I am curious how would you explain the way it made you feel. If you were to illustrate it how would it look? I just received your box with my books. Thank you so much for the additional Paulo Coehle book. Have you read any new books? I would still strongly recommend *the Master and Margarita*. I have written you more so I hope that they do not take as long to be received. I believe that your negative environment and mine must have served some greater purpose. Or you and I were having sympathetic experiences. I agree completely about the negativity and you are right its inherent intention is to make actions impossible. I will always love to hear you complain, so please be forthright and don't hold back. If you can't vent to the ones you love then who can you vent, and besides I am assured that you are awfully sexy when you are angry. You are certainly not one of those women who with anger lose her sense of mysterious beauty and her frail conception of purity. For the glimpses of their anger are only the vein leading to a greater quantity of turmoil inside. Your anger is completely honest and innocent, which makes your shameful expression that much more appealing. I can see the blush in your cheeks mounting as you express your hostility towards your co-workers. Frustration is certainly a charm and not a fault. With every detail trivial or meaningful you give me more to love. Tell me anything you like or think. You are so sincere in your life. I admire all of you. Whatever limitations have been sold to you they have done so with the greatest cruelty for you are perfect. Your sadness, frustration, ambition, charity, love, and honesty are all equally beautiful. I don't see parts, because they are incomplete. Your true beauty is in the whole. Even in misery so much beauty can exist. I can only pray that you don't ever limit the amount of love you give me. Life is a dream forever, a symphony to play with diligence so that we may feel the music of our soul. The music elevates us from all that is base. The more instruments played the more complicated and passionate the music becomes. I would love to hear everything and dream so sweetly of you. This is how I would describe your words to me, music. I love you.

When you dance do you feel people watching? Do you feel like they might witness something entirely personal something so open that it could penetrate your core. Caught with your hand in the cookie jar. You feel like you are the light from out of the darkness. Do you feel bashful or do you feel liberated? Liberated people feel the surge of energy from moving to the rhythm of their soul. Greater forces exist in this world than what we see. Do you think that they see God existing inside you? God created you and exists in you. Should we hide what he has given us? He calls to us from the Garden of Eden, but we emerge clothed in shame. What are we if we are not ourselves? We are his instruments for his symphony. Dancing is natural to those who are honest and sincere. For these reasons I love it.

I carry you in my heart, Charleston
September 30, 2005 – Charleston,

I am so happy to come home and have an email from you! I'm sorry about the confusion when you called. I had just fallen asleep so I was not really conscious when I answered. Unfortunately it is not that uncommon. I could carry on a full conversation in that state but make absolutely no sense. The best part is that I think I make sense. Just a warning.

Your letter brought back so many memories of the little things that truly are the most important. You are amazing. The detail with which you remember things is unbelievable. I think about those things all the time and to know that you do too is comforting. It made me feel so loved. Don't think that I don't always feel it because I do. It was just that I hadn't had any communication with you until the night before. I really missed you and I was so happy to talk to you, and then get the letter. It was very emotional.

I've read some of the history book you gave me. I also started reading a book that Niki gave me called *Emotional Intelligence*. I just started but I will let you know what it's like. I have the Master and Margarita but I have not read it yet. I've been bad about reading lately.

For as long as I can remember dancing was a huge source of anxiety. I always felt that people were watching me. I never had confidence in my abilities or myself; therefore I rarely danced. I still have these tendencies. When I take classes I don't feel self-conscious for possibly a variety of reasons. The majority of the people are also learning. I am learning steps and not dancing freely. And, I have a partner. I don't know exactly why I feel less self-conscious. I do know I feel liberated in the class. Maybe that will stay with me in other situations.

I tried looking into a music program for you. SAE seemed to be more of a technical school. I looked at the LA Music Academy. It could be a possibility. I emailed someone from the national association of music education but I still haven't received a response. I will continue to search.

I love you!!! Talle

*

QUESTION
October 3, 2005 – Talle,

Painfully I still feel that I am soliciting your opinions and thoughts. Even though I am confronting you with this my intention is certainly not to upset you. Presumably I thought of this carelessly until today when my friend Tim sparked this thought. He asked questions about you in his email. Most of them I couldn't really answer. I didn't take notice; until my reply was that we are still very much in the early stages of our relationship. I was upset stating this, because I don't think it is true. I couldn't explain to him through email how I cared for someone so much but knew so little. His questions sparked my thought on this and I don't like it. I don't know your opinions on a variety of issues. I don't know what you think about on a daily basis. I know only through observation certain things you like and dislike, but I don't know why you like them. I don't really know what upsets you or makes you feel happy, except for on what I have witnessed and taken detailed notes. Today, I had the unfortunate feeling that you have shared nothing of yourself with me. I asked myself if this was my doing. If I have in some way discouraged you from sharing your thoughts and feelings. I don't feel like that is true, but this is a question that only you can answer. My goal has always been to make you feel comfortable enough to share. I have even asked you about issues that I thought would perk your interest. This question is probably better discussed in person, but not any time soon. If I have in anyway prevented you from sharing, then I have deeply wronged you and myself. You must see that knowing your thoughts, opinions, dreams, desires, experiences, memories, the total compilation of your personality is more important to me than anything. If you think for whatever reason you have nothing to say or write then you could not be any more wrong, because you presume what is insignificant to you is insignificant to me. This would be plainly cruel. Please think on this.

Love, Charleston

?

October 4, 2005 – Talle,

Did I upset you? If I did, then I must reiterate that was not my intent. I love you terribly. This you can be certain.

Love, Charleston

QUESTION

October 5, 2005 – Charleston,

I'm sorry I haven't gotten back to you. I've had a lot going on and I wanted to be able to devote my full attention to you. I am upset, but not at you. It breaks my heart that you think I haven't given anything of myself to you. I don't feel this is true, but if you do, then I have to do something. Let me explain. I'm not exactly sure when I lost the ability to fully express my feelings. I know that I somewhat have, but I wasn't always this way. There could be different reasons. I gave everything of myself in my past relationship and it was completely taken for granted. I suffered through a lot of pain but for some reason was to weak to change it. When I finally had enough and moved to California I started to put up walls. Everything changed. I became stronger and more independent. I never really thought about how that would affect my next relationship. Another reason could be how I feel I am perceived. For whatever reason people have always "taken care" of me. I was always the shy, sweet girl that people wanted to take under their wing. No one ever took me that seriously and as one of my friends told me last night- I am the type of person who always fades into the background. These things anger me because I'm not that person. I might have been that person, but I am not anymore.

Unfortunately people around me still see me this way. The point is other people have always dominated conversations with me. A lot of times when I spoke up and said something I was talked over. After a while I guess I decided I didn't really have anything that important to say. When I did decide to say something and I got the attention of the people around me, I would get nervous because I expected no one would listen. So, I would lose my train of thought and wrap it up quickly. I became a really good listener. It is hard for me to write this to you. I am so envious of your natural ability to openly share your thoughts and opinions. It is one of the most attractive things about you. It also makes me somewhat intimidated because I know that I don't do it well. On top of that I am not the best writer. So, my insecurities really come out when I try to do both. Charleston, you open my mind to so many new things. I want you to know everything about me. I am not scared of that. No one has ever cared enough to really know my mind. There are two things I want you to understand. One- I opened myself completely to you when I gave you my lists of must-haves. While that may not seem like that much, for me it was. Thinking about things and putting them down on paper are two very different things. It was a good experience for me; I had to let my guard down. I put in words things that are very important to me and I let you see them. You have to understand that was a big step. Two- I don't always know what to tell you. Nothing that I am doing compares with what you are going through. I don't ever want to seem insensitive. I understand what you are saying about assuming things are insignificant. I will consider that when I write to you.

I love so many things about you. You are thought provoking, intelligent, sensitive, sincere, intuitive, open, and honest. I want to be as open with you as you are with me. Please understand that I want that. It is not my intention to hide anything from you. I can only ask for your patience. You have done absolutely nothing to make me uncomfortable. You are perfect. I love you with all of my heart.

Love, Talle

I LOVE YOU!!
October 5, 2005 -

Whooo, now I feel a lot better. I thought you were torturing me with your silence. It was horrible. I was tried, committed, and sentenced to anguish in purgatory. It sucked!! You have to understand that I am wrong to imply that you have never shared any of yourself with me. I know that you have and you have never attempted to hide anything from me, because if you had, then I would have really pried. You just don't really divulge anything. I do understand how difficult writing those "must haves" was. I wrote down everyone. I think that you explain yourself perfectly and to be honest I can't help but smile. I feel that I understand you so much better now. You really clarified so many questions for me with this reply. Though you did lie to me...

Regardless, I won't be saying that I want to "take care" of you. I can't believe that you have been trying to be taken **seriously** all this time!! I am sorry for laughing. I do it out of love, but you are going about it all the wrong way. People never take women seriously, especially not beautiful women. I am certainly not trying to be chauvinistic. You need to understand your problem completely. I can't help, but smile because this is an easy one to fix. If you permit me I can show you how in person. But your explanation is right. The result is people talk over you, dismiss you into the shadows and take you for granted. God, I love you!!! You must realize now why I asked you to read the *Celestine Prophecy*. We have a purpose. I was just waiting for you to discover yours. If you are wondering, then you should know that your problem is not fixable. God made you how you are and you can't change that but you can work with it. You can't change that you are a beautiful woman and for many people that is a problem. Men rarely take beautiful women serious. However they can respect you. Women will either envy you or dismiss you. Keep doing what you are doing, except please let me know what you are thinking. I have a plan. I will ask your permission, but I believe you met me because you had changed or were trying to but had found that people were still treating you the same. I told you that you had a lot of strength inside you and this took a lot of strength to admit. This will take some time, but I promise no man will ever take you for granted and no woman will dismiss you in the end.

Oh and who gives a crap whether you write or express yourself well. I don't care. Besides, this just comes with practice. I have been practicing my whole life and I still suck at it. Mostly it is a matter of judgment, which comes with time. This is why you confide in people who love you because they don't criticize you. I do care that you have been angry about something the whole time that I have known you and I have never known. I want you to understand how important this is for me to know you. I don't want to be a victim of your last relationship. I think that it is fair enough to have walls. Everyone does. Honestly they will help you develop strength until you are strong enough to live with out them. Just keep that in mind. Tell me whatever you want, any urge you have. If you are holding back or outright dismissing something because you think that it is unimportant, then you are wrong. If you love someone, then everything should matter. You will never appear insensitive. Once I love someone that doesn't end. I love you so much.

Love, Charleston

How's the dancing? Have you ever done any acting...?

October 6, 2005 – Charleston,

Thank you for understanding. I apologize again for making you wait. I hate that you felt tortured. I know how that feels.

Will you explain how I lied to you, I don't understand.

I don't think I realized that I was angry with people not taking me seriously until the other night. I was having a conversation with my friend Michelle and she took the opportunity to explain her perception of me. No matter what I do in her mind I will always be below her. We would not be friends if it weren't for her. A decision would never be made if not for her. I understand where she is coming from. She was the first person I met when I came to California. I was not in a very good place in my life. So, I see why she thinks she chose me as her friend and has been taking care of me ever since. I don't need her to take care of me. I just want her as a friend and an equal. Anyway, I guess I realized many of my relationships have been this way and it bothered me. You have never made me feel like I was below you. You've always seen me for who I am and what I can be. Another reason I love you!

Work has been awful lately. The last day of the month was on Saturday. I did not make it. I was so disappointed. I really put a lot of effort into making this a successful month. At one point I had a 30% increase. To lose it all was such a let down. It was really hard for me. I feel like a failure because no matter what I do my business continues to suck! On top of that I had a situation with the store secretary that pushed me over the edge. A Code Adam had been called in the store. A lost child was reported. Kim saw the child so she went and helped take care of the situation. Our procedure when that happens is to guard the doors. I went and stood by the door for a couple of minutes. I got word that the child was reunited with her parents. I started walking away from the door and it was confirmed, again that the child was fine. I walked towards alterations because I was steaming something for a customer when it happened. When I got into customer service the store secretary and a HR person were standing in the doorway. The secretary started questioning why I was walking around and why I wasn't standing by the door. She had the most appalled look on her face and was rolling her eyes and wouldn't even look at me. First of all she completely questioned my integrity. Second, she has no right to speak to me the way she did, especially not in public. I was already stressed about work and this pushed me too far. I got so upset. I wish that I hadn't but I could not help it. Not to mention, when I walked out of alterations a couple of minutes later she was in front of me ranting about it to someone else. I have had problems with this person before. She is one of the most negative people I know. I needed her help a couple of times in the past few weeks and it was impossible to get. It was really bothering me so I went and talked to HR. They said mine wasn't the first complaint they'd had today and did I want them to talk to Janet. I said no, that I would rather do it. Well, they did tell Janet. I happened to be walking by her office right after they told her. I didn't want to tell her because the two of them are very close and they have the same attitude a lot of the time. I was so surprised by her response. She basically told me that she knows I am the type of person who always has honorable intentions and that if I feel something is inappropriate then she believes that it is. She said if it were someone else she might not have addressed it. She made me feel so much better and it was reassuring to know that she feels that way. However, she told me I have to confront her. That was awful. I made her cry, Charleston. I know she made me feel awful but I really did not want her to be that upset. Anyway, things are better now. I'm glad I did it but it was not easy. So, we started a new month and it isn't going very well. I don't really know what else to do. Not to mention the Irvine Spectrum Nordstrom opened last week. That does not help things. Enough of that. I'm on vacation now so I'm not going to think about it for a while.

I was thinking about sending pictures the other day. I don't have any new pictures but I am in Ohio now so I will take some and send them to you.

I'm glad you got the package from my grandma. I called her to let her know. She was very pleased. She is so sweet! She loves doing the shoebox greetings. I think it's great.

My dogs are driving me crazy. They are locked in the attic with me because a lady is over talking to my mom. It is already hot up here and they keep getting in my face with their heavy breathing. They are both just staring at me. They are so weird!

Dancing is fun. I went to the salsa class again last week. I love it! We basically learn a couple of steps and try them with different partners. I get the steps and can do them by myself. It's really fun when you get a leader who knows what they are doing. I can usually keep up! I think we will continue to take salsa lessons. There are ballroom classes before salsa so if we ever get out of work in time I think we will try one of those as well. As for acting, I don't think so. I'm not a very good actress.

I love you so much! Talle

October 6, 2005 —

You're in OHIO!!! Why didn't you tell me?!!! — Charleston

*

October 6, 2005 — Talle,

Don't worry sometimes I need a little torture. I will explain how you lied to me, but first did Michelle really say this. She must have been feeling good about herself that day. Oh, how silly girls can be. If you ever want me to expound on Michelle, then please let me know. Is she the one whom we met at Beach Fire with her boyfriend? The boyfriend is a little uncomfortable with himself wears glasses. I don't intend to criticize, but if you believe you are below Michelle then you are one of three things: very foolish, lonely, or don't know yourself. I am sorry to turn this on you, but this is very upsetting. You are an exceptional person, certainly better than me!! I think if I heard Michelle say those things I would be very disappointed and tell her to stop hating herself. Most people, who are caretakers, are actually dependents. They need the people that they supposedly take care of. They need someone good in their life to feel better about themselves. Yes, this would be a repetitive relationship process, because most people cannot stand themselves. Now I really wish that I were there. Certainly I believe that you must see some of this. If you had a choice of no company or bad company, which do you think that you would choose?

This is a tough one to explain on paper, easier in person. I told you that I saw more inside you than you were displaying to everyone else. Well let me back up. This is probably going to come out odd, but I think you already know this. Everyone acts. Very few people are true to themselves. In fact most great books on literature are centered on this plight of men to be of true character. When I am with someone I see who they are. Their eyes reveal everything. I see the person that is true to themselves, true to their soul. People can be very confusing, because they can act one way, think another, and be someone completely different. They have no trinity in character. After seeing their soul, I can observe how they act and understand what they think. This helps me understand them better. Anyone who believes in themselves can do it. My previous comments were directed at your soul and character being out of balance; even though, you told me outright that you thought that was not true. However, you wrote that you couldn't openly express yourself for a variety of reasons. Expression comes from your roots. You have layers that prevent you from expressing your true character. I didn't know previously that you desired to be taken seriously. I didn't know this was an aim. Anyone can see the fire smothered, the light subdued, the love exhausted. Underneath all the coats on top of you, you are a person full of passion for life, joy for others, and endlessly loving. You have a fascination of trying new things, traveling to different countries, and helping people. You told me. I can see you clear as day, which is why I love you. You just got burnt out absorbing so much. This happens to everyone, but instead of actively rejuvenating yourself you have immersed yourself in work. I love you dearly. You are perfect! I am happy that you are home. I am sure that it makes you happy to spend sometime with your family and weird dogs. As for the girl at work you did the right thing that took a lot of moral courage to confront her. A strong leader once told me you have to love your men. You have to punish them when they screw up, but you always have to love them.

I think that you've gone off the deep end with salsa. You're going to be a better dancer than I am, which is not saying much. Don't be expecting too much. I tend to go to my own rhythm. You will have to teach me a few things to refresh my memory. I am really glad you love it. Dancing comes from your soul. I sent flowers yesterday to California...

I love you, Charleston

October 7, 2005 – Talle,

Two questions: I can't remember the day we met. Was it April 9th? I remember that it was a Saturday.

Did you receive the package with my books? I love you. Send my blessings to your family. Charleston

October 7, 2005 – Charleston,

I can't believe you! You sent me flowers!!! You are so sweet! Thank you. Now I will have something to look forward to when I get home!

You actually have not met Michelle. Marianne is the girl from Beach Fire. I do not feel like I am below Michelle, but she perceives me to be. She didn't actually say that, but she did say the other things. The reason it came up was because I told her that I talked to Carrie (the girl from work) and she was surprised that I was able to do it. In explaining why, she told me these things. Michelle went to a leadership conference a few weeks ago. When she came back she was enlightened to why she chooses people to be in her life. She told me she chose me to be in her life because she could take care of me. Even though she knows I don't need her. It doesn't stop her from trying. Don't think I just sit there and take it from her. I tell her like it is. She can try to boss me around but I don't listen. Maybe she will eventually see me for who I am. To answer your question I would choose no company over bad company. Michelle is not bad company. To be completely honest I think she was jealous that I was able to confront Carrie. She would not have been able to do it herself.

We met on May 15th. It was a Saturday night but it was after midnight so it was the 15th.

I did not receive your package before I left.

My mom is waiting for me so I'm going to go. I love you very much!!! Thank you again for the flowers. I wish I could have been there it would have been such a pleasant surprise!

Love, Talle

October 7, 2005 –

Oh well I feel stupid.

Are you sure that it was May 15? I really think that it was before that date. You're positive that it wasn't in April? I am sure that you are positive, but that doesn't make sense. Losing mind.

Love you, Charleston

I LOVE YOU SO MUCH!!

October 6, 2005 – Talle,

I have to re-iterate how happy that you have made me. I really feel like I understand you more. I read over your must-haves as I do from time to time. While I know they are very important I don't think that I fully understood them because I didn't know your mind so well. Without knowing your personality I couldn't envision what a word like trust means to you, or an idea like help people, etc... Your personality is a reference point from which I can see you. Does that make sense? This is part of the reason for all the questions.

Your grandmother sent me a package. I was astonished. I am extremely grateful. She sounds magical. I would love to meet her.

Love, Charleston

PICTURES

October 6, 2005 –

Oh yes please send pictures!! I miss you. – Charleston *(Photos 10 – 11)*

FOOLISH

October 8, 2005 – Talle,

I have to admit that I feel very foolish over the last few emails. I can't help feeling that my emails may have come across the wrong way. Please forgive me if they have. I was honest when I said that you are a better person than me. I love you in a way that is suffocating. I think of you often, and when I do my heart holds its breath. Your image is emblazoned in my mind. I can see your smile so vividly. I love you and love you. Thank you for loving me in return.

This will be my last e-mail for a little while again. We will be in transit for a couple of days. We are offloading soon. Please know how much I love you, believe in you, and admire you. You are an incredible person. If I could grant you a wish what would it be? If I think of you too much my heart overflows and I have to do something.

Love, Charleston

October 8, 2005 – Charleston,

Please don't ever feel foolish. I don't even know why you would. You're e-mails have made me really look inside myself and that is a good thing. You are the most wonderful person I have ever known. I am the luckiest person to have you in my life and your love in return. I am constantly thanking God for bringing us together. It truly is amazing! Are you asking what wish you can grant for me? If so, the only thing I want right now is for you to come home safely. Please just be safe. I love you too much. You are constantly in my thoughts and prayers. I've thought of you so much this past week. I've relived so many of my favorite memories. We went back to the town I grew up in and where I went to school. We went to this apple orchard that I loved going to in the fall. We also ate at my favorite hamburger place. It is a drive-in and I used to spend a lot of time there in high school and college. I realized how much I want you to be a part of these things. And how excited I am for you to come back so we can make more of our own memories. I love you more and more everyday. I will be anxiously waiting to hear from you. Take care of yourself and be safe. I will send you pictures as soon as I can.

I love you!!! Talle

BACK AGAIN
October 9, 2005 – Talle,

I am sending another box with some books, empty DVD cases, etc... If you would not mind putting those in my house I would appreciate it greatly. I enclosed some articles for you that I thought you might find interesting. Don't e-mail this address for now. We are going back to Iraq. I don't know how long we will be. Right now everything but our destination is uncertain. I really love you. I will carry you with me everywhere. Thank you so much. I can't say it enough. I love you. I will get in touch with you.

Love, Charleston

*

KUWAIT
October 11, 2005 – Talle,

We just arrived in Kuwait. I tried to call you. I love you very much. I was really happy just to hear your voice on the answering service. This will be my primary e-mail address for the next couple of weeks. We are in transit, but I should be able to check often.

I finished Paulo Coehle's book, which you sent me. I am curious about what you were thinking when you sent it to me. I love you for sending it. This meant a lot. I will remember it as a very special book. Did your friend give it to you, because she was hoping that you would learn something from it? I really thought that it was a beautiful story, simple, but poignant. I liked the emphasis on the magic of life. The spiritual journey reminded me of the *Celestine Prophecy*. I thought the feminine Goddess was a little underdeveloped. I didn't finish fully understanding that portion. I did like the balance that he was making between man and woman sharing a path. The description that love is a total surrender is accurate. Do you think people would be willing to give up so many of the "rules" and "roots" they have or are establishing in life? Do you think people could just cut themselves off to the world in order to pursuit a life without reason only heart? Give up being practical and symmetrical? Allow the world to consume them with all its chaos and wonder... Do you think that a person could give up the world if they did not have someone to give it up for?

Please tell me about your time in Ohio. Tell me about your family and work. Did you see any old friends? How did it feel returning home? Had you returned recently? Is work still negative? What excites you when you wake up in the morning now? Any new dreams?

I love you so much. I can't think of you too often. It is beginning to hurt... I will look forward to seeing you soon.

Love, Charleston

October 11, 2005 – Charleston,

I was sick when I saw I missed your call. I hope you will be able to call again soon. I'm so relieved to hear from you. Your last e-mail kind of scared me. I didn't understand what was going on. It's hard for me not knowing where you are. I love you so much!

My trip home was wonderful. I haven't been back in a year. My parents live in the Cleveland area, which is about an hour north of where I grew up. They have an amazing old house on Lake Erie. It is actually across the street, but close enough. We found out after they bought the house that my grandmother's aunt lived there at one time. It is a really neat house and it's my mom's dream home. My dad was in Baltimore the first couple of days I was home so I just hung out with my mom. We went into Hudson (the town where I grew up). They redeveloped the downtown area. It is a historical town and the downtown is a really cute street with shops on one side and a park on the other. Behind the main street they built a whole new area with shops, restaurants, a new library and grocery store. I saw the mother of a friend of mine. I haven't really kept in touch with her since high school. I guess she is a nurse, which is good, but pregnant, not good. She didn't divulge any other info but it doesn't seem like the best situation. That was my only contact with friends. I don't get to spend very much time with my family, so I took advantage of this time. My best friends no longer live in that area anyway.

We drove through Kent. It's still the same. It's definitely not the prettiest place. It brought back a lot of memories, good and bad. I felt happy that I was no longer there. The last time I went back it was a little painful. I'm proud of the steps I've taken in my life to get where I am now- emotionally and in my career. I'm not quite where I want to be and it may take some time to get there but I'm happy.

The first couple of days were beautiful! The last couple were cold and rainy. I didn't mind. It was fun to bundle up and sit next to the fire. My brother came up from school on Friday and my dad came home that night. I got to meet Mark's girlfriend. She's adorable, and very sweet. No one is used to him dating this type of girl. I am very impressed. The funniest thing is that she works in petites at Nordstrom! They live about two hours away from each other so I don't know how long it will last. They seem to really like each other so we'll see. My aunt and uncle live down the street from my parents so I got to spend some time with them as well. The trip was mellow, which I needed. I really enjoyed being in Ohio with my family. I like the feeling of it much better than California. I love season's especially fall. The people are so much more down to earth and normal. Not so materialistic and self-absorbed. The people here drive me crazy sometimes. Not that there aren't the same type of people everywhere, but here it can be overwhelming. It was hard to come back. Especially since I knew what I would find at work. I've got to get to my yoga class but I will continue writing when I get home.

I love you, Talle

October 12, 2005 – Charleston,

I'm back from yoga. It was good today. The instructor is new, but she is getting better each time. I feel better. I've been stressed out and the yoga really helped relieve some of that. Work is the same. I was so disappointed when I came back. After one week I was down $13,000. That is virtually impossible to make up. The whole store is down because of the Irvine opening. It just sucks because I am going against a decrease and this could have been my opportunity to have increases. Petites is such a weird business. I really don't like it but I will not be able to get out of there until I start having increases.

We had a bake sale at work to raise money for United Way. I was in Ohio but I made some buckeyes before I left. Apparently they were a big hit! I guess people were fighting over them.

What excites me when I wake up in the morning? As much as my job irritates me I still love the merchandising process. I get excited to go in and see the new merchandise and re-work the floor. I think of you. Whenever I think of you my heart is happy. It helps me keep things in perspective for the day. I typically start off my day with a positive attitude.

I haven't had any dreams that I remember lately. What was your dream? You told me on the phone that you had a dream.

I don't think Niki had any motives for giving me the book. She has read many of his books and thought I would enjoy this one. Probably because it was a love story and she knew I had fallen in love. I think it would be very hard for people to pursue a life with only their heart in mind. This type of life would have so much risk involved that it would be hard to imagine someone doing it without love. Sacrificing your world for someone you love seems easier to me. If you have to choose what would you choose? People are the most important in my life. If it came to it I would sacrifice my world for someone I love. I'm trying to think of a way to answer your question of what I was thinking when I sent it to you. I know the answer but it is something I would rather talk about in person. I don't know how to express it through writing and it has evolved as I give it more thought.

Camilla has to do her homework. I love you tremendously. I hope you will have a chance to call again soon. Please take care of yourself and be extremely careful!

Love, Talle

October 12, 2005 – Talle,

I loved what you wrote about home. I am so happy that you had such a revitalizing visit. I think it is almost therapeutic to visit the places of our past, similar to the novel. Hudson sounds like an enchanting place to grow up. You describe it so vividly, but now I am wishing that I could see those colorful leaves. Was their snow on the ground? I agree about the seasons. This is something that I do miss. I remember growing up in Massachusetts. My childhood was so much more fulfilling because I was raised there. Everything has a procedure to make it more meaningful. I remember my falls were spent at the Topsfield fair. I loved all the animals and the rides. It always took place around this time, near Halloween. I think for children having seasons makes everything magical. California is shallow, but it has its benefits as well. I can't say that I have the same impression about the locals, but I don't know as many as you do. Marines are different and they consume my life, so I guess that I live in a microcosm in California. I also find that I don't really pay attention to people that I don't like. This was the hardest part about returning last year. When I came back I didn't want to be around civilians. It was so uncomfortable. I didn't like them and I could only really enjoy myself around Marines. Certain traits that you grow to respect become unbearable if not present.

Mark's love sounds very exciting. I hope that something as little as two hours could not deter a courageous heart from love. I would expect more and I know that 6 months away on the other side of the world could not deter me from you. Love is so worth it to be exhilarated every day. When you write that following your heart is risky what are the risks? Don't you find it strange that you have to dare to be bold? Our passions alone are not enough. We must also be courageous. I would choose to surrender myself, because I know that at the end I would have no regrets. I am being cut off but I will call you soon. I wish you would tell me instead of waiting in person. I am patient, but memory is faulty. I need to say more, but will finish later. I love you.

Love, Charleston

PICTURE
October 12, 2005 – Charleston,

Someone from work just sent me this picture *(Photo 4)*. It's not very clear but it's something. I love you!

Love, Talle
October 14, 2005 – Talle,

Oh so that is what your parking lot looks like at work!! I would have never guessed. Thank you so much for the picture. You look stunning as always. Definitely a little fuzzy, but that just leaves a little to the imagination. I can't wait to go dancing with you. Every time you talk about it I get excited. I don't think anything turns me on more than dancing with someone who loves it and of course thinking of you.

You should know. You have done everything on your own. I promise you that. A little encouragement can help, but you have to face all your fears in the end. Most people are never willing to break their mold. Their fears inhibit them too much. I know because I have tried with other people and no amount of encouragement could help them. They were satisfied with their circumstances and afraid of change. You are the courageous one. I just told you what you already knew in your heart. I don't think you give yourself enough credit sometime. You really understand a lot that most people wont. You are far more special than you think. I sent you more stuff in the mail. I really hope that it arrives soon.

I thought about what I will need here. Mental distractions are the most helpful. I would say pictures are great, prayers are reinforcing, and stories work wonders. They can be about anything, because it just helps to think about something else and know that you are a part of something that isn't war. Nothing is too silly and I promise you the sillier the better. Also please don't stop writing if you don't hear from me. I will see you soon.

Love you, Charleston

*

THE HEART
October 12, 2005 – Talle,

I apologize for the abrupt cut off. I had to run to a class on Improvised Explosive Devices (IEDs). Their tactics have not really changed since last time, so the brief was rather boring. I wanted to finish writing to you. Tangent, This becomes problematic, because when I write you letters but also e-mail. I feel like I am discussing subjects after the fact. Subjects, you haven't read yet. So it's difficult to explain things on top off subjects that I have already written to you. I hope that you receive my mail shortly. You should have received the box with books that was mailed before that letter.

We have discussed a lot through emails and letters that I wish we could have shared in person. This deployment has brought out sensitive and important issues that I would not have wanted to postpone. I feel like even though we are apart we are still growing, learning from and of each other. While I completely agree that I wish that I could speak in person it is worth it to me to share now when it has arisen. I will explain my answer through a story.

When I was 19, I went to India with the complete intention of never coming back. My heart had been pushing me, burning to go for sometime. I eventually became so overburdened with trying to keep back my passion that I exploded almost literally. I spent my whole first year in college wanting to escape. I had an urge that had to be satisfied, but going the practical and proper path I had to wait until the year was over. Meanwhile issues kept mounting; little problems prevented me from following through with my passion. I had to help my family. I had summer obligations. I had to attend my sisters' college graduation. I attempted to suppress myself with simple joys, but eventually during the last couple of days of my sisters' graduation. The explosion happened, not a physical outburst, but a spiritual one. I could not contain it. I walked back to my sister's apartment where I was staying. I packed up my belongings and went to the airport. I got on a plane and went back to Florida. I left my family behind in Baltimore. She still had three more days of ceremony, packing, parties, etc... I couldn't wait any longer and my family suffered. When I returned home I spent two weeks doing nothing but research and preparation. At the end of those two weeks I got on a plane to India. My mother cried convulsively told me that I was breaking her heart. She did not want me to go, but I couldn't be stopped. I had to go. I had disappointed and hurt everyone, but they knew that I loved them and that it was not my intention. They are my family and therefore understood my need. I told my mother that I might not come back for a while.

When I was in India everyday was honestly an adventure. I will tell you about my adventures if you like sometime. I met wonderful people and truly experienced miracles. When I was there I never felt more complete more harmonious with my surroundings. India felt like a second home and the people took to me as much as I took to them. I worked in a Hospital, but did not like the politics of the doctors. I worked in a primary school and loved the children. I went off into the Himalayas by myself and that was when I discovered something. Something I won't be able to completely explain in writing without serious thought. Nonetheless you already know it. People are very important. We thrive off of a mutual energy, of which love is the most pure. We feel this energy every day during common tasks and interactions with the cruel attendant, the happy salesperson, the negative co-worker, and the loving priest. We are all connected with this spiritual energy. Humans require this connection. We can have a communion with nature and our spirit, but it is like a circuit that is not completed or closed. It does not endure perpetually. As I began to experience these mysteries and have these journeys I realized how important it was to share them with someone. How important it was to love people. When I returned home, I vowed that I would return to India someday, but not alone. I was there for less than 3 months. I learned that I wanted to follow my heart and that a life in society could be very fulfilling if you always followed your heart. I have moments of fear and weakness, but eventually my heart overcomes them. I cannot suppress my passion. I have learned everything in my life from the moments when I didn't control them. To live your life out of control is to find your true self, to live a true life, to have exhilarating experiences. I think that you risk too much if you don't follow your heart, because then you never live at all. I attempt to seize every opportunity to live devoid of fearful thought, but I don't do it perfectly. I have the same temptations, but I am aware of them. Maybe this will explain why I wanted to know what you were thinking when you sent me that book.

If you give up everything and follow your heart, God will protect you. You only have to have faith. I wish that you could have shared my experiences. I see the passion inside you, but maybe you are not ready to unleash it. Life can be as wonderful as you make it, but you have to choose to make it wonderful. I didn't learn to write proper sentences until I came into the Marine Corps and as you have read I am still having trouble, but I realized that my fear came from feeling incompetent at it. I realized that it didn't matter if I was a bad writer, singer, slow reader, horrible painter, etc... Who is judging me? What competition am I in? So many people restrict their lives fearing they will lose a "prize." The only thing that matters is to DO, and the only "prize" we lose is the experience, nothing else. If you do it and fail do something else. If you do it and succeed then a world of possibilities are opened.

You have to love what you do. You have to believe in what you do. Your passion gives your actions purpose, which inspires your soul. I learned to write decently by writing. I will learn to paint by painting. I learned to love by loving. I will learn to live by living. Everyday we have an opportunity to do what we choose.

I already asked you. You just don't know it yet. I want you to come with me. I don't know what destinations are in my future, but I can feel the passion that has been swelling over the last 4 years in the Marine Corps and I know that I am going to have to travel. I don't know where in the world but to live an adventure. Serving in the Marine Corps was a result of that passion, but I am coming to a close and moving on to something else that has not been fully realized yet. I cannot see anything with certainty or paint a picture with clarity. I have plans, but I have to let my heart decide not my head. My heart has not decided what and where yet, but it has decided that I want more than anything for you to come. I wish that you could have had an experience on your own before hand, because you will be encountered with so many new and possibly uncomfortable experiences that it might be difficult for you and I would be the object of your frustration. I want you to know without me. I know that I will always be confronted with challenges, which is why I had reservation at Disneyland. I would be tortured with you suffering through my choices. I know that I can handle a lot of discomfort and I know that I can move quicker alone. If you were to detest me for putting you through something you didn't understand before hand I would hate myself. Absorbing any negative energy from someone you love tears the flesh of your heart apart. I would never want that to happen. I must impress upon you that I don't want to take care of you in the sense that you have described before. I want to share life with you. I love you. My heart knew that it loved you the first day. I can't fight it.

Love - Charleston

October 12, 2005 – Charleston,

I love that you shared this information. It means a lot and it helps me understand. I really would love to hear about your adventures. You are such a unique person. What is it that sparks this desire in you? Have you always had such passion? I know you follow your heart. I just wonder how it makes these decisions. I fully agree with you that we have grown and learned from each other during this time apart. I don't think I anticipated that would happen. It can be difficult to explain how I feel through e-mail. Even on the phone I have a hard time. I would always prefer being in person. It helps me to see your facial expressions and hear your voice. It can be difficult to accurately depict your true meaning in writing. Even though you are very good at describing your emotions and I feel like I take things as you mean them. Reading your emails gives me time to digest what you are saying. Writing has helped me to describe my thoughts more clearly. I feel very close to you even though we are far apart. I'm really looking forward to the time we will spend when you return.

My heart was racing when I read the words that you are asking me to come with you on this adventure. It means so much that you want to share this with me. I can think of nothing I would rather do. This requires a lot of changes for me and I'm not going to pretend that it doesn't scare me. I understand that you have spent your life following your heart. I wish that I could say the same. I never really gave it much thought. I usually just did what I thought I was supposed to do. I always tried my best to make others happy. I've succeeded at this. I've never really given anyone reason to be disappointed or hurt. I did well in school, I went to college, I stayed out of trouble, I got a job, and I support myself. I've lived a very conventional life. I'm assuming this journey would not have a time frame and that I would have to leave my job. As I think about this I feel like I couldn't do it. As I think about it a little more I wonder why?

This is not the job I want. I never wanted to be a manager. I know I am working toward a goal but what is stopping me from going somewhere else and accomplishing it? I know that Nordstrom is a good company and there are a lot of things I like about it. I know eventually I will get a buying position, but when? 5 or 10 years from now? Realistically that is possible. I really don't want to wait that long. I know I stay out of fear of the unknown. I am comfortable in my job. I know the people. I know what I'm doing. I have a routine. I've always dreaded change. But in all honesty there is nothing holding me to this job. I admire your courage to stop at nothing to pursue your dreams. Knowing that I was hurting my family would be a hard burden to bear. I don't want to disappoint them. I have to hope they would understand. My real concern is my financial situation. If I am to go away how am I going to pay my bills? I have rent and a car payment.

Whatever savings I had is gone due to the accident. I will eventually see that money but it's not a significant amount. That is something I have to think about. All of this aside I am honored that you have asked me to do this with you. You mean more to me than any of these things. I am very excited to think of the adventures we could have. Please don't worry about me taking frustrations out on you. I'm excited at the thought of experiencing new things. If I am in an uncomfortable situation I will be in it with the understanding that I made the decision to go with you. Knowing that it was a likely possibility. You may have to be patient. I could slow you down. I'm not the toughest girl you'll ever meet.

I don't think I fully realized why I sent you that book. I didn't want to say this because I'm not sure how it will be received. Nor can I fully explain in writing. Remember when we were at Disneyland and we had an argument about what you were going to do when you came back? I realized that you were going to live your life always following your heart and pursuing your dreams. I was scared that I would not have a place in your life. I think I wanted you to read that book because in the end they followed their dreams together. I wanted you to want me to be a part of your dreams and adventures. I knew and know that I want to be with you at any cost. There is not much keeping me where I am. I am ready for something different. I started realizing that about a year ago. Not until you emailed me about the book did I realize the similarities between the main character and myself. I've learned a lot about myself these past few months. Thank you for really wanting to understand my character. You've opened my eyes to so many new things. You even got me to explain this to you. I love you with all of my heart. I'm really excited right now. Please take care of yourself and be safe. I cannot wait to see you!

Love, Talle

October 14, 2005 – Talle,

After reading this, my heart is racing with enthusiasm. I almost wish that I were closer to coming home before discussing, but if you wait for every moment to be perfect than sometimes it doesn't happen. You have to have faith in God. We have so much to do. In life obstacles always exist. We simply have to realize that a solution always exists as well. The more faith and the more creativity you have the easier the solutions will come. Looking at what obstacles are ahead of you makes me even more excited, because I know that you are looking at this realistically. One would have a very easy time accepting such an offer without ever really committing. You have made me so happy because I know your acceptance is genuine. Please don't take the planning process, which is working through the details to be laboring. They are part of the excitement of adventures. How am I going to find a solution to this problem? And with a little faith and creativity sure enough the problem goes away. Your obstacles: apartment, furniture, car, car payments, sister - roommate, job, family and friends, any debt? These all need to have a resolution and some take time, but that is Ok. Everything works out the way it is suppose to. Do you foresee any obstacles that I am over looking? How would we solve each one? I am once again amazed. Didn't you find it interesting and odd when you recognized that you didn't know why you were feeling like you couldn't do it? Didn't you catch sight of an inconsistency and were struck with this feeling of imbalance? Once you have recognized that the first time you will become aware of it more often. You will see it in everyday occurrences. Why did I not say that when I wanted to? Why did I say no when I wanted to accept? Why can't I learn to dance? Why am I eating something I don't want? We spend are adolescence learning to control our energy instead of learning to harness it. I am so proud. This recognition is a seed that will grow tremendously with time. You will see. All you had to do is be willing to ask yourself why. Are you physically not able to do it? The idea is absurd. A way always exists. I am too excited now. I love you. I don't want to mislead you. Adventures require a lot of physical, mental, and spiritual endurance. I am not worried about you keeping up or being the toughest girl, because it is not a question of that. It is a question of giving up, quitting, or seeing no way out. This is the idea that fuels a conventional life. We can't imagine anything else. We think we have no other choices, but why? God has given us everything we need to follow our hearts and choose our own path. We just have to listen to him. Conventions bind us because we can't see any way out. I need you to read *Siddhartha* by Herman Hesse. You will see that with a little bit of sacrifice and suffering you can accomplish great things. I have a copy in my house, if you want to borrow it. I sent you a magazine from wilderness travel. Has national geographic like pictures? I don't intend to use it because I am not the tourist type, but I want you take a look at the pictures. I remember asking you if you could go anywhere where would it be. You suggested the obvious Paris, but also a place with beautiful green water. You didn't know where that would be. You didn't have a picture of it. Tell me what pictures draw you in. Inspire you to explore.

I love you so much, Charleston
October 14, 2005 – Charleston,

I think you covered all of the obstacles. I don't yet know how we will solve them. I believe that the answers will come. This is all very exciting. I get butterflies thinking about it.

I've found myself asking those "why" questions over the past few months. It's amazing to me how much you know. I'm glad you planted this seed; it is opening my eyes and helping me do things I've always thought about but never done. My life is more fulfilling and I am happier. Who would have thought I'd be taking salsa lessons. I'm not going to be able to go for the next couple of weeks. I have to close on the nights it's offered. We are going to go on another night and learn some other dances. I'll keep you updated on what I learn.

I'm excited because I am going to the spa tomorrow for Marianne's birthday. I think I'm going to get a facial. I've gotten one at this spa before and it was amazing! I'm supposed to go out with her afterward. I'm a little hesitant because the last time I went out with her and her boyfriend it was a nightmare. They got into a huge argument and he left without her and she was a mess. They said they were breaking up. Which would have been for the best. They are awful together. But they live together and quickly fell back into their routine. It is inevitable that if they go out and drink any amount of alcohol they will argue. I always get put in the middle and it's miserable. I guess I can hope for the best.

I loved hearing your voice last night. I can't wait for you to come home! I miss you terribly!

I love you, Talle

*

SPAS
October 14, 2005 – Talle,

Everything about you makes me smile. I really love you. Even when I write you I have to hide my stupid grin from all the Marines around me. As you know I grew up with my two older sisters and my mother, so I have been a victim of spas. Two worst experiences Violet had me do this foot scrub with her. I had just finished Marine Officer Boot Camp and my feet were pretty tore up. I have never been in more pain in my life. I felt like such a baby. I squealed the whole time. The worst part was that my feet were so sensitive I couldn't walk on them for weeks after until they toughened up again. On another occasion my mother sent me to the spa and I thought I was getting a massage when they laid me on my back and put steam on my face. She told me to relax so that it would open my pores. Little did I know she was going to start gouging my face!! I have to say though I don't know how you would be able to tell a good facial from a bad facial. I mean a great massage is easy to distinguish, but a facial sucks any way and they go until everything has been exhumed! I did get a comment that I had a very good complexion. I think she was just kidding with me.

The obligations of friendship can be very taxing. This is something I have a lot of trouble balancing when to tell my friends no and when to go out of my way for them. I wish that I could go with you, because then I know we would both have fun anyway. Just enjoy yourself if they fight so be it. At least if you expect it you won't be disappointed when it happens. I'll pray that it doesn't happen. I hate not being with you, which is making my job very difficult. The happiest parts of my day are reading or expecting your e-mails. I love it when you just tell me the most random things or anything at all. I love sharing everything with you. Oh ya I had a conversation with this girl from Ohio. She is from the Cleveland area. I told her my girlfriend was from Hudson. She said it was beautiful and that all her high school friends went to Kent.

Have I told you that you are perfect lately and very sexy?

I love you, Charleston

Ps. Question: What is all this controversy over Supreme Court nominee Harriet Mier? I saw some headline that the President is suffering because of his nomination?

October 15, 2005 – Charleston,

I love this email! I love thinking of you trying not to smile when reading your emails. I would not be able to hide it. I smile so big when I read emails from you. I can't help it. It's also my favorite part of the day reading your emails. It's the first thing I do when I get home. I'm sorry to hear about your traumatic experiences at the spa. I've only had one facial. It really was amazing! I agree it can be painful but they give really good neck and head massages with it. I did have this bump on my chin and I never figured out what it was. The girl tried squeezing it and it was unbelievably painful. Aside from that I loved it! We didn't end up going to the spa yesterday. Maybe tomorrow. We did go out and it was fine. Her boyfriend didn't come. It was just Marianne and one of her friends. We went to Javier's for dinner. Then we went to Hennessey's. I haven't been there since we met. It made me happy thinking of how we met. I was a little sad though. I really wished you were there. I miss you terribly. I also had missed your calls and I was feeling awful about it. I'm so sorry about that. I wish we could have talked. Your mother left me a message today. It was so sweet! I am very thankful.

Harriet Miers: people are concerned that she isn't qualified. She lacks experience, as she's never been a judge. Sorry, but I don't know much more.

I had such a bad day yesterday. My regional merchandiser came to the store. We were talking about my business and how awful it is. As you know I take it personally. As if I don't feel bad enough she completely made me feel inadequate. She made the comment that how can South Coast be having an increase and you and Santa Ana be down? You're all in the same area. I wish I had the answer. I really don't know what they want me to do. I am trying my best. I am so fed up. She says the merchandising is fine it must be my crew. They are all new and don't have the necessary personal trade. I had to build a team from nothing when I got there. They all work so hard and it is going to take time to see the results. I just really didn't need her to make me feel like crap about it. While this was going on security was placing "bombs" around the store to see what we would do. Of course they put one in my department. I was running around working with my regional and the visual team and paid absolutely no attention. They set it up so that someone would come over and tell me there was a suspicious bag in my department. When she told me I looked at it and assumed it was the maintenance managers stuff and walked away. They were watching on the camera the whole time so the girl couldn't say anything. A couple of minutes later she motioned for me to come in the back. She told me it was suppose to be a bomb and I needed to call security. So, I called and told them but I took to long and they were mad. It was kind of funny afterward but not at the time. Hopefully if someone does decide to leave a bomb in my department I will react a little quicker.

It's kind of cold today. I love it. I'm excited to curl up in my blanket and watch some girlie movies. I love you and I hope you are doing well. Take care of yourself!

Love, Talle

RAINY DAY

October 16, 2005 – Charleston,

It was really great talking to you last night. I was having a hard day and it helped to hear your voice. I'm glad you arrived to your destination safely. I love you.

It was a rainy, cold day today. It was kind of nice for a change. I didn't end up going to the spa. Marianne never returned my call. Oh well. I ran some errands and did some things around the house.

I sent you a CD from the iTunes store. I don't know if it will work or not. I thought I'd give it a try.

I was wrong about my mom's email. Sorry!

I'm sending you some things. Hopefully they won't take too long to arrive.

I wish you were here with me right now. I really want to kiss and hug you! I'm counting on these next few months going quickly. I am about two weeks away from another sale. Once that starts time should fly. I hope it will go quickly for you. Do you think this is harder than you thought it would be? How did you think you would feel? I knew it was going to be hard for me. I was scared we wouldn't have as much communication. I'm so happy that we have email and occasional phone calls. I love hearing your voice. At first I get really excited and sort of nervous. I get major butterflies. After I calm down I feel so relaxed and reassured. Whether you want me to or not I worry. There is no way to avoid it. Please continue to let me know if there are specific things you need or want. I love you!

Love, Talle

October 18, 2005 – Talle,

You are so perfect. Thank you for the honesty. I couldn't love anyone more. You know I dream and think about you often. I smile just thinking about it. I love talking about you and when I do I can't help but get excited with a silly grin. I think that I must be a little crazy. I expect that I over developed my imagination from years struggle and loneliness. However, I think that if I didn't have such developed mechanisms to deal with it then this separation would be unbearable. I can talk to you. I can feel you in my heart. I can visualize you so well that I can pacify myself. I was riding on a bus last night thinking how glad I was to have met you and how hard it would have been if I had met you earlier. I could never have left you twice. Not like this when I can't return when I want. This is becoming harder than I expected. I fell asleep last night holding my sweatshirt as a pillow thinking how nice it will be to hold you again. That first night how overwhelming it will be just to fall asleep with you in my arms. I can see it. I can see your smile with the edges of your lips down turned. You kiss my hand and I think how perfectly we fit together. Every email buys more time, restores some energy, and provides more faith. A Japanese quote states, "the blossom that grows in adversity becomes the most beautiful of all." I believe that was in a movie too, but I know that our love will be so much stronger because of this adversity and that makes me really happy. Because if your going to love then I believe in loving greatly. My love can only grow stronger.

     Love, Charleston

GOOD DAY
October 18, 2005 – Charleston,

     I feel so much better about work today. I never had a chance to speak with Janet when I got back from vacation. I wasn't sure how she felt about my terrible business. She has always been supportive but I wasn't sure. I've had so many consecutive months of decreases. I was so relieved when she was walking toward me this morning singing "have I told you lately that I love you". I had to ask her why. I've done nothing that should make her love me. She was very reassuring. After being brought down by my regional merchandiser, Cheryl, it was comforting to hear her encouragement. I told her about my experience last week and she was so angry. She's given me another assignment. I have to confront Cheryl about her negativity. I don't know why I am always getting myself into these situations. I don't have a problem doing it because she needs to know how she was perceived. Her visit certainly didn't inspire me to come up with new ideas to generate business. However Janet's understanding helped me out of my slump.

     I had class tonight. It was about bookkeeping and taxes and all that kind of stuff. I followed while the teacher did her portion. When she brought in the CPA I was lost. She spoke in general about a few things but nothing in particular. There are some people in the class that already have a business. They asked questions and she basically had conversations with them about what they needed to do. None of it made sense to me. Accounting is not my forte. I have acquired some useful information. I think the class would be really beneficial if I was going to start my business now. Regardless, I have gotten some good information. I have a binder that goes through all the things you need to think about when writing a business plan. I like knowing what I can expect. She talks about the pros and cons of making different choices. I have a more realistic view of what it takes to run a business.

There was the most unbelievable thunderstorm last night. I felt like I was back in Ohio. I've never seen or heard anything like it in California. There was one thunder that scared me to death. I couldn't even move afterward. It was so loud. I couldn't believe it. And the lighting lit up the entire sky. It was crazy!

I love you so much!!! Talle

October 18, 2005 – Talle,

Janet sounds like a boss who knows what she is doing. She must understand you very well. I like her from what you have told me. I am glad that you are back on your feet because you have told me your ideas before and they are impeccable. Cheryl couldn't develop a better plan herself.

Fortunately I am pretty good at accounting. It is really only following a math worksheet. If they made it sound complex then they were exploiting technicalities. The basics are pretty easy. You have a great approach to new things. I never understand everything the first time. I have to listen, stew on it, and eventually it will make sense to me. When you are actually doing it you will see a lot more. Learning is one thing. Doing is another, but at least you know what to expect. Additionally you can always hire an accountant, which the experts recommend anyway. After all, CPAs take a lot of classes to earn that credential. I love you. You are amazing!!!

Love, Charleston

BLESSING

October 18, 2005 – Charleston,

I'm so grateful everyday that you are a part of my life. You are a blessing. All day long I see people in miserable relationships. Some of them admit to the misery and others make every excuse to cover it up. It's so sad. I can usually relate to the feelings these people have so I understand. From you I've learned how a relationship is meant to be. It is such a warm and wonderful feeling to be assured that the person you love loves you. They would never disrespect or intentionally cause pain. I know there are not many people like you in this world. I have to believe that people can have loving and kind relationships. They just have to choose not to settle for anything less. I love you. I'm just so happy to think about you. I absolutely cannot wait for you to come home.

I wish I knew what you were doing. It probably would be worse if I knew. I guess I hope you would tell me it isn't as bad as the pictures in my head. I love you, and you are always in my heart and prayers.

Love, Talle

October 19, 2005 – Talle,

Please don't ever forget how much you are a blessing in my life. You are so special and I have tried very hard to find someone with half the amount of love you have. You have no idea how much that meant to me when you told me without hesitation that you would come with me. You have displayed such an incredible sense of sacrifice. You are absolutely right about people. They must choose. I believe most people don't understand they have a choice. They believe that they are victims of love and for those that do not choose for themselves they do become victims of love. I also believe that most people don't know how or what it means to love, which is far more disturbing than not choosing. Love is supposed to be selfless. You love to give energy to other people, but most people only believe in taking it away. I wish you could see how easily this has come to you and how many people could not understand that real love is about sacrifice. You amaze me everyday. I love that about you. Try not to think too much on what I am doing. This is hard, but this is when you must have faith in yourself and God. Everything God does serves a purpose. God is in every one of us, picking us up when we are down, hugging us when we are lonely. God will be there for you if you let him. I will be gone for a couple weeks. Don't stop writing if you can. I will let you know when everything is fine. I don't have to have you to love everything about you. This alone gives me strength.

Love, Charleston

October 20, 2005 – Charleston,

I will be praying for you even more these next couple of weeks. I love you. Be safe.

You were in my dreams last night. It was wonderful. I wrote about it in a letter. It has stayed with me all day. I feel energized as if I was really with you. It truly will be amazing that first night to fall asleep in your arms. I am so happy thinking about it. I wish there was another way I could describe the way I love you. I feel like I say the same things over and over. When I am sitting here at the computer I am so overwhelmed with love for you that sometimes I can think of nothing else. I am amazed every day with how much I love you and how much love I feel in return. It's the greatest feeling. You are amazing. I love you!

Love, Talle

*

FEW MORE DAYS

October 21, 2005 – Talle,

I wake up every morning and my first thought is you. Except this morning it was holy shit it's cold, but immediately after that thought it was you. We have moved 6 times in the last 10 days and we are still on stand bye, waiting. We were supposed to go and now are held up for a couple of days. The unit's frustration level is pretty high. We had our first memorial service yesterday. Reminded a lot of people who were here last year how much this sucks. Life has actually been easy for the last couple of days, but it is honestly too easy. A stagnant military is not a good thing. Too much time to sit gives too much time to let your guard down. We will become complacent.

My sister wants to throw me a party. The idea is detestable. She sent me a list of the people that she wanted to invite. I couldn't have been unhappier about having a party. Just thinking about it gets me heated. I don't know why I have such strong feelings. I know that I would like to see some of my University friends, but I feel so far removed from them. I feel like this is a problem that I wish I could change, but having been gone has changed my life perspectives. I have constantly been engaged in war for the last 3 years. Even when not at war the Marine Corps is at war and war has reduced my life to very simple principles. I value a simpler life. One that is certainly less grandiose than my University days. I worry that I would have little in common with them. My life has taken such a different direction than many of them. Worst of all I fear that I would be hostile towards them. I think this stems from the same problem that I had when I returned last time. You become so hostile towards everyone. I hope that you won't frown upon this. I know this is a bad outlook, but it is the truth. Please forgive me.

On a happier note, I was so happy to read that you had a wonderful dream. Your e-mails have changed a little bit in the last week or so. Your tone has altered. I feel so in touch and in love with you. I am waiting for the moment to hold you again to be reunited with my sexier half. Have you received any mail? I hope all my mail did not get lost. You are so perfect. I love you.

Love, Charleston
October 22, 2005 – Charleston,

Why do they keep moving you around? If they cannot figure out what they want you to do they should really just send you home. You know you will never wake up cold with me!

Please don't apologize about your feelings. There is nothing wrong with feeling the way you do. I can't even begin to understand the things you go through while you are away. Let alone having to come home and readjust to the people and things around you. You need to do it at your own pace. If you know you will not enjoy a party with old friends right away, don't let her have one. When you are ready, maybe you should have one, but there is nothing wrong with not wanting it. At least you understand how you are going to feel when you get home. The situation would be much worse if you thought the party would be a good idea and ended up being miserable. The intent is to welcome you home and let you relax and have a good time. Does your sister believe that you really don't want to have a party? Will she organize it regardless of what you say because she may think you are just saying you don't want a party?

I still have not received any mail. I hope it is not lost too. I get excited every day to check the mailbox. I've sent you a couple of letters. Hopefully they won't take too long. I feel very connected with you. I think it has become easier to write. I've let my guard down a little. I love you so much!

I had very a rewarding day today. We were getting judged today for the v-award, which is an award based on visual elements in the store. My department was judged. This means I have to work closely with the visual team making sure everything meets their standards. This is potentially a good thing because they will come in and move the floor around and give it a fresh, new look. They were supposed to come Tuesday morning and work with me. It is absolutely crucial that I am there when they move my floor. I understand their concepts but in the end it is my decision. It's my floor. I'm on it everyday. I know what will and will not work. So, last night they decide to move my floor without telling me. Luckily, I was there helping with an event that was happening in the store. I had to leave the event, which I didn't feel right about but I had no choice. My biggest concern was that one of my buyers was coming in the morning. If my floor does not make sense she is going to blame that for my bad business. I will not let that happen because I work hard on my floor to keep it in order. I know that it is not to blame. It all worked out because I was there to give my input and I was happy with how it looked. My visit with my buyer was fabulous! She was so supportive. She told me she really only came to encourage me and congratulate me on a great event last month. I had chosen a vendor to focus on and ended up having great results. She said a lot of great things about my leadership skills and the floor presentation. I was blown away. She is my dress buyer and I have consistently had huge decreases for her. To know that she understands how hard I am trying is such a good feeling. I even received compliments from Janet and Cheryl today. I feel revived. It is much easier to go to work when you know you are appreciated.

I love you. I'm constantly thinking of you. Please be safe!

God Bless, Talle

October 23, 2005 – Talle,

I think my sister wants to do something special for me. I don't know if what I tell her will stop her. My sister knows if I don't want to do something then I won't do it. You are right they should send us home!! Makes sense to me. I actually think about your body heat a lot, because you are so HOT!! I don't think that I have ever met someone else who puts off as much heat as you do, which is great because the temperature is always perfect. I honestly had that same thought last night. I was shivering in my bag and was like damn if Talle were here then this would be a perfect temperature. You know now that I think about it. I have grown to despise cold weather environments, but I think that I could endure them with you. I guess that I wont entirely rule them out.

What do you mean that you have only let down your guard a LITTLE!!? That's not good considering I am pretty defenseless at this point. I love that you foiled their attempts to go behind your back and you should be praised for your leadership. You are great leader, exceptionally caring and decisive. I would think that it would be very rewarding to work for you. Your planning is very creative and instinctive. These are not attributes that come easily. Well I think amazing sums it up.

I was talking with a friend. He has seen pictures of you and we have talked consistently throughout the deployment. You haven't met him, but he is probably a closer friend than most. He is pretty quick witted. I was talking to him about you, as I love to do. I explained to him that I asked you to come with me once I take off when I return. I told him how blown away that I was since you accepted without hesitation and were actually willing to sacrifice so much. I told him how important this commitment was to me. He asked me some details and I explained that for me real love is sacrifice. I told him that I was concerned because I knew that you had some obstacles. He replied, "Ok so you asked her to leave everything behind, basically dump her sister, quit her job, leave her friends, and give up her belongings. Bold move you jerk!!" I laughed, because he is right. Now I really feel like a jerk, but I couldn't take it back. I love you too much.

Love, Charleston

October 22, 2005 – Charleston,

You could never be a jerk! I am willing to make these sacrifices because of you. You are worth it all. I'm assuming we are not going away forever. People and things will be here when we get back. The only thing that may not be is my job but I am capable of finding another. Besides, I am really excited to go. I want to experience new things. I want to do the unconventional thing for once. I want to be with you. It could not be more appealing.

I took a waltz lesson last night. It was fun. We practiced a couple of steps and then tried it to music once. It's different with and without the music. I don't know how I would do with the music. It really depends on the leader. As long as I know how to do basic techniques I will be fine. I'm assuming you know how to waltz. Your mother told me I should learn it. It just so happened they were teaching it last night. I was excited. It will be amazing dancing with you. I cannot wait!

I checked the mail today and I have a package at the office. It was too late to pick it up but I will get it tomorrow. Hopefully it is your books. I'll let you know tomorrow. I'm going to Disneyland again. This time Michelle's husband Mike is with a mutual friend also Michelle. They are a lot of fun together, so I'm looking forward to it. I love you!

Love, Talle

PICTURES

October 24, 2005 – Charleston,

Here are some pictures from my apartment and before you left *(Photo 3 & 6)*. We had a fun day. We rode the new Space Mountain. It was re-done for the 50th anniversary. It is basically the same thing. They made a few changes to the music and the effects, and it is a smoother ride. We went to the Haunted Mansion. It was decorated for Halloween with Tim Burton's *The Nightmare Before Christmas* theme. It was amazing how elaborate the decorations were. I got this thing called a pineapple whip. I've never seen it before but I walk by the stand every single time I go to Disneyland. It is pineapple ice cream with pineapple juice and a cherry. It was so good! I can't believe I've been missing out for all these years. I hope you enjoy the pictures. I love you!

Love, Talle

*

THANK YOU

October 26, 2005 – Charleston,

I received two boxes from you yesterday. One was with the books. You don't have to worry about that any more. The other was the rug. Thank you so much for sending that to me. I am touched. I put it next to my bed and said a prayer for you last night and will do the same tonight. The letter enclosed with the books was intense. I wrote you a letter about it so I won't go into it now. You consistently amaze me. I love you.

I finally went to the spa. I had a wonderful facial. It was very relaxing and not very painful this time. The neck massage was great. I wish I could give you one I'm sure you need it.

I'm so proud of my mom. She found out somehow that there was store near her that sold local artists work. She went and talked to the owner about the bracelets and handbags that she knits. The owner told her to bring them in and she would decide if she liked them. My mom made some extra pieces but was so nervous to take them into the store. It was sad because she was really scared of being turned down. She finally decided to take them in and the girl loved them. She bought one for herself right away. It was cute and she was excited. I'm proud of her.

I took the books over to your house today. Everything looks good. I love being there, but it will be better when we are there together.

I love you! Talle

October 26, 2005 – Talle,

I love you. I could not write it enough. I am glad that you liked the prayer rug. I thought that it might be nice. They didn't have too many interesting items to send. Thank you for your prayers. I really think they are helping, because I have felt considerably better the last couple of days. I don't know if the box with the books was the first one that I sent or the second one. What was the postmark date? If it had the book on Attila it is the first one. If it had a book on the *Brother's Karamozov* then it was the second. I am pretty sure that I enclosed letters in both of them so I don't know which one.

I received one of your recent letters. You write beautifully. I couldn't stop smiling for at least twenty minutes. I felt like such a goof. For me I can only write so much and then I have to do something. I have to show people that I love them. I can't wait to show you how much that I love you. I am writing a response to your letter as well. I love you. I will need a lot of prayers for the next two weeks. God bless. Keep dreaming!!

Love, Charleston

October 26, 2005 – Charleston,

I'm happy to hear you have been feeling good. I will say even more prayers for you if it helps. I love you. I can't wait to show you how much either. I get butterflies thinking about it.

I got the first box of books you sent. It had Attila and it was from the end of August.

I love you so much. I can't even think of anything to write right now. I'm just picturing you. Imagining what it will be like when you come home. The things we will do and how it will feel. I don't think I've ever anticipated something so much in my life. I hope I will see you in my dreams tonight. I feel very close to you. Be safe, take care of yourself, and stay warm. I love you!

God bless, Talle

October 27, 2005 – Hello my love,

I had wonderful dreams of you last night. Even though I was freezing and waking up every 2 hours, my dreams were vivid. I received your card about your dream and my dream was a re-enactment of yours. It didn't take place in a mall, but your family arrives in the end. The dream was a little odd, because when they came in my pants were down. I was like oh that's embarrassing. Great dream. It was definitely good spirited. This was by far the most vivid too. I think that is because you are having dreams now as well. I love that because now I know that I am in your soul, as you are in mine.

We went out on the town all seems very quiet. This was the joke last year. Whenever I would go out, peace would break out. Needless to say, God looks after me. Seems to be encouraging.

Have you decided on a costume yet for Halloween? You have to do something fun and inventive. Is your sister going to partake? I wish that I could enjoy it with you. I can already envision all the fun different things that we could do. Scary movies, costumes, parties, fairs, trick or treat, pranks are just a few choices. What do you think? What would you want to do if I was there? That would certainly be an exciting thought.

You are soo hot! I can't stop thinking of you.

Love, Charleston

October 27, 2005 – Charleston,

I can't stop laughing about your pants being down when my parents came in. That would be very embarrassing! I'm glad you were able to have a good dream despite the terrible sleep.

I love that there is peace when you are around. That is very reassuring. I hope it will continue to be that way.

I haven't figured out Halloween. None of my friends are doing anything. Camilla is going to a party on Friday with people from work. I could go but it's not that appealing to me. Who knows something could come up at the last minute. We have a sale starting next week so I wouldn't mind getting some extra rest. Now if you were here it would be a different story. We could carve pumpkins. One year I got a kit that had outlines for different faces. I carved the coolest looking pumpkins. It was easy but it looked complicated. Then we would have to toast the pumpkin seeds. They are delicious. Have you ever had them? My mom used to always make them for us. I love passing out candy to the trick-or-treaters. I love seeing the little kids in their costumes. It reminds me of my dad taking us around every year. I think he got more excited than we did. I always loved that. Even when I got older and everyone went with their friends I preferred to go with my family. We could watch scary movies under a blanket, next to a fire. I would love to cuddle with you in a warm house when it's cold outside.

We could go to a costume party. What would we be? These months are my favorite time of year. There is such a warm happy feeling everywhere. I wish we could be together but you are in my heart.

I was MIC tonight at work. I swear the weirdest things happen when I am in charge. A customer found $700 in cash in the pocket of a jacket on the sales floor. She wanted to let me know but then she didn't want to give me the money. I think she wanted to be a Good Samaritan but she also wanted to be rewarded by getting to keep the money. She ended up giving it to me. I was able to research the SKU and find the phone number of the person that returned the jacket. I haven't called this person yet. I'm not sure how to word it. I think I'll let Janet make the final decision. It was nice of the customer to bring it to my attention. She very easily could have kept the money.

I love the tone of your e-mail. I can't stop smiling about it. It put me in a really good mood. I love you so much. I would be happy to research these cities. I'll just need a little bit of time.

Love, Talle

October 28, 2005 – Talle,

My pants were down. This was weird. I was walking toward the door trying to pull up my pants and your dad just came right in. He passed me with my pants down didn't even take notice. He walked toward you. The rest of the family caught up. I looked at my pants and was like that stinks!! You and your family were walking on ahead. No one really cared, except for me. Very odd must be "symbolic?"

What creativity!! Well, Halloween is planned for the next couple of years. I think that you chose enough great ideas. They all sound exceedingly fun!?? Warm covers, kinky costumes, cool candy what else could a man ask for in a fantasy... I'll just keep dreaming. What costumes would we wear matching or separate? Are we the mysterious hot couple or scary movie revival? I don't think that I have ever eaten roasted pumpkin seeds, but I have had pumpkin pie, one of my favorites. Oooh we should cook treats too, because that would be fun, pie, candy apples, what else? We would have to throw a haunted house for the kids in the neighborhood, because that would be awesome if we got kids to pee their pants!! What do you think? I think that organizing something in the community would be really cool in order to centralize all the kids and have fun functions. They could gather at a community center were they can get costume aid and face painting. You can give them organized routes for trick-or-treaters and have planned tricks. You can even give the pranksters missions that have to be carried out with stealth and have a counter plan in effect to catch them. That would be really exciting!! If we were in Boston, then you could expect to carve pumpkins, get tackled in the leaves, eat brown donuts and apple cider, pick apples, dip them in caramel, go to really scary haunted houses or have our own and do the hibbty bibbty (no comment) ;)

I hope that you have fun no matter what, or you can save up for next year!! I read men's health the best place to pick up women is a clothing store. I'm going to have to start hanging out in Nordstrom's more to hit on the women. Know any good spots? I bet you get hit on every day, damn girl!! I better keep telling you how much I love you. I love you. I love you. I love you. Have you ever seen 7 brides for 7 brothers? Random

We were talking about Thailand because we may port there. I think that I might have to stay on ship the way they talk about it. Everywhere is brothels and women selling themselves. I think that a massage would be enticing, but was laughing because I don't think that it would lead anyplace good. Better off handcuffed to the ship or locked in my room. The whole country ain't got anything on the petite's section at Nordstrom, where the players are at. I love you. Big hug. Big kiss.

Love, Charleston
October 28, 2005 – Charleston,

You are amazing. I've probably told you that over and over again but it is true. I love you so much! For our costumes I think we should be matching and definitely the hot couple. Caramel apples sound yummy! You should know because anyone who has been around me lately is constantly reminded how much I love anything pumpkin. Pumpkin pie, pumpkin lattes, basically anything that I see pumpkin flavored I have to have. You probably remember the obsession with pumpkin ravioli. I actually had some in Ohio. I went to a huge market in Cleveland. My dad was really excited to take me there. They had a pasta stand with every imaginable type of ravioli. We got some and my mom made it before I left. The haunted house sounds like a great idea. I'm not sure how I feel about the kids peeing their pants. Although it would be rather funny! I love the idea of organizing something in the community. I always loved that sort of thing as a child. Did you like haunted houses when you were younger? I was always scared. I wanted to go anyway, so I would go with my friends. Most of the time I would stay outside. If I actually got the courage to go through I usually hid behind the person in front of me the entire time. I would probably do the same today.

I had never thought of it but it does make sense that clothing stores are a good place to pick up women. We certainly spend a lot of time there. I don't get hit on regularly so thank you for the "I love you's" but you do not have to worry. Last year, a balding, overweight, old man, did hit on me. I felt bad for the guy so I couldn't be mean. I gave him my work number and he called all the time asking me to lunch. It was kind of creepy. I eventually had to tell him I had a serious boyfriend and he left me alone.

I never realized men were so obsessed with prostitutes! It is disgusting to me. Are they attracted to the idea of it? Or do they really want to partake in these activities? I know I can be naive but I had never heard of guys getting so excited at the thought of hookers. It's gross!!!

We had a little meeting at work today. Janet picked a couple of managers to attend. The company wants to do $10 billion dollars next year so they are getting opinions from the managers to find out how we can increase our volume. They asked a lot of questions. What would you continue to do if everything was taken off your plate and you were only responsible for driving volume and developing your team? What would you stop doing? What do you dislike? One of the biggest problems universally is that everyone enjoys the culture and stays there because they enjoy what they do. Pay is the biggest drawback, but it was funny because none of us brought this up. So, Janet did. All of the notes are going to corporate. Maybe they will realize that their pay is not competitive. It would be nice to make more money, and I feel that it was an effective meeting. There were good suggestions that I hope will be taken seriously.

I love you so much. Big hug, big kiss back at you!

Love, Talle

HALLOWEEN

October 29, 2005 – Pumpkin,

A new term of affection arises!! Matching costumes is a bold move. I don't know if everyone would be able to handle the heat. We may have to tone it down a bit. Don't forget about our horoscope. This is very important, because together we exude a palpable magnetism, charming and alluring. I strongly believe that no coincidences exist. Can you imagine how magnetic we would be together? I think you would mesmerize people. You are dazzling, sexy, and full of energy and love. Who could resist you? I know that I couldn't. Everything that I wrote in the letter is already been foretold in our horoscope, strange how things are obvious if you pay attention. I love the pumpkin obsession, so trendy. We should have everything pumpkin one day! Do you think your favorite color will become orange? I like orange. Community would be fun. I think kids would love you and I could make them pee their pants, perfect combo. We will have to organize something in the future. Will start planning. I loved haunted houses. They were great. I often hid behind my eldest sister. She loved horror and mystery. So if I am hiding behind you then whom are you hiding behind?! Oh and you definitely wouldn't be staying outside, cause that is some bullshit!! You are coming with me.

When I was little in Boston we had a house with a sunroom. The room was all glass hence the sun shined in. We had a big fireplace in the room and it bordered with our forest. It got pretty spooky at night. My eldest sister always loved watching *Friday the 13th*, *Nightmare on Elm St.*, etc…in the sunroom. We would be sitting on the couch with all our friends over watching a scary movie with a roaring fire. Mid way through the movie they would all be sitting on my sisters side of the couch and here I was this little boy sitting on the other side of the couch alone trying not to be scared. That was horrible!! It definitely scarred me for life.

My question about the clothing stores is that all the women that you would want to hit on are in the sections or stores that no man should be. Why would I be wandering around the petite section? I mean I can't just walk around certain stores that would be a little weird wouldn't? You have a serious boyfriend? Well, you better tell your serious boyfriend that you're other boyfriend is coming home soon!!

I have figured out my whole deployment: Hookers and Fighting. I don't get it either. They do say that physical aggression leads to sexual as well, so maybe that is part of the obsession. I know that I have only one butt to chase, and damn yours looks good. I bet yoga is paying off. Did I ever tell you that you have a perfect posterior? I can't even think of it without making me crazy...woo!

A lot of topics to cover: The whole retail industry is going to have a good year, so that makes sense about attempting to capitalize this year. However, as an industry they have a very low average wage. In fact I believe it is the lowest. I did some research comparing our national industries and the retail industry is the worst to work in. I don't know if realistically Nordstrom's could raise the wages of its employees significantly. Does it pay that much less than comparable jobs in retail?

I got to go. Have a happy Halloween. I love you. I want to huuuugggg you. I want to ruuuuubbbb you $%#@**. I mean kisssss you.

Love, Charleston

October 30, 2005 – Charleston,

I love pumpkin! It is so cute! You are so cute! I ended up going out last night. Niki invited me along with her husband and some of their friends to a club. It was mainly a Persian party but it was different and fun. I didn't have any time to get a costume so I wore the one from last year. The costume is supposed to be a sexy witch but it looks nothing like a witch. It is hot pink and black. It sort of has a corset top and a tulle skirt. There is a witch hat but I didn't wear it. Niki was a dark angel. Her husband, Amir, wore the scream mask and scared everyone the entire night. I got to do some more Persian dancing. It was a fun night. I kept thinking about how much fun we would have had together. People would be mesmerized.

I'm very disappointed because my Uncle Barry, Aunt Lauren, and Brian are going to Aunt Mindy's tonight for dinner. They are going to carve pumpkins and do Halloween stuff with Brian. I haven't seen Brian in so long and I want to be a part of it. I have to go into work because I have so much to get ready for tomorrow. The sale starts on Wednesday and all the markdowns are taking place tomorrow. Practically my entire floor has to get marked down and then I have to re-set the fixtures. It is going to take forever! I also have to do some serious cleaning because my mom is coming next week. She is coming on the first day of the sale which is horrible timing. I will hardly have any time to spend with her. My dad is going to Palm Springs so she is coming here. He will come for the weekend. I'm really looking forward to seeing them. My mom will just have to come into the store for lunch everyday. The shop owner that my mom took her knitting to called and asked her to make ten more bracelets. She wants to take them to a show. She is excited. It's really good for her. My cousin, Mike proposed to his girlfriend. They are going to be married next November. I'm really happy for him. His fiancé, April, is a teacher in Philadelphia. He works for Lockheed Martin. Right now he is spending the weeks in San Diego and the weekends in Philadelphia. I don't know how he does it. He is my Aunt Betsy's son.

You're right about never being in the stores with the women you would want to pick up. You could get creative and pretend you were shopping for a gift for your mother or sister. Just ask the girl her opinion about something and there you go. The other thing is that there are usually hot girls working in trendy men's departments or stores. The problem with that is they get hit on all day. It probably gets old. Niki works in men's furnishings and gets hit on all the time. She hates it but she is also married.

The retail industry really is the worst to work in? That stinks! I've never seen any facts showing that other retail stores pay more. I have heard that some do. I will have to look into it more before I can say for sure. One of the comments made in the meeting was that Janet could go manage a Home Depot and make significantly more money.

I hope things are going well. You seem in good spirits. It makes me really happy. I love you! God bless.

Love, Talle

Oh yeah, I kicked my bed this morning and re-injured my toe. I don't know what my problem is lately! It's getting ridiculous!!!

LOVE ;)

October 30, 2005 – Talle,

I can only be truly happy, when I am writing you. Not much else to do around here that is exciting. I love you. Just had to tell you. God bless.

Love, Charleston

October 30, 2005 – Charleston,

Thank you for such a sweet note. I love you so much. At least you are more than half way through your deployment. Can you even imagine what it will be like when you get back? It will be so unbelievable. I absolutely cannot wait! God bless.

Love, Talle

HAPPY HALLOWEEN!!!

October 31, 2005 – Charleston,

Happy Halloween!

I had a surprise visit from my dad tonight. He flew into LAX and was suppose to have dinner with a co-worker. It ended up being canceled so he was able to have dinner with us. I didn't even know he was coming into town tonight. It was a very pleasant surprise. We went to Javier's at the Spectrum. My parents really miss Mexican food. There is nothing like it in Ohio.

I received a few letters from you today. I was really excited! One of them you told me you received the package I sent you. I was very confused about the Jimmy Choo receipt but I finally figured it out. When I took your books from your house to my house they were in the Jimmy Choo bag. When I took the books to the post office I gave them the bag of books and they packaged it. The receipt must have been in the bag and they put it in the box. I didn't mean to send it to you, sorry!

A Beachfire is opening in Ladera Ranch. It seems strange. The building looks like a clubhouse. It will be interesting to see what they do with it.

I love you very much. Thank you for writing such beautiful letters. They mean so much to me!

Love always, Talle

**

Part Three

Have patience. This all sounds well in theory, but without practice you cannot apply this to your life. We must be proactive and patient. Like yoga, step-by-step we become more flexible. We become stronger and soon can combat the challenges that test our very nature. We knew this wouldn't be easy. Love is hard. It requires perfect people, who can find their way through the storm of life and don't compromise for anyone. They are fearless, feeding love with every ounce of their soul. Unfortunately we are not perfect.

Have faith. The greatest trick the Devil ever pulled was convincing people he existed. Couples in love have both individual and relationship fears that they must overcome. Just saying they will combat them is easier than actually doing it. Yet we do it every day and prevail. We have the power to decide. We decide whether to let fear run our lives. We find our way out of the forest. We correct the errors made along the way. We choose to have faith in our instincts and we learn to make our own magic

Make magic. Life throws you a lot of curve balls, but you have the power to make the best of it. If we remembered one thing this was it. Free will allows us to choose how to live. We chose to accept each other despite our faults. We chose to make sacrifices despite the risks. We chose to be in love despite our circumstances. We were making magic with every word, surprise, poem, and gift. They nourished the love we had. Love inspired all these acts, but it also grew from them. We were writing our story and no one could write if for us.

SALE

November 1, 2005 – Charleston,

Tomorrow is the big sale. I just finished with the set-up. We were done in a record breaking 30 minutes. I am so happy that part is over. My day doesn't seem too big tomorrow. Hopefully we will be able to make it. I haven't made the first day of a sale since I started in Petites. I'm really hoping to change that.

I'm going to go to bed. I love you very much. Take care of yourself and be safe! God bless.

Love, Talle

FINALLY!

November 2, 2005 – Charleston,

I finally did it!!! The first day of the sale was a huge success! I made my day in by 3:00pm. Everything went perfectly. I am so happy! I had the largest increase for petites in Orange County and was one of the few to make it in the store. I am so proud of my girls. It was such a great day. I am so tired though. I am going to go to sleep. I love you and miss you.

Love, Talle

MISSING YOU

November 9, 2005 – Charleston,

I'm sorry I haven't written. It's been a stressful week. I'm sure it does not compare to yours. I've been saying extra prayers for you. I hate not knowing what you are doing and that you are okay. I have faith that everything is fine but I cannot help worrying. I love you with all my heart.

The sale and my mother's visit took a lot out of me. I had to work long hours and wasn't able to spend much time with her. I was stressed about it because work was demanding and I just wanted to be with my mom. When I was with her I was tired and irritable. I think that I resented her in a way for being there and I feel awful about it now. She went home today and I feel really sad. I wish I could have spent more quality time. I was able to spend one full day with her, which was like old times. It was fun. We went to lunch and shopping.

We went to the Montage in Laguna Beach for lunch. It is unbelievably beautiful but the prices were obscene. There is no salad worth $21. We sat outside overlooking the ocean. We both had a glass of wine. It was a fun splurge.

Camilla was talking about what she wants to do next year. This was very sad to listen to her. She wants to have the college experience and she knows she has to move to do it. She has tried living on campus before and wasn't happy. I think that she is comfortable and happy here. I don't know why she would want to do it. She has the ability to commute and get her degree. I am concerned for her. If she really feels compelled to experience college, then I want her to have that opportunity, but I don't want her to be unhappy.

She recently decided against medical school and is now considering psychology. These are really tough decisions. I think some experience will help her decide. I love Hunter and know that if they are meant to be it will all work out in the end. I just hope that she doesn't hold her self back from pursuing her dreams.

My grandmother got a letter from you today. Thank you so much for doing that. I cannot even tell you how much that meant to her. She is very happy! You are amazing. I wish I could squeeze you and give you a big kiss!

I miss you terribly. It's been four months! I hope you are still on track to come home on time. It's getting closer and closer. I cannot wait. I was envisioning your arrival during yoga last night. It was a wonderful thought. I love you! Take care of yourself!

God bless, Talle

BIRTHDAY
November 10, 2005 – Charleston,

I heard that today is the 230th birthday of the Marine Corps, so happy birthday!!! I love you!

I'm ready for you to come home. I get more and more excited the closer it gets. It is starting to become more of a reality than a dream. I love you so much. I cannot wait to spend time with you.

I have a predicament at work. One of my salesgirls is consistently performing below the expectations. I've been lenient with her because she is a great employee. I recently asked her if she enjoys selling. She admitted she doesn't like it any more. I gave her other options and she chose to interview with customer service. She is such a sweet girl but is quiet and never looks happy. Customer service won't hire her. I feel bad. She is sensitive and I don't know how she will take this. I don't want the company to lose her because she is a hard worker, but I can't keep her on my floor and she didn't like any of the other options I gave her. It's a difficult situation. I'd rather not be in it. I just hope she will understand and be willing to try another option.

I love you much! Take care of yourself and be safe.

Love always, Talle

HAPPY VETERANS DAY

November 11, 2005 – Charleston,

Happy Veterans Day! I just want to remind you how much I respect and honor everything you do for this country. You are an unbelievable man. Even though I don't understand all you do I am amazed at the thought of it. You are such a selfless man. I've never seen anyone care so much about the men he leads. You are an inspiration. I am proud to love you. You and your men are in my prayers. I love you.

My salesgirl Katie found out today that she did not get the customer service position. She was so upset. It was heartbreaking. After some time she became open to the idea of being a stock person. She has two interviews tomorrow. I pray that one will work out.

I had two interviews today. My first instinct about the first girl was no. The interview ended up going really well and I could see her being successful. One of my concerns is that she hasn't kept a job for more than a year. She seems outgoing and personable, which I want, but I need someone with enthusiasm. My team is relatively calm and down to earth. My regional manager (Janet's boss) made a comment about making sure there is excitement in the department. This has been in the back of my mind, so I am having a hard time deciding. The second interview was perfect. She is exactly what I was looking for in a candidate. I know she would be perfect. I wish I could hire both of them. I don't know what to do. I guess it's a better problem to have than not having any applicants. I've been here before. I wish I could get your opinion. I would love to know your thoughts.

Happy Veterans Day! Thank you for all of the sacrifices you've made. I love you with all my heart.

Love, Talle

THOUGHTS
November 12, 2005 – Charleston,

I love you. I cannot stop thinking about it. I just want to tell you over and over. Everything makes me think of you. You are my first thought in the morning and my last at night. It amazes me that I feel so connected to you. I really feel you in everything I do. Our love is special. Sometimes it blows my mind to think about it. I really miss talking to you. I hope you will be able to write soon. I haven't had much time for anything other than work lately. It is exhausting. It's a constant roller coaster. One amazing day followed by a huge loss. I never seem to break even. The only difference is that now the rest of the store is in the same situation. I am actually number one in Orange County for petites, even though I have a 5.9% decrease. Oh well, that counts for something! I am off tomorrow and I'm really looking forward to it. I think I will go to a yoga class in the morning. I've never been to this one. I usually go to church. I will attend a later service so I can try the class. I cannot wait for the day that we can do these things together. I love you so much! God bless.

Love, Talle

DISNEYLAND
November 14, 2005 – Charleston,

I just got home from another trip to Disneyland. It was a very short trip. Michelle called me this morning and asked me to go after work. I had been planning on going to Pilate's but she talked me into going with her. We got there at 7:30 and the park closed at 8:00. We probably should have thought about that before we went. We rode Space Mountain and then had dinner at Downtown Disney. The park was all decorated for Christmas. I loved it. I have always wanted to go when they make it snow. I think they start that after Thanksgiving. I'm excited!

I had a good day at work. I got a lot accomplished. I sent out a game plan of events and contests for November and December to my buyers today. I had completed it a while ago for Janet so that I could get prizes from her. I don't know why I never sent it to my buyers but I decided to today. I am excited because my Dress & Coat Buyer emailed back and offered to give me two $25 Nordy bucks (basically cash that is taxed) to be used for a contest involving coats or dresses. They are already sponsoring a contest for December. I really appreciate their generosity. I also found out I won $120! There was a contest in October for managers. The buyers gave $10 for every day that we made our sales goals but you had to make at least 10 days. I made 12 so I won! I was excited. I never win contests. I'm hoping to win the coat contest we have for the next two months. My team and I created a really cute contest. Every girl has a stocking. Every time they sell a coat they get to choose a stocking stuffer. I went to Target and got all kinds of little things. At the end of the month the girl with the most stocking stuffers gets $50 Nordy bucks. Everyone gets to keep the stocking stuffers they accumulate, in a way everyone wins. Anyway the buyers really liked the idea so I had some points with them. I just have to make sure we sell enough coats.

Sorry I just rambled about work. I really love you. I can't wait to hear from you! I hope all is well.

All my love, Talle

WORRIED

November 16, 2005 – Charleston,

I'm worried about you now. I hope you are safe. I hope you are not a part of the things that are going on. I love you so much. I'm constantly saying prayers for you. I cannot wait to hear from you. I just want to know that you are safe.

I was in charge of the store last night. It was a rough night. Nothing major happened. There were just so many little things that kept going wrong. Luckily the store had an awesome day. It's not fun to be the MIC and miss the day.

I went to yoga this morning. I like going in the morning. It is offered on Sunday and Wednesday morning, which is perfect. My body feels so much better when I do yoga. It is especially helpful this time of year because of work. It will be great for you when you get home. I'm really excited to go with you.

I love you! I miss you! Take care of yourself!

Love, Talle

LOVE

November 18, 2005 – Charleston,

I just got so excited because I logged onto the computer and I had 5 emails. I thought for sure one would be from you. Unfortunately they were all junk. I really miss hearing from you and I cannot stop worrying. I love you so much! I cannot wait for the day when this is over. I just want to be able to touch your face and kiss your hand. To look into your eyes while you hold me in your arms. I would give anything to have you here right now. I love you with all my heart. I pray that you are safe. I pray that you will feel my love and that it gives you comfort.

I love you, Talle

RELIEF

November 22, 2005 – Charleston,

I am so happy you called last night! It was such a relief to hear your voice. I wish you were feeling better. I hope it will all be gone today. I love you so much. I cannot wait to talk to you again.

I love you! Talle

*

HOPE

November 22, 2005 – Talle,

I am so grateful for all the emails and letters. This means so much to me. Thank you for loving me. You really are perfect. Your love has given me so much strength and hope over the last three weeks.

I am glad to hear about Yoga. I love the ending when everyone passes out on the floor. Envisioning you doing Yoga is a big turn on. I am looking forward to that moment. I love you. I am going to call you so I will keep this short.

I can't wait to see you and hold you.

Love, Charleston

THANKSGIVING

November 25, 2005 – Charleston,

I love you so much. It has been wonderful talking to you. I hope the rest of your Thanksgiving was nice. I saw on the news that they were serving pumpkin pie somewhere in Iraq. I was really excited at the thought of you getting to eat some pie. I hope you were able to. I made the pumpkin pancakes. They were good. I had a nice day. The food was delicious. I loved seeing the twins. They are so rambunctious. I swear they never stop moving. They are sweet and constantly smiling or laughing. Heather and Kevin are moving to Virginia next summer. I don't know how often I will see them so I have to take advantage of this time. Everyone sends their best. I got to talk about you a lot. It was very enjoyable. I feel happy when I'm talking about you. I hope you will have the opportunity to call again. I love you with all my heart.

Love, Talle

WARMTH

November 30, 2005 – Charleston,

I love you! I hope you are doing all right. It has been wonderful hearing your voice! My thoughts and prayers are with you as you go out again. I wish you didn't have to do this. You should be on your way home! I've been sending warm thoughts your way. I hope you can feel my warmth and embrace. I love you! I cannot tell you enough.

I got some information for your men today. I will send it to you. There is also a card for a realtor they can email for additional information. Let me know if you need me to look further into anything. I can get more information, as it gets closer to your arrival. I'm excited thinking about it!

Camilla turned 21! It's hard to believe. The two of us went to Javier's in Laguna Beach for dinner. The waiters sang to her, put a napkin crown on her head, and fed her flan. It was hysterical! She is planning a big celebration this weekend. Originally she was going to get a limo. She decided it would be impossible for everyone to stay at our house afterward, so now she wants to get a couple hotel rooms. It should be exciting! I'll let you know how it turns out.

I love you very much. Take care of yourself. God Bless.

Love, Talle

BIG NIGHT

December 4, 2005 – Charleston,

I love you so much! I am constantly reminded how lucky I am to have you in my life. As difficult as this time may be it shows the strength of our love. I cannot wait for the day that I can touch you. Knowing the day will come is all I need to get through this. I'm glad that my love gives you strength. I hope you will always feel it. I pray everyday that you will be filled with my love. You are perfect. I admire you for your strength and positivity. It takes an extraordinary person to do what you do. I love you.

Last night was the big night. Camilla decided to get three hotel rooms in Dana Point. The plan was to go out to dinner and then go to Hennessy's. My friend Michelle came. I was really excited because she never goes out. Dinner went well. We ate at El Torito. Then it was time for Hennessy's. It was an unbelievable experience! The bouncer would not let her in. They claimed the person on her license was not she. A couple different people looked at it and all agreed. They confiscated her license! It was crazy. Of course she lost it and was sobbing. Everyone was yelling at the bouncer's. It was a nightmare. I went back to the room to get her credit card and school ID to prove that it was her. I guess before I got back one of the other bouncers recognized her from high school and confirmed it was her ID. The owner came and apologized and offered to buy everyone drinks. I just felt so bad for her because they were so disrespectful. It was an infuriating situation. She bounced back quickly and ended up having a good time. She only got sick once and is hanging in there today. I had fun. Though, I was really missing you. There was a lot of dancing and you really should have been there. I love you.

Love, Talle

December 16, 2005 –

Funny you got to talk about me during thanksgiving. I love talking about me too. Just kidding. I get all giggly and stupid when I talk about you. Really is embarrassing, so I mostly try to keep it to myself.

I don't know about the birthday party doesn't sound like hotels and limos is going to end up right. Sounds like strippers and tequila will be involved somewhere. Whenever we had a limo I came home with twice as many strangers. I am always wondering who are all these people are. They all just pile in the limo, weird!! I can't wait to find out what happened. I sure hope the computer is fast, unless you kept me hanging.

Love you, Charleston

December 16, 2005 –

Wow this was definitely worth the wait. I can't believe they wouldn't let her in. That is so unreal. I can't believe it. What a nightmare. I am glad that I wasn't there. I wouldn't have bounced back so easily. Nothing upsets me more than people who don't have manners. What idiots.

What are you doing the 24-29 January?

Love you, Charleston

RAINDROPS ON ROSES

December 8, 2005 – Charleston,

I was driving home and I heard *Raindrops on Roses*. It made me think of you and smile. I sang it in honor of you. I will never forget that night. I love you! I miss you terribly. I cannot wait to hear your voice. I pray you are safe and well.

Love always, Talle

December 16, 2005 –

Now this really is a great Christmas present. Nothing makes me happier than thinking of you singing. When I look at the picture of you on the tire swing. I wonder what you were thinking in your head while swinging so gleefully. You must have been singing something sweet.

> Whiskers on kittens...
> Brown paper packages...
> I love you, Charleston

MISS YOU
December 12, 2005 – Charleston,

Oh I love you so much! I cannot wait to hear from you. I hope you are doing well. My life consists mainly of work and sleep lately. I haven't had energy for much else. Work has been good the past couple of days. I will hope it continues. You know how that goes. I've been trying to continue going to the gym. It helps my energy level. I am going to Pilate's tonight. I think I will go early and do the elliptical as well. I didn't have to work today so I was able to get some extra rest. I hope you are able to get decent sleep and stay warm and safe. I love you and miss you terribly. You are constantly in my prayers.

God Bless, Talle

NEED TO VENT
December 13, 2005 – Charleston,

First I want to tell you I love you, miss you and hope you are well. Now I need to vent. Something happened at work today that really upset me. It doesn't surprise me but I am fed up. Let me give you some background information. Everyday at 4:45 there is a meeting with the department managers and the closer from each department. We review every department's sales for the day and how they can meet their goals before close. We started this when business became tough. The idea is to keep the day momentum going into the night when most managers are off. Janet runs the meeting. She wants everyone to yell, scream and be excited. I was the night MIC. A couple of minutes before the meeting she tells me I am running the meeting alone. After having a momentary anxiety attack I think, okay I can do it. Public speaking is not my forte. She knows I am not a cheerleader. I am quiet. I am perfectly capable of having the meeting, but I am not going to yell, scream, or jump up and down. Don't get me wrong I can have enthusiasm and energy, but probably not to her extent. Anyway, I started the meeting. She wasn't there. I read the store's stats for the day and then asked each department to share their sales. We were having a good day so it was exciting. I was as energetic and enthusiastic as I could be. Once I was about halfway through she came in. The first thing she says is "Is it just because Talle is giving the meeting or do none of you have any zip in your do-da's?" I just stood there and turned bright red. As if it wasn't hard enough for me to be in front of my peers in the first place. She humiliated me. Everyone was enthusiastic and clapping. I guess it just wasn't good enough. I felt like how could it ever be? She knows me. Why did she make me do it? It's just Janet's way.

I know her insecurity makes her lash out at people, often humiliating them in the process. This not the first time she's done it to me or anyone else. I think this is ridiculous and intolerable behavior. Unfortunately salespeople are seeing her true colors. I think this should not happen and is poor judgment on her part. Only managers should be exposed to her negativity and even sometimes cruelty. Both salespeople and managers made comments tonight, which set the tone for a bad night. Any confidence I had going was shot. She made me feel like crap.

Janet is a good manager. Maybe not the nicest person, but she is supportive of me, which makes my life easier. If you are on her bad side, she can make work miserable. There was a time when Janet did not love me. I will never forget the way she made me feel then. It can be awful. It is unprofessional to behave this way sometimes. I wish she could see that. I'm sorry I rambled. I love you very much. Thinking of you and remembering I will see you soon helps me to deal with these frustrations. I can't wait to be able to come home from work to you. Nothing else will matter. I love you. I pray that you are safe and warm and that my love will help you through.

Love always, Talle
December 16, 2005 –

Zip in your do da's?? On a whim I made it to a place that has Internet. This is the first email that I read. Bottom line I agree with you completely. She must be insecure. You certainly don't need to be more enthusiastic. You are not a "cheerleader," and that is ok. Besides few cheerleader-types are genuine. Honestly I think your style is very dignified and respectable. I don't care what Janet thinks. Not everyone needs to be a "cheerleader" to motivate their people. How do you think Grace Kelly, Audrey Hepburn, Elizabeth Dole, or Jackie Kennedy would act in your situation? Could you see any of them jumping on seats screaming?

I think you have 3 good points from your email. One she was unprofessional not just for what she said, but for showing up late and then interrupting you after asking you to lead the meeting. Either, you are running the meeting or not. I wouldn't task one of my men to do something and then interrupt him while doing it. Leadership doesn't work like that. In the Marine Corps we delegate down to the lowest level and trust in our Marines with our ultimate goal being mission accomplishment. We provide them with our Commander's Intent to convey how each task accomplishes the larger mission. Knowing our intent enables them to adapt to the chaos of war and accomplish the mission in their own way. Second, just because Janet runs the meeting like "girls gone wild" doesn't mean you have to. If she asked you to run it then you need to run it how you want, in your style, with what suits your personality. Every person has a different leadership style and you have to be true to that. People are far more responsive to sincerity. Don't compromise your self for her sake. If you are in charge THEN YOUR IN CHARGE. Third your peers or Janet shouldn't ever, ever, ever intimidate you. Honestly, you probably intimidate them. You are an intelligent, sexy, respectable lady. You are extremely enviable and in a class all your own. No one controls you or makes you who you are. If it is your choice not to run those meetings a certain way then that is your choice. If you do run a meeting then I am absolutely positive that you will find your own talents and way with people that will be admired and respected. Just follow your instincts, but don't ever compromise your choices. You are certainly no one's puppet. Don't let anyone treat you like one. I'll give her something to worry about. Love you.

Ran out of time, Charleston

December 19, 2005 – Charleston,

Thank you for the email I always love to hear your comments. I appreciate your support on the Janet thing. I agree that I should not change who I am for her. That was part of what made me so angry. She knows me why couldn't she let me do it my way? She tries to mold people into what she wants and a lot of people fall into it. I have always loathed that. I never wanted to be that type of person.

It was wonderful talking to you today. I am so glad you were able to call. I love you so much! I would love to come to Hong Kong in January. I looked at flights. They start at around $800. I have two concerns. One is the cost. Two is that I don't want to jeopardize any time off when you get home. It would be amazing to see you that soon. That is in a month!

Take care of yourself. Be safe. I love you.

Love, Talle

*

BLANK

December 21, 2005 – Charleston,

Thank you again for getting those phone numbers. You are amazing! I called them today. Both are brokers. I left a message but was not able to get any information. I looked on the website for one of the brokers. There was a listing of all the businesses for sale in the area. There were a few in San Clemente and Laguna Beach. It did not show any information about exact location. I requested information for a couple of the listings. They mainly seemed to be gift and furniture stores. There was a clothing boutique in Dana Point. I requested information on that as well. I just finished making Buckeyes. They are going to be my Christmas gift to people at work. I also tried making my mom's lemon bread recipe. It's so good but I've never made it because it is tricky. It seems to have worked but I have not tasted it yet. That will be the true test. I love you so much! I am so thankful to have you in my life. I really miss you. I am so excited for what the future holds. Take care of yourself and be careful.

I love you! Talle

December 25, 2005 – Talle,

I love you sooooo much. I am holding my breath till I see you again. Merry Christmas.

Love, Charleston

MERRY CHRISTMAS

December 25, 2005 – Charleston,

Merry Christmas! I love and miss you! I hope you were able to have some type of celebration. I pray that you are not in harms way. Maybe you are on your way home?! Wherever you are and whatever you are doing you are on my mind and in my heart, as always, but in a special way today. I cannot imagine what it is like for you to be there, away from your family, in awful, unsafe conditions. I am counting the days until you return. I love you very much.

Thank you so much for the beautiful earrings, necklace, and bracelet. They are absolutely beautiful! I love them!!! I do not own any pearls. I am so excited to have my first set. Thank you. I received many compliments! Your mother is wonderful. I appreciate everything she has done for me. She has been so generous and kind.

I had a very nice Christmas. I got out of work yesterday at 4:30. Janet let us go early, which was a pleasant surprise. I went down to Mindy and Jason's for dinner and spent the night. We ate dinner then watched the movie Love Actually. Uncle Barry, Lauren, Brian, and Granny were all there. My cousin Mike also came for the night. Today was a very nice, relaxing day. This morning Aunt Mindy, Uncle Jason, Mike, and I got up and opened presents, had breakfast, and took a walk on the beach. Later on we went over to Uncle Barry's for dinner. Aunt Betsy and Uncle Scott (Matt's parents) got in around 6:30. There was a lot of family around and it was a helpful distraction. It is hard for me not to be with my immediate family. I have so many wonderful memories of holidays spent together. It is heartbreaking being apart. On top of that my longing for you became even stronger.

I am so happy because you just called! I love you so much! You are on your way home!!!!!!!!!!!!!!! That is the best gift! I am so excited!

I love you, Talle

December 27, 2005 – Talle,

Ok so here is the time line and I am using military time. We pack up at 2400, load buses at 0100, pack the airplane at 0200, stand in freezing cold till 0700, Board plane land in Kuwait 0830, load buses 0900, drive to Naval Base arrive 1100, wait for boat drive boat to bigger boat, then drive bigger boat 6 weeks stopping in Dubai, Singapore, Hong Kong, Hawaii, and finally to YOU!! I am so excited that I am going to go back out side and shake for another 3hrs. I feel like a shriveled marshmallow... Love you miss you. Will write you from ship. We are on our way home.

Love, Charleston

December 27, 2005 – Charleston,

I love the time line. Thank you. I'm sorry you have to be so cold! I will warm you up when you get back! I am happy, relieved, and excited that you are beginning your journey home. I love you! I cannot believe I missed your call. I was in the mall and I felt my phone vibrate but by the time I answered it went to voicemail. I quickly went back to the store but just missed that call. I was sad. I would have loved to talk to you. Thank you for the sweet message. Good luck with your travels. I hope you will warm up on the ship.

Love, Talle

LOVE YOU

December 30, 2005 – Charleston,

I love you. Right now I hope you are on the ship making your way home. I just woke up from an unexpected but revitalizing nap. I went into work this morning. At 11:30 Janet called and asked me to go home and come back at 5 to be MIC. She is paying me extra so I do not mind. I am looking forward to having the next two days off. I do not have any new year's plans yet. I will probably go to Michelle's. It will be mellow which is fine. I am trying to go snowboarding one of the days. Hopefully that will work out. Other than that I need to clean, organize, and catch up on life.

Hunter picked Camilla up from the airport last night. We all went to dinner. They wanted sushi so I decided to give it a try. I have had it before and the last time was in Ohio. I did not love it but I could see that I could get used to it. Well, I tried the crunchy rolls and they were great. Since I was feeling so adventurous I tried one of Hunter's rainbow rolls. Not so good! That was not easy to get down. At least I gave it a shot. For now I will stick with crunchy rolls.

I told Camilla that I would be living with you when our lease is up. She expected it and was fine. That was a relief. I was having anxiety about her reaction. She does not know where she will live but she has some time.

My mom received your letter. She was touched. You write and express yourself beautifully. Reading your words really moved her. She has always been worried about me in love. I have not always made the best decisions. I am sure she had concerns about our relationship as well. It has moved so quickly. She was relieved to hear your side of the story and to understand how much love we have. Thank you so much for writing. I love you very much. I am so blessed to have you in my life. I cannot wait for you to come home. I have been thinking so much about the things we will do. My heart races at the thought. Take care of yourself and I hope to hear from you soon.

Love, Talle

TESTING
December 31, 2005 –

I have to find your email. I hope this is it.

Love you, Charleston

December 31, 2005 – Charleston,

This is the right email. I wrote you yesterday but I sent it to your other address. I forgot about this one. You probably cannot check that one can you? If not I can forward it to you. I love you and I am glad you are on the ship. I will write to you later. I am going to see a movie with Michelle.

Love, Talle

HAPPY NEW YEAR
December 31, 2005 –

Ooohhh I Love you, a bushel and a peck, a bushel and a peck, and a hug around the neck... You have inspired this completely original song. Happy New Year!!! I love you and wish that I could be there with you. I am dying to see you. I have developed this crazy disease where I can think of you at any moment and then once I do I can't turn it off...

My Marines are very grateful for the Real Estate package. It was perfect. I have your book *The Purpose Driven Life*. I was planning on reading it on the way home and as I began to read I noticed that he suggests reading it with a partner. Since you sent it, I will put the question to you. Would you like to read it together when I return, or would you rather me read it on my own? I would like to read it with you, but I know that you have already read it. I love you.

Love, Charleston

SEE YOU SOON
January 1, 2006 –

I miss you too much...
Traveling to Hong Kong Talle Gilmore
Tue 24-Jan-06
Total distance: 7284 mi (11722 km)
Total duration: 16hr 20mn

Traveling to Los Angeles
Sun 29-Jan-06

*

January 1, 2006 – Oh my God!

Are you serious?! I love you so much. You are absolutely amazing! I opened this email and almost passed out. You know how I get with surprises. I am shaking I don't even know how I am typing. This is incredible! I cannot believe I will see you so soon! I am so excited. How did you even have time to do this? My mind is racing. I cannot think straight. Thank you. I love you and I am so happy!

Happy New Year! I knew this was going to be a great year. However, I was not expecting the first day to be so exciting! I am looking forward to the things this year will bring. I really missed you last night. It was the hardest time I have had dealing with our separation. We went to Mark's in Costa Mesa. It is a really nice seafood and steak restaurant. Being in that setting reminded me of you and that started the longing. Not to mention I was with three married couples. It was a nice dinner. I had a delicious fillet and afterward we played poker. I do not have much interest in the game but that was the plan. It was a nice evening. I really missed you and could not wait for the night to end. Anyway, that is over now. I have moved on to more exciting things! I am so excited to see you in Hong Kong! This is incredible. I honestly cannot think straight right now.

I love the song you wrote for me. It is adorable! As for the book, I would love to read it with you.

Happy New Year! Thank you. I love you. Talle

HONG KONG
January 2, 2006 – Talle,

I have to see you.

I apologize for the surprise. I know it was a bit sudden. Additionally, Hong Kong is a very special place. Returning to Hong Kong will be an important moment for me and I would like you to share it. This year will be a challenging year for both of us, one that I am very excited to undertake. I must comment on your enthusiasm, because you are truly remarkable. Your sincere excitement is enchanting, which makes loving you surreal. If you have questions about Hong Kong, then I would recommend speaking with my mother. She has a more practical understanding of the city. I am more in tune with its magic. I love you. God has blessed us with each other.

Love, Charleston

SPICE?
January 3, 2006 – My love,

I am overwhelmingly in love with you. I am having anxiety attacks waiting to see you. When I think of it I have trouble thinking straight. You are going to have to excuse me from all ridiculous actions when I see you. I don't know how I am going to handle it. I might pass out or explode. I just don't know... I don't know if this puts it in perspective, but I have so much internal energy thinking about it if the military would let me go I would. I would jump off the ship, swim however far it took to get to shore, walk as far as it took to transportation, get to an airport, fly home, and find you wherever you were at exactly that moment, and hug you until I passed out. Ok have to stop thinking about it.

I just finished the book your mother sent me *Off the Planet*. I enjoyed the book and thought it was interesting reading about space, but was a little worried. She sent it because the author reminded her of me. Well I started reading the book and he came off really arrogant, didn't get any better by the end. I was laughing but concerned wondering if she was implying anything. I really hope that I didn't come off arrogant when spending time with her. That would be disappointing.

I recently read an article about kinky sex and now am a bit curious. 2,000 women were polled. 70% said that they have tried kinky sex and 90% said that they wanted to partake in some form of it. I thought these numbers were inflated. Have you secretly been feeling kinky all this time and I have been oblivious? Did I miss all the signals? What a fool I must have been to your hidden desires for a bit of spice? Obviously I am joking. I love you. I have idolized you for 6 months. Even in the midst of serious combat operations I will have brief mental lapses where my thoughts turn to you. You must know that I find you incredibly attractive and love you possibly to a fault.

Maybe I haven't communicated this enough.

With all my love, Charleston

January 3, 2006 – Charleston,

I don't know how I am going to handle seeing you either. I can relate to your feelings. I haven't been able to think straight since I read that email. I knew the end was in sight but it was taking so long! To think there are only a couple of weeks separating us is incredible! And we are going to be in Hong Kong. I never would have dreamed this could be reality. We might have a problem if you think you might pass out because you know this happens to me all the time!!! I am so excited!

I am glad you enjoyed the book from my mom. She does not think you are arrogant in any way. I have not read the book, so I know little about it. I think her implication was about the drive or accomplishments of the author. I know it was not about arrogance. She would tell me if that were the case.

Kinky sex huh. Those numbers seem astronomical to me as well. The kinky stuff is a little beyond my imagination, but who knows what the future will bring! ☺ Anyway you are perfect. I love you.

Love, Talle

January 3, 2006 –

Oh I love you, so much. I am typing this with a silly grin on my face. I really appreciate and love your honesty. I can't think of you often, because every time I do I revert back to a silly high school kid. The knots and butterflies in my stomach start acting like a wind tunnel. Once it is turned on, I can't wipe off the filthy grin. I don't think that I even acted silly when I was in High School. You are so wonderful that the excitement to see you more than makes up for Thanksgiving, Christmas, New Years, Valentine's Day, and my Birthday. You are the most perfect present that I could ever receive, but containing the excitement is just too difficult like a present you have to open. I could say I love you endlessly. I feel like I'm taking crazzzy pills.

I'm glad you agree about the kinky sex, because I really thought I was missing something. I do believe you, because I know that you are completely honest with me, and I love that about you!!! Oh don't worry about any hidden meanings in the undertones from me either. I was mostly just playing with you. I believe that intimacy should be both fun and playful, but you must define that as a couple.

If my heart hurts writing you, then what in the world will seeing you do? Charleston

January 3, 2006 –

Today, we are porting in Dubai. The city was an oil rich country that ran out of oil and poured their profits into making a Las Vegas in the Middle East. They have out done themselves in a completely unrealistic scale: in door skiing, water parks, camel rides, gambling, dancing eastern Europeans. Dubai is like one giant Middle Eastern Theme Park. When the Marines get off the ship we call it Liberty. Liberty is a tricky process, because the command wants to give them free time but risks having the Marines get in trouble. The day begins with about four different briefs on the liberty policy and staying out of trouble. The highlights are you are representatives of your country and the armed services don't discredit yourselves. You have three more liberty ports to go if you screw up you wont see anymore. And, make sure your buddy is with you at all times. No matter what Marines will be destructive. It's Genetic. My first priority is to call you. Do you see how dedicated I am to you? I am madly in love with you. I can't even think of anything else.

Love, Charleston

FUN IN DUBAI

January 5, 2006 – Charleston,

Are you excited for the water park? I am excited for you and I wish I were there.

It was a very warm day today in the 80's. It was kind of strange.

I went to the dentist today. My jaw has been bothering me. I am embarrassed to say that I had not been in four years. I was very nervous about going. I prepared myself for bad news. I deserved it after delaying the appointment for so long. I cannot tell you how relieved I am. I did not have any cavities and everything was fine! I have a TMJ problem but I can deal with that.

Work is unbelievably bad. I cannot even comprehend how my department could be failing so miserably. It is now the fifth day of the month. In five days I have taken so many returns that I am in the hole over a thousand dollars. It is part of retail to take returns especially this time of year. But this is outrageous! I am the only petite department in the negative. It is embarrassing and discouraging. It is so difficult to remain positive in this situation. I really do not know how to handle it.

I loved talking to you yesterday. I was so giddy! I could not stop smiling for hours after we hung up. I really really love you. I am so excited to see you. It is overtaking my mind. I hope you have a wonderful, fun, relaxing day today.

Love, Talle

16 DAYS!!!
January 8, 2006 – Talle,

We finally have left Dubai and the count down begins. Dubai didn't really turn out as expected, especially since we were not allowed to leave the pier. Maybe you would be interested in returning with me some day. This is just a thought;). The enthusiasm is going on a strong boil otherwise I may not make it. I have way too many ideas, thoughts, and questions to share, ask, etc... I think that I have overloaded my brain. I finished the other book you gave me *The Weight of Water*. I liked her description about kindness, which is the result of having an abundance of affection that you are capable of sharing with others. This is poignant to describe the scrooges as lacking affection. You must have been sending me an abundance of affection because I think that I might be overloaded. I thought Anita Shreve had wonderful prose and exceptional fluidity, but I thought overall lacked in substance. The only really tragic moment was the child dying in the end, which is brought on you abruptly; otherwise, the story is relatively predictable. I think she overloaded it with two parallel stories and too many themes. She didn't really bring one overriding theme, idea, or topic out in the story. The end doesn't leave the reader with one resolution or epiphany. I think she has some insight into the female psyche, but doesn't fully develop her awareness. I am curious what a female perspective might be? Maybe I am missing the intricacies because I am not a female.

You have two choices. Do you want to be included in the process of selecting activities in Hong Kong or would you rather just see it as it comes? Just to state it plainly: I am happy to entertain either choice. I am so excited for our reunion that I would love to show you around, but in the end and always I want your participation. I leave the choice to you. Let me know and I will send you some already gathered information or not...

I included a picture of Marines on the ship that you might enjoy *(Photo 9)*. I love you, Charleston

*

January 8, 2006 – Charleston,

I am glad to hear you have left Dubai. I wish it could have been a better experience. It seems like a very interesting place. I would enjoy visiting Dubai with you some day. I would love for you to show me around Hong Kong. I want to do and see the things that are important to you. I do not know much about Hong Kong other than what I have seen on the Internet and gathered from conversations. Some of the consistent recommendations include Victoria Peak, shopping, and harbor cruise. These things sound appealing. If you would like my input I will be happy to give it but ultimately I want to understand Hong Kong's significance to you. I am up for anything. I love you and I am excited to be with you!

I decided to go to church last night. I like to do yoga in the morning and I had things to do today so I knew I wouldn't make it this afternoon. I am glad I went because I learned of an amazing story. Fifty years ago this weekend five American missionaries in Ecuador were speared to death after attempting to make peaceful contact with the most savage culture ever known. The son of one of the men and one of the tribesmen that killed that man's father came to the church to speak. The son, Steve Saint, spoke about what it was like when he found out his father had been killed. And later having the opportunity to live with the same men that were responsible for his death. The tribesman, Mincaye, spoke while Steve translated. He told a little bit about the first encounter with the missionaries and said a prayer to the church. It was incredible that these people were able to fully trust and forgive each other. Steve Saint wrote a book that I purchased and there is a movie coming out at the end of the month. It was incredible to listen to these men talk. I will bring the book to Hong Kong so you can read it.

I have been thinking a lot about the first two days we spent together and how I felt. I get butterflies every time. I remember getting the massage and thinking is this for real? over and over in my mind. I was blown away and that was only the beginning. I am still amazed at how you pulled it all off. Everything was so new and I expected to be nervous but it all seemed so natural and comfortable like I had known you for years. Then to think about how quickly our feelings developed into love. And now at the end of this separation thinking about all of the possibilities ahead of us. It is incredible. You are more than I could have ever hoped for. I love you with all my heart.

Love, Talle

TWO WEEKS NOTICE
January 10, 2006 – Talle,

I am sending you my two weeks notice. Our current relationship is not working out. I cannot stand it when I have to communicate with you through this plastic key-typing pad. The abominable process of sending emails and waiting for replies is entirely too slow and has been wearing on me for some months. The physical abuse of carpel tunnel, finger lock, and wrist cramps are justifiably outrageous. On top of which my emotional fortitude has been continually weakened with your insistent professions of love and adoration. I can no longer tolerate our separation and am forewarning you that I will seek other prospects of instant gratification. In two weeks, I will be rendezvousing, if there is such an activity, with an incredibly sexy, smart, and funny lady in the former British Principality Hong Kong, otherwise known in the ancient Chinese description as Charleston and Talle's Playground - Charlle. Please do not fuss or cry over my departure. You will be fine. I may have some moments of incredible hysteria, sexual deviance, and mental breakdowns, but "I will survive" - quoted from the original survivor Gloria Gainer. My new pursuit will be exceptionally witty and energetic, giving me the tingle of excitement throughout my core. However, this is to be expected and desired with new adventures. We shed the old and consume the new. This will be my final goodbye and admonition of love. Your former sex god – Charleston

ADDITIONALLY
January 10, 2006 – Talle,

Just in case you failed to see the sense of humor in the first e-mail, I still love you...A LOT!! I am just a little bit too excited knowing that I will see you in two weeks. One of my friends had a book on

Hong Kong, which I memorized yesterday (I am obviously very proud of this achievement). I have planned our complete itinerary. I had a lot of trouble finding enough time to schedule room service with cuddling, but in the end I was able to pull it off. Don't worry about seeing Hong Kong. I scheduled ample time hugging in front of the hotel window and I am sure we'll have to see the lobby at some point. In my planning I didn't find it feasible to actually leave the hotel without you receiving grossly public displays of affection or "G"PDA, so I just figured we would forego it.

As you can see I have lost my mind and will spend the rest of the day looking for it. I love you. Tell me if you're in the mood to criticize some poetry could use a fresh perspective?

Love, Charleston

January 10, 2006 – Charleston,

You are too much!!! This was the perfect ending to my day. I will go to sleep smiling thinking about our rendezvous in the hotel room!

I would love to read your poetry but you have to remember that criticizing is not my specialty. If you wrote it and it comes from your heart I will have a very difficult time finding anything wrong with it. I know this bothers you and I understand your point but try to see mine. Regardless, I would like to read it.

I have a question for you. Will both your roommates be living in your house when you get home? I am trying to help Camilla figure out where she will live. The topic is getting sensitive because her options are dwindling. She won't talk about it because she doesn't want me to feel bad but I can see she is upset. I am pretty sure that they will be there but I just want to have all the facts.

I love you, Talle

12 DAYS TILL CHRISTMAS

January 11, 2006 –

On the 12th day of Christmas my true love gave to me...

Well I know that this is not Christmas for everyone else in the world, but it will be for me. This will be a time to celebrate the love I have for those special people in my life or just celebrate the love I have for you and you alone. I have music playing in my heart whenever I think of you, but words can only be carried so far. The idea of making you smile, feel light on your feet, or just fall into a dream keeps me breathing slowly, patiently waiting for that day to come. The day I watch the energy of life flow into your heart will make my love feel relieved with peace. I will be with you...

Please, do not feel this way. You love me very much. This I know. I could not be frustrated or hurt with you, because my love for you is too great. I only could be hurt if something happened to you. How you or the world affects you will always do more damage. Criticism doesn't have to be destructive. I only want to know how it makes you feel, of what it makes you think, what images does it create, how it affects you - emotionally, mentally, etc... No right answer exists it is purely a personal response and opinion based from you reaction to it. Maybe it will not inspire anything and that is good too. Maybe it will make you depressed, sleepy, laugh, smile, sad, remember all of this is good.

I will contact my roommates to find out for sure. We will figure out something. I don't want Camilla to be upset either.

Derby Days
Imagine a night with heavenly spite
Where the cries are hollow and nothing is right
One tiny sip will make the marshal tip

A hell of a day short tempered and cruel
So tense and frustrated I just want to duel
Although give me a drink and this all might sink

Now that's an idea, look at her beauty
But I'm so lonely, tired, and full of duty
A might gulp without even sucking the pulp

The stools are hard, round, and swervy
So inviting that I just may be tempted
Until the freedom of standing is detected
And I am able to endure the day's derby

Unraveling Dreams
Imagine a tonic, which makes the world have no end, so many tastes
they are difficult to comprehend. You can become what you want fat,
fairy, and free. You only have to taste and give up your grace. Say you
desire just anything at all, then sit back and swig you'll have a ball.
Your heavenly request is being sent with my best. You'll have nothing
to fear it can make you disappear and all of your dreams fall apart at the
seams.

I love you, Charleston
January 12, 2006 – Charleston,

Your poems seem sad. It makes me wonder how you have
been feeling. They make me think of a sad, exhausted man in an Irish
pub. I like the flow of *Unraveling Dreams*. *Derby Days* was sort of hard to
read. Thank you for letting me read them. It means a lot to me.

I have been spending a lot of time preparing for this trip and
your return home. It is so much fun and I am so excited. I really cannot
believe it's happening. It always seemed so far away. We are going to be
together in less than 12 days! This is amazing!!! I am choked up
thinking about it. The thought of being with you affects my entire
body. I really might pass out. I feel like jumping up and down and
screaming and then I feel like crying. I am a mess.

I guess Camilla is going to move in with Hunter and two of his
friends. I am confused because I had a conversation with Hunter the
night before about why they should not live together. I am not sure
what happened for him to change his mind but apparently he has. As
long as things continue the way they have been it will be fine. I just
don't want her to feel trapped. They have tried living together before. It
wasn't necessarily bad but it wasn't great either. Well, she has a plan and
that relieves a lot of stress.

Are you going to Singapore next? Are you almost there?
I love you! Talle

*

THE COUNTDOWN BEGINS: 10
January 13, 2006 – Talle,

Tomorrow will be in single digits. This will be such a relief.
Now that I have become fixated on making it to Hong Kong...a mess
we will be indeed.

I watched an interview on Nordstrom's Diversity initiative. I
thought was pretty interesting. Do you really think Nordstrom's is that
diverse and as a result the stores have been more successful? They
commented that it has always been noted for superior service, well I
can attest to that. The female representative was a very good speaker.
I was impressed.

Tim hasn't replied to me yet about Mikey. He only told me
that he got a puppy, German Shepard. It will be nice to have a dog in
the house. I am sure it is pissing everywhere. At least I am not there I
have dealt with my share of pissing around the house. Are you sure
that Camilla is going to be all right living with Hunter? I don't want
this to put either of you in a harder situation. Just let me know what I
can do to help. I know lots of possible male roommates, but I don't
think that helps at all.

I loved, and loved your commentary. Everything you said was
perfect!! You are brilliant. I love what you wrote about the sad,
exhausted man in an Irish pub. I think you were absolutely right. They
were both about the fascination, but deleterious effects of drinking. I
have a tendency to fool around with rhyme scheme, which was the
product of the first one. I would agree it does come off choppy, but
hard to recognize when I wrote it. The second one was purely stream
of consciousness and tonal. I based everything on how it sounds, but
really not much thought goes into it. For whatever reason when I do
that they read easier. This has been so helpful. Thank you so much.

I love you...Rendezvous in 10 days!! Charleston
January 14, 2006 – Charleston,

Speaking of puppies I have one sitting on my lap right now.
One of Camilla's future roommates was given a puppy for free but has
nowhere to keep it until they move into their house. Somehow we were
volunteered. I originally said no. We are not allowed to have pets and I
don't want to ruin anything a month before we move out. Now that I

have seen the baby I love him and he has to stay. He is so small. He is a mix of Siberian husky and something weird that I cannot remember right now. He is black with a little bit of white and blue eyes. He is so sweet!

I found out today that my Aunt Betsy has breast cancer. We are hoping for the best right now and will find out more details next week. Will you please pray for her? Will you give me an idea of the type or amount of clothing you will need. I am trying to get everything ready. Do you have anything or do you need clothes for each day? The type of clothing will also help me because I still don't know what I am going to pack. 10 days. I can't wait! Why can't it be today?

I love you, Talle

The dog, which does not yet have a name, is sound asleep in a ball on my lap. It is the cutest thing ever!

THE COUNTDOWN CONTINUES: 8
January 15, 2006 – Talle,

8 days till its all over...

I told Tim that you might stop at the house. I don't need much clothing. I only need a nice pair of shoes for going out, a nice shirt and a sweater. I have my dark grey jeans. If you want to dress a little more formally then I need a suit to match you. Otherwise I have a blazer. However, I do need a couple of notebooks if you can manage it. They are in my bookshelf: a small leather bound, small black hard with Chinese character, large green hard cover "life 2004-2005", and medium hard cover with reds and golds if you open this one it says finance on inside cover. If this is too much don't worry about it. I have one more favor if you don't mind. When you drive to my house heading south on Camino el Real from the Coffee Bean on the left, past my turn, is a tire center for lease or sale. I am curious how much sq feet is posted on the sign. I can't remember.

You on the other hand need shoes for swimming, dancing, walking/hiking/shopping, and dining. I'll leave the clothes to match with you. I can't wait to see what you choose... I would recommend that you dress comfortably for the flight, because I think it will be long. I also would be careful about packing too much, but I'll pick you up at the airport so you only have to make it to there. I love you and can't wait to see you.

I am so sorry about your Aunt Betsy. How did they find it so suddenly? I will pray for her and the rest of your family. I remember how much wonderful energy she had in her smile. I will pray that it stays that way. You must feel awful. Please let me know if I can do anything else.

Love, Charleston

January 17, 2006 – Charleston,

I am so excited about coming to see you. I love getting ready it makes me happy. Of course I will bring your notebooks. I will probably stop by your house tomorrow afternoon. I hope it will be all right.

Aunt Betsy noticed a lump and went right to the doctor. I guess it was missed in her last mammogram so it was very lucky she felt it. They are opting to have a lumpectomy rather than a mastectomy. The results should be the same. I think she feels better after seeing the doctor yesterday. He was reassuring that she would recover. We will just pray that is the case. Thank you for your compassion.

I never answered your question about Nordstrom. There is a lot of diversity. I don't know that I would attribute it to making the company more successful. On the other hand we are always directed to have a diverse selling team. The reason is that you want to have a salesperson for each type of customer, which shops on your floor. The customers will be more comfortable shopping with someone they identify. I never really thought about it but that could be part of our success. Was the interview talking about the store level or more about the corporate structure? I think the main reason Nordstrom is successful is because of the return policy. We will pretty much return anything and give you your money back. Any way you want it. That is a great selling point.

I have inventory tonight. It sort of marks the end of this separation for me. I remember thinking about this day coming and knowing that it would be just about done at this point. Even though originally I thought I wouldn't see you until February I always had hoped you would come home sooner. Well, you are not but I am going to see you in one week! That is incredible! I love you so much! I'll see you soon.

Love, Talle

6 SWEET DAYS
January 20, 2006 – Talle,

We arrive in Singapore, today. I will call you. I am so sorry about your Aunt. Could you send me her address? Never mind maybe that wouldn't be appropriate. I will certainly pray for her. Thank you so much for picking those things up, but please don't take it if it is too much.

About Nordstrom's diversity, for me personally I don't think it makes a difference. I would agree completely in theory about wanting to purchase something from whom you relate, but honestly an older black woman with a charming personality could convince me of spending more money than a young man in his twenties. Maybe she is with whom I relate??

I have another poem and I hope you don't mind.
Pillow Thoughts
Every night comes with a moments thought
As my pillow softens to my face.
Closing my eyes opens our heart
To a flurry of music with strong bass.

An image so vivid I can hold
Wrap my arms around the warmth
Trace the line over your hip down to toe
Squeeze every inch covered in filth.

This relief is all that I need
One touch and its done the trick
A glimpse of hope as I breathed
Keeping you close through the week.

I lay my head down to rest
Sigh a smile for the day's success
Sing a tune when the beat begins
Happy the heart has filmed our sins.

I was working with unusual rhymes, attempting to not be predictable.

I love you. Can't wait to see you, sooonn.

Love, Charleston

January 21, 2006 – Charleston,

I love this poem it is perfect. I like the way you did the rhyme. The last part is my favorite. It made me smile and then want to cry. I have gotten pretty used to this reaction. You have a way of bringing it on quite often. I love you.

Aunt Betsy had surgery on Thursday. They removed the tumor but lymph nodes were involved. That is not really a good thing. She will start radiation shortly and possibly chemo. It is a relief that the doctors have reacted so quickly.

I think I am all set to leave. I can hardly get through the days. Work is excruciating. I love you and I will see you in 3 days!

Love, Talle

4 DAYS

January 20, 2006 – Charleston,

I am so upset I missed your calls last night! I hope you had fun in Singapore. I love you very much. I cannot wait to see you. I am trying to get everything ready. I went to your house today. No one was home so I did not get to meet anyone. I got some clothes and your notebooks. Seriously, I cannot believe we are this close to seeing each other it seemed like it would never come! My mind is going a million different places I cannot concentrate right now. I love you and I will see you in four days!!!!!!!!!!!!!!

Love, Talle

3 DAYS

January 21, 2006 –

I love you... Just in case they give you any trouble at the airport. These are the numbers for the booking. Let me know if you have any concerns. I will see you soon.

Expedia.com itinerary number: **114968312601**
Expedia.com booking ID (flight): 2LJ744 (1)
Main contact: Talle Gilmore

JUST ANOTHER DAY
January 23, 2006 – Talle,

Well now, I can't sleep at all anymore because of the enthusiasm. I just lie in bed waiting, which really sucks. So I may be a wreck by the time I get to the airport, but then you may be too so we can be a wreck together. You should be leaving tomorrow and we should be arriving in Hong Kong about the time you are leaving. I can't wait to see you. I hope you have a safe and comfortable journey with not too many kinks? If you need to get in touch with me email will be the best way. I love you and will see you soon.

Love, Charleston

*

I MISS YOU ALREADY
January 29, 2006 – Talle,

I really miss you already. How was your last day? No trouble traveling to the airport I hope. Thank you so much for coming and spending that time with me. I am jealous that you are already home without me and anxious to see you again.

I looked into Aspen a little. I think flying out of Orange County is almost $200 cheaper. Tell me what you find.

I don't want you to think that I have given up faith or been disappointed. You could never. I don't want to change you or make you something you are not. I am just asking for you to not be afraid or unwilling to share yourself and be who you are with me. I want your instincts, raw emotions, feelings and opinions without thought or preconceived notions. I will not be upset, hurt, or disappointed. You can't be afraid of your true self. If you want to slap me for something I said then slap me. I would be upset that you restrained yourself. If you want to wake me up because your excited then wake me up and let me share in the enthusiasm. This is the last that I will say on it. I don't want to push you too much. Have faith in your instincts. The ones God gave you.

Love, Charleston

January 30, 2006 – Charleston,

Thank you so much for everything in Hong Kong. It was an experience I will never forget. I loved being there and being there with you. I really enjoyed walking around and experiencing things as they came. I love that we randomly went through that market. It was so real. I loved walking in and out of stores with no real purpose other than to look. I liked the feeling of being in a big city. It is so alive; there is so much energy and so many people. I enjoy being in that environment. I loved the Felix. The view was incredible. Just being there made me feel special. It definitely gave me the feeling that we were in a "cool" place. I love that there was mystery to it as well. Not knowing what was upstairs or behind the wall, even the bathrooms. Hong Kong will always have a special place in my heart. I hope we will go back.

It was much harder to say goodbye than I had anticipated. After you left I was left to my own thoughts. It was difficult. Remember my difficulties with change. They can spark from something as small as not having you in the room we just shared together. I was alone again. It was what I did with this time that was different from what I have done in the past. Yes, there was a lot of crying. I felt a lot of pain. I still do, mostly as a result of personal disappointment. I started making a list of things I needed to do when I got back. It turned into a journal. I wrote about the things in my life that I was not happy with. I wrote down my thoughts on why. I wrote about how I can change them. I took all the things that were in my head and tried to make sense of them. I prayed. What it all boils down to is exactly what you always say fear.

I have made a decision not to let it run my life. I do have to take it one step at a time. If I think about all the things I want to overcome or do I get overwhelmed and depressed. In yoga they tell us to have patience with ourselves. We may not be able to do all the moves today but overtime with practice it will get easier. I need to apply this in my life. I need to have patience with myself. I know that I have the ability to change things. For now my focus is on overcoming fear. Once I can train my mind to think before reacting out of fear I will be able to do the things I want to do and say the things I want to say. You have my list of things to do. They have not changed. Without ever considering what I wrote to you on that list I asked myself what I want to do. I came up with the exact same answers. Of course that makes sense because those are things that are important to me. However, when you were asking me what I want to do my mind was going blank. I had so many walls up. I had to ask myself the same question. When I realized I wrote the same things it was an awakening. I do know what I want. So why the walls? That is the part that kills me.

We have had the same conversations in the past. I understood and agreed with everything you've said. I took your theories applied them to things in my life and became optimistic about my possibilities for growth while you were gone. After a while, I felt like I was living my life more fully than I had been. I started to get comfortable. I had not forgotten about the things we had discussed but I was only applying a small amount to my life. When we were together again it all came back. I have let you and myself down because I forgot about the most important thing. Sharing my feelings and opinions seems so simple. It really is simple.

I needed to spend some time before I left breaking down my walls. I was just so excited all I could think about was seeing you. I wasn't thinking about allowing myself to open up. I have been pretty shut off to people these past few months. There is not that many people in my life I feel like sharing with. The few that I choose to never really understand so I have kept a lot of the thoughts to myself. Most of the time I listen to other people talk. I needed to readjust before I came to see you. I know how important it is to share with you. I want it just as much. I am glad that you pushed me and would not back down for two reasons. I know you love me and see things in me that I have not allowed myself to actualize. Two, you are pushing me to face up to and act on things that will make me a better, happier, more fulfilled person. I appreciate everything that happened this weekend. The good because it was amazing and the bad because it was strengthening and enlightening. Thank you for not giving up on me. I never want to let you down. I respect and love you too much.

I still have things to say so I will write more later. I need to see a doctor. I don't know what's going on with my tailbone.

I love you! Talle

January 30, 2006 – Charleston,

The doctor did not have much to say. He took x-rays and there was not a fracture. I knew that because I never fell. Anyway, they gave me muscle relaxers, which I will not take. They said to ice it so I will give that a try and hope it goes away.

I went back by the tire center. There is not a for sale sign up. The only signs on the building are no parking. I will still try to find the square footage for you.

I cannot remember if the dates for Aspen are the 17-21 or 18-22? I looked it up both ways. It is cheaper to fly out of Orange County. I was surprised because that is not usually the case. The cheapest flight I found was just under $400. That is good compared to some other prices I found. I will get those tickets when you confirm the dates.

My last day in Hong Kong did not go according to plan. I woke up and got ready. I was still emotional which delayed my departure. I wrote a little more in my newfound journal. I went back over to Times Square because I wanted to find things for my family and friends and get some breakfast. Everything was closed because of the New Year. I went to Starbucks and got a muffin and read for a little while. Since I wasn't able to do anything there I decided I would go to the airport, check my bags in and take a taxi to the Buddha. I went out to get a taxi, which was confusing because you have to take the right color taxi. The person I spoke to did not understand what I was asking so it took awhile to figure out I needed a blue taxi. I waited and waited for a blue taxi but they never came. The guy kept calling to get a hold of someone but never did. I don't really understand why that happened but it was starting to get too close to risk leaving the airport. I was disappointed. That promised to be a good experience for me to have on my own. I got a couple of souvenirs for my family and waited for my flight. There were no problems after that. No passing out or throwing up. Everything was fine. I really wish you could have come home with me. I know you will be home soon but now that I've had a taste of you I just want more. Falling asleep the first night and waking up the first morning I felt pure joy. Lying in your arms is the most comforting, warm, safe place I've ever known. What is it like to be back on the ship? I hope these last 20 days go by quickly for you. I will be counting the days. I love you.

I am about half way through *Rich Dad Poor Dad*. So far I am very intrigued. I've got the whole book marked up. So many of the things he talks about are relevant not only in finances but life in general. He makes really good points about fear. At a time when I am trying to overcome many of mine this book is hitting home. Our conversation at Felix is making more sense and I am seeing the majority of the world in a different light. I don't know what will happen in the future but I know I never would have looked at money in this way. Just like most people I was brought up to do well in school and get a good job and work hard. I never would have seen the different ways to go about making money. I still do not know how to apply this to my life but at least I am getting the knowledge. Good recommendation. I will let you know what I think when I finish the book.

I love and miss you! I've got to ice my butt! The doctor asked me if I had a significant other to hold the ice for me. I said I had just seen you but you were not here. This gave him an idea...he asked me and he actually used these words "Not to get too personal but did you have sex doggy style?" It took so much restraint not to laugh out loud. He was serious and I didn't want to disrespect him, but this was such an outrageous notion. It was too funny!!

I love you! Talle

January 31, 2006 – Talle,

I love you. These emails were hilarious and perfect!! I couldn't stop smiling for hours. Did the Doctor really ask you? You articulated everything so clearly and genuinely. You didn't put any "thought" into this when you wrote, because it feels like fluid emotion. I have to resolve these two comments...

I have let you and myself down

Thank you for not giving up on me. I never want to let you down

You will never let me down. This isn't a test where you get a pass or fail. Your struggles are with yourself not with me. I will love you no matter what you choose, because that is the only way I know how to love someone. I really feel connected to you through these emails. Thank you for trusting me with your genuine feelings. I can't say that I will always understand, because people can have different perceptions and points of view, but I will always want to understand through discussion and sharing. You are an incredible person, who has a tremendous amount of strength. I don't think you have ever tried to use it and maybe you are even afraid of the power that you could wield. We are all a little bit afraid of our destructive capability, but it can be a powerful energy if harnessed appropriately. You are becoming exactly who you are, nothing more. You only need to have faith in your instincts and feelings. Thousands of years of evolution and spiritual energy have developed them much greater than our mental faculty. We all should use them not guard them, but many people are afraid that we would be monsters. We would become primal and savage. My compassion for humanity doesn't come from my head, because according to sound logic helping someone really doesn't help me. My emotions come from my heart. This is where I feel the sensational urge to do good and right with selfless action. Our minds are juvenile in comparison. I like your Yoga analogy and I think it is accurate. When you are stretching you think about the technique and your breathing. Constantly positioning your form to perfection and slowly overtime you are touching your toes. Even in Yoga classes they address fear. I have had instructors talk about the tension in our muscles as our fear of letting go. Our bodies' reaction is to fear the pain and tense, but if we actively calm ourselves, breath, and let go our body relaxes and we can stretch deeper. This allows the body to become more flexible, stronger, and powerful. Yoga is a good start and I am expectant to do it with you. I think that it will probably work out the kinks in your butt, since I can't hold the ice pack.

I am glad that you are enjoying the book. I think this is the most information that you have ever given me in response to a book. It is exceptional feedback. I am glad that you really like it. I had the same feelings. I think both applicable to life and finance. I have read most of the books on the back cover that he suggests, but the only way to really learn how to apply it is to try it. I think for me the biggest lesson was having faith in yourself, be flexible and creative, and you will always find a solution or someone who can help you. I really love you. I really miss you. Ship life is horrible. I miss having you in my arms and waking up with you. Holding you. You know I couldn't believe it, but my first reaction when I went to sleep on the ship was how much colder it was without you. I think you are the only person that I have ever met that produces as much body heat as I do. I think you actually produce more. I may be inaccessible for a couple of days. I love you.

Love, Charleston

*

SHIP
January 31, 2006 – Talle,

I am flying over to another ship. I don't know if I will have Internet access. If you don't hear from me I love you...

Thank you for looking into the Tire Center. Is it operating again? Did it still have a fence around the compound? Someone may have bought it or temporarily took it off the market. Well I love you for trying. I really hope that you like the book.

How is Camilla? I have more things to share with you when I return. I am very excited.

Love, Charleston
January 31, 2006 – Charleston,

The tire center still has a fence around it. There were a lot of tires inside. Were they always there? It does not look operational.

Camilla is doing well. I had dinner with her and Hunter after they picked me up from the airport. They are still looking for a place to live. There are going to be four boys, a dog, two cats, and Camilla. I'm not sure how excited she is about all of that. However, I am very excited. What more do you have to share?!

A miraculous thing happened to me today. It was my first day back to work and I walked into a mess of things on my desk. The thing that stood out the most was a card with my name on it. I thought "how nice of someone to give me a card." While I was checking my voicemails I was looking at the handwriting wondering whom it was from. It looked familiar but I thought there was no way. Sure enough when I opened the card it was from my old friend Julianne. I could not believe my eyes. She wrote me the most incredible letter. She wrote about this past year and all of the things she was proud of in her life that she would not change. She wrote about our friendship and the role she played in it ending as the one thing she would change in a heartbeat. She went on to say other things about our friendship and what it meant to her. She said that she did not expect anything from me but wanted me to know she thinks of me often and misses our friendship. I was blown away. The thing is I always knew she felt this way. I guess because I put myself out there once and it was ignored I needed her to take this step. I was always blown away that she let it go. In the end it is just as much my fault as it is hers that the friendship ended the way it did. That was a brave thing she did and I give here a lot of credit. We are taking steps to re-kindle our friendship. I don't know that it will ever be the same but I do now that I am happy and unbelievably relieved to have peace. It was absurd to me that we worked in the same space yet avoided each other at all costs. This week has been an emotional roller coaster. You asked me if I liked roller coasters did you foresee all of this? I feel like I am going to explode! I wish you were here. I really want to talk to you and I really need a hug maybe even a kiss!

I hope you will have Internet on the other ship. I really miss you!

Love, Talle

February 2, 2006 –

I finished one ship and am back, but I have one other ship to go. I would agree that she was brave in making that card, but I would also ask why now? Strikes me as a little odd. Why did you two originally end your friendship? I realized something too. Those mornings waking up I thought that my headaches were due to drinking, but that also seemed ridiculous given the small quantities. I had the same problems when I got back on ship and if I took naps during the day. My dreams were so intense and vivid that pulling out of them, waking up was so difficult it was like pulling my mind out of concrete.

I guess in a way it felt like a hangover, but different. They seem to have gone away recently but some were very violent and not related to war.

I don't know if I feel comfortable with Camilla living with all those men. Are you sure that she is going to be ok? Thank you for the info about the tire center. It could have been sold or taken off the market temporarily. I love you and miss you. Charleston

February 2, 2006 – Charleston,

It seems crazy that your dreams were so intense they gave you headaches! Have you gone through periods where you consistently had these types of dreams before? Do you think they are happening for a particular reason?

The last few weeks of my friendship with Julianne were difficult for me. She was starting a relationship with her now ex-boyfriend Eric. She was severely infatuated with him but he was playing hard to get. To keep her mind off of him she was dating other people. I guess what happened was she had so much going on (a lot of which I did not agree) that it consumed our relationship. This was the start. It ended when she became exclusive with Eric. There were a series of events where the three of us were involved. It was as if I were not there. To the point that they were groping and making out as I sat there with them. After the first time I told her how it made me feel. She truly did not understand, at least that was the impression she gave me. It was like talking to a brick wall. When it continued to happen I was over it. I became distant because I felt disrespected. She just let it go. There are things about Julianne that I know. First, she has never maintained a female relationship. Second, if she sees something as a challenge she is going to do her best to overcome it. The first thing made our bond special because I was the first female she ever let in. However, I could not be surprised that our friendship ended. I knew her history. What I could not believe was that she was faced with our challenge everyday yet chose to ignore it. At any time I could have confronted her. I chose not to and that was my decision right or wrong. I think she brought it up now because she is facing new challenges in her life. She is really looking at who she is and why. It was a good step.

I really do not know what it will be like for Camilla. It does not seem like the ideal situation but for know it is the choice she is making.

I know she doesn't feel like she has any other options. I just hope she does not end up being their maid. I can see that happening. However, the alternative is worse. From what I know these are not the cleanest of boys. I hope for the best.

I love you! Talle

February 3, 2006 –

The alternative is worse? What do you mean the alternative for Camilla is worse? I don't understand...

I remember what you told me about Julianne, now. Her description sounds familiar to other people I have met. I have met dozens of people who easily drop relationships for what they really want. These relationships can be frustrating because they are in the relationship for themselves, not for the relationship or the other person. They aren't necessarily selfish just weak. They give up something without understanding its significance. I can never fully befriend these people. They lack loyalty. In the end they prove their weaknesses with their actions. True character can be so difficult to embrace, but when confronted with our weaknesses we see our humanity. People treat reality as cruelty and harsh words, but I would rather know the truth. Most people are not willing to believe that they can be so fallible. I think my imperfection and its recognition is my greatest source of strength and confidence.

I had my dreams again last night. A lot of murder mystery... I don't know what to make of it yet. He has visited me before and He could be trying something. I'll figure it out.

Charleston

*

MAKING PLANS

February 1, 2006 – Charleston,

I love you. I want to run some things by you. I need to turn in my vacation request. This is what I was thinking. You come home on the 19th a Sunday. I will take Sunday and Monday. I have to work Tuesday and Wednesday. But then I will take off Thursday, Friday, Saturday, and Sunday. Let me know what you think. I planned something for your birthday/valentines day and I am really excited about it!!! If it will work for you, then the best days for me are Saturday and Sunday the 25th and 26th of February. I cannot wait for you to get home! It is going to be great.

I love you, Talle

February 2, 2006 —

The only thing I would change is Thursday the 23, because I will have to work that day and Friday part of the day. I don't know if you could take the following Monday or Tuesday, which I think is the 27/28. I am so excited, but I thought I was gonna be able to plan Valentine's? I am so jealous. I can't wait to see you, but it is not much longer. AAAAaaaahhhhhh!!!!

Love, Charleston

February 2, 2006 —

Okay, I will probably take Monday and Tuesday. That will work out to be the same amount of vacation days. I'm so excited!

Love, Talle

February 2, 2006 —

Oh I didn't think of it. I know that you want to be there when I return on Sunday the 19th. If you are just going to work a normal day though and be done by 5pm then it might not be worth taking off a whole day, because I know the Marine Corps and I guarantee that by the time we have unloaded the ships, gotten everyone and everything accounted for dealt with the chaos of everyone running everywhere it might be really late like definitely no earlier than 3pm and could be as late as 10pm. So if you take off a whole day then it might not be worth it. Think on it. It is your choice, but I would rather not waste the time I could have with you, like an extra morning waking up with you just so I can see you when I first arrive which might happen anyway.

Love you, Charleston

February 2, 2006 —

Actually, that is a really good idea since it is a Sunday I would only have to work until 3:00 and it counts for a whole day. But...let me know if you think you will get in early because I want to be there.

I love you, Talle

February 3, 2006 —

I think that if you are going to be done by the 3pm go to work. I can promise you even if we arrive early that I will not be done before this time. You would be just sitting around waiting, which will suck for both of us. Just come after work. That will be best either way or at least that is my opinion. I think you will probably be there on time anyway.

Love, Charleston

SWEET DREAMS
February 3, 2006 – Charleston,

The alternative for Camilla is to live in filth. Hunter's current apartment is so bad he doesn't stay there anymore. I don't want her to have to be the only one that cleans but living in a disgusting house would be worse.

I received my settlement check today. It is a huge relief. I am so happy to pay off my debt! The check was for almost $18,000. I never thought I would get that much money. It's incredible. I need to figure out what I am going to do with the rest of it. You started me thinking a lot about my car. I don't know what I want to do with it. I'd like to talk more about it when you get home.

I will work Sunday. This way I can be off Friday through Wednesday and take the same amount of hours.

I hope you start having sweet dreams!

Love, Talle

LESS THAN 2 WEEKS
February 6, 2006 – Charleston,

Okay I really miss you! I am ready for you to come home. Are you getting excited or just trying to focus on your work? Less than two weeks. It is hard to believe.

Work has been pretty consuming. Nothing is really going on I just had to work a lot of days in a row. I had Sunday off which was nice. I went to a party on Saturday night. A guy from work quit and threw himself a going away party. It was not much fun. I went with Marianne for about an hour. That was all we could handle. It was in a house with nothing in it except a stereo and alcohol. I went to yoga in the morning, which was great. The Sunday morning class is always difficult. The instructor is a little more advanced than the instructor on Wednesdays. It is faster pace with more cardio. Not really aerobic but it does get your heart going. Marianne was going to come over sometime in the afternoon. While I was in Hong Kong the kitchen manager at work was in a terrible car accident. He had been in critical condition but I heard today that he was able to go home. Anyway, we have been doing different things to raise money for his family. We had a bake sale today. Marianne was going to come over and we were going to bake together. She and her boyfriend broke up and he moved out. This is a hard time for her and she tends to hibernate. I was excited that she wanted to come over but she didn't end up coming. I had even made a super bowl dinner. I had chili, salad, and bread. Camilla and I ate it together while reading magazines and "watching" the super bowl.

I can't wait to talk to you. I love you so much!

Love, Talle

MISS YOU
February 8, 2006 – Charleston,

I finished *Rich Dad Poor Dad*. I am really glad I read the book. There are still some things that are hard for me to comprehend. The investment stuff is an area I know absolutely nothing about. He also says he would not encourage anyone to start a company because of the failure rate. I understand the odds so is it really a smart idea to open my own store? That confused me. I like the way the book is written. It is really easy to understand even for a person that does not have a lot of financial wisdom. He repeats important topics, which helps me remember them. It's funny how when you are focusing on one aspect of life and everything around you seems to synchronize. I started reading this book. I received a large sum of money, the topic at church last week was money, and then I was reading in a magazine about a new book about money and women. I bought the book. Hopefully it will help me to avoid common mistakes women make with money. I am going to invest the remaining money from my settlement. I would like to get your opinion on some options when you get home.

I started looking at storage facilities. How much space do you think you will need? I have a lot of stuff. Most of it is not big but there is a lot of it. I also started getting information about apartments. I have not looked at anything but I have listings.

I am really excited for you to come home. Is there anything you really want to do or have when you get back? I love you and miss you a lot! I hope everything is okay. I miss hearing from you.

Love, Talle

Will you tell me the dates for Aspen? I want to turn in a vacation request.

BLANK
February 10, 2006 – Charleston,

I am getting concerned. I can't figure out why you have not been able to write and it is making me really nervous. I hope everything is okay. I miss you and love you very much! I am anxious for you to come home. Your mother will be here on Friday the 24th. I'm not sure of any other details I have not been able to speak to her. I can't wait to hear from you. You are in my prayers as always.

I love you! Talle

February 13, 2006 –

I thought of what I would like to do. I was having my dreams again. Only this time I was teaching myself stuff. I was reviewing dancing, doing work, creating very weird worlds but very difficult to wake up from. I would really like to go dancing and have dinner with my roommates even if just at home. I would like to go to church, yoga, and one other thing. You asked what cravings I have. I have only had one craving since I left that I would really like to do... I love you and will see you soon. Charleston

February 13, 2006 –

Okay. Sounds perfect. Are you intentionally not telling me the other thing?

I love you. Happy almost Valentine's Day!

Love, Talle

Oh, the apartment I looked at was not so good. It is in a beautiful location but the actual place is pretty run down. It is really

small and it is one of three other apartments that share the same space.
February 13, 2006 —

Oooh I like fixer uppers!! But if it requires anything beyond paint and furniture I think it might be out of my expertise. I wouldn't go less than 800sq/ft prefer a 1,000. How small is small?

And, you already know the other thing. I talked about it before I left.

Love you, Charleston

HAPPY VALENTINE'S DAY
February 14, 2006 —

Ok, I am only saying Happy Valentine's Day, because I couldn't not. But am seriously disgruntled about it. I refuse to admit that I am missing Valentine's Day with you as well, so I am postponing it until I return. The holiday is taking a rain check. I hope that you don't mind. In all honesty can there really be a Valentine's Day without the one you love. The idea is absurd. I know that I am destroying a certain sentiment, but I really must object! And since I am soon to be home I have enough defiance to hold out until then. I love you and will see you soon. Charleston
February 14, 2006 — Charleston,

Happy Valentine's Day! I love you. This valentine's day I am celebrating our love. Whether you are here or not, you are in my heart. So even though I cannot be with you I know you are out there and to make it even better you are on your way home. I do anticipate the rain check. It will be wonderful to be with you again. I can't wait to see you.

Love, Talle
February 15, 2006 —

Thank you for the beautiful flowers! I received them late last night, after my romantic dinner with Hunter. Camilla had class so we decided to go to Chili's. We forgot it was Valentine's Day. It was funny. You are going to be home in four days. I cannot believe it! I love you!

Love, Talle
February 15, 2006 — Talle,

I love you so much. I can't wait to see you. I think that I will be singing at the top of my lungs!! I just finished reading Dostoevsky's *the Idiot.* The book is beautifully written. It literally tore out my soul to finish it. I can't even say anything else. I am becoming an emotional idiot myself. I am going to see you in three days and a wake up!! I was told today that we actually might be finished at 1300, but I don't have a lot of faith in that and I would much rather wait for you to come then have you waste a whole day off, which can be spent together. I love you hugs and kisses.... Charleston

*

RETURN
February 15, 2006 – Talle,

This is the Return Information. They don't give any details, but the exit you want to take is the same for San Onofre if you were going to go to the Power Plant, but instead you go east. The Info says once inside the gate signs will be posted. I will probably be able to talk you on once I arrive. Don't worry about the timeline. I would just show up when you can. I mean that honestly. Don't stress over this one, please.

Love you, Charleston

February 15, 2006 – Charleston,

Thank you for the information. I'm not sure how I feel about not being there for you though. I understand the desire to have time together later I want that too. It seems like such a special welcoming and I would hate not to be there. I am really excited and I don't know how I am going to get through work anyway. Maybe I can leave at 2:00 instead of 3:00. I don't know. If that is an option I would get there at 2:30. What do you think? I love you and I cannot wait to see you!!!!!!

Love, Talle

February 16, 2006 – Talle,

I am speaking completely honest. I know that no matter what I say an impulse to be present for my initial return is going to exist. No matter how much I assure you that this is not what is important it almost comes across as a test. Example, "well its not important, but lets see if she really loves me enough to come!" This is not the case and is ridiculous. You and I have waited 7 months to be together again. I really don't believe two hours or a half an hour is really going to make a difference. I will be so excited to see you when it happens. I also know that the idea of the homecoming sounds really special, but I remember last year. It is different for officers. Last year it was pandemonium running around trying to ensure all my Marines had all their gear, making sure all the equipment was going to be accounted for and turned in, meeting everyone's friends and relatives because they want to introduce you. If I was just a Marine I would only have to turn in my rifle and check out and I would be done in 10minutes, so it would be great. But I know that I will have to run around or at least stay put until everyone and everything has been taken care of. It's not a big deal it just means that I won't be able to run and give you a hug at the sight of you. I am still going to have responsibilities.

These are my opinions on it. I don't want you to stress. Come whenever you can. If its 10pm, that would be nothing compared to months. If you really want to be there for yourself (not for me) that is fine and I don't want to deter you. Again this isn't a test!! I just don't want you to think that I am telling you not to come, or don't come, or I don't want you there. This would not be true. I love you. I am going to see you in two days and a wake up!! *(Letter 1)*

Love, Charleston
February 16, 2006 – Charleston,

I understand. I will most likely work. If I can get out a little early I will. I absolutely cannot wait to see you and it feels very real as of today. I met Mike, Tim, and Buddy. They came home while I was in your house. I wasn't able to do much so I am going back on Saturday night. I brought your car to my house. I guess it has been getting a lot of tickets. It should be fine in my parking lot. It is so strange to walk outside and see your car. I love it! It feels like you are here. I can't believe that in less than three days you actually will be. How are you doing? Are you going crazy? I certainly am!

I love you! Talle

BIG BEAR
February 16, 2006 – Charleston,

When I spoke to your mom she mentioned staying the night in Big Bear on Saturday. I looked into the hotels and there are only two and both are booked. There is one other place I found but it is seems a little out there. It is a "snowboarder hotel." It doesn't look like a place I would take my mom so I'm not sure what to do. I could also look for cabins. I also wanted to make sure you were interested in staying the night. Just let me know what you think.

I love you, Talle

February 16, 2006 – Ok,

I am definitely going crazy. Especially now that you told me my car has been getting a lot of tickets!! That's no good. Last I checked it was in my garage and it doesn't get tickets there. Roommates are in big trouble.

I can't sleep anymore. My schedule is all messed up. I am running off of naps. I try to go to bed and I toss and turn for hours. My brain is going into overload with the idea of coming home finally. I think that I turned it on too early. This week is going by quickly just not quick enough. I love you miss you, but also might overload when I see you. I feel like an animal locked in a cage and I can feel a lot of violence swelling. I really need to channel my energies elsewhere.

I think my registration has expired, so be careful driving the car. I don't know what to say about Big Bear. I know that it's not worth it to me to force the issue. Is another day available? I don't expect you to be doing all this work. I am seriously in need of distractions...

Love you, Charleston

February 17, 2006 –

Yeah I don't know what to say about your car. Tim said he has been paying the tickets. I wish they hadn't decided to move it. I hate that you are going crazy. I will do my best to keep you distracted. If there is anything in particular you need or want me to do please let me know. It will be such a relief when this part is over. I love you terribly. I am not going to work on Sunday for my own sanity. I will be a mess if I am sitting at work, being useless, knowing you are here, and not able to see you. It will also give me some extra time. See you soon!!!!!!!!!!!!!!

Love, Talle

HAPPY BIRTHDAY

February 18, 2006 – Charleston,

Happy Birthday to you. Happy Birthday to you. Happy Birthday dear Charleston. Happy Birthday to you!!!!!!!! I will actually sing it for you tomorrow. Because you will be home! I cannot believe it! I wish you were here today but it just means we'll have to make up for it tomorrow. I just want to give you a big hug and a kiss. I love you so much! I will see you tomorrow! Happy Birthday!

Love, Talle

February 18, 2006 –

Extra time... are you up to something!? I do really love you. I wish that I wasn't going crazy. Working out is helping, but I really need to do something. This is very odd, but it's only when I return home. I went through the same emotion last year. I didn't feel comfortable around civilians. I always had this animosity, almost rage. I couldn't only talk to Marines and I had these incredibly destructive urges. I expect this sounds scarier than it will be, but... Containment will probably be in order! Anyway tell me a story, a joke, or something because otherwise I might jump off the boat and start swimming. I love you big hug. Charleston

February 18, 2006 –

Containment sounds good to me! I have a very short story that I cannot explain in full but I was very excited about. The other day I was looking for something that I had pretty much decided I would never find. I needed to give it a shot anyway so I went to one place and didn't find it. The second place I tried actually had it! I practically jumped up and down over it. I really could not believe it. You are going to be happy!

I love you, Talle

February 18, 2006 –

Very short story...with no details but good lesson in FAITH!

FW:DIRECTIONS TO HOMECOMING

February 18, 2006 – Talle,

This is some more direction. I will call you once we hit the beach. I love you and can't wait to see you. Charleston
February 18, 2006 – Marines and Sailors,
The information below was provided to the KV network. Please ensure your family members and friends have the information.

Subject: Directions to Homecoming

Ladies,
Below, you will find the directions for families to get to the Homecoming at the Parade Deck behind the 13th MEU Command Post. There is road construction this weekend so the bridge into Camp Del Mar from the Main Gate is inaccessible. The only entrance/exit to Del Mar will be through the Del Mar Gate. If you have any questions, please let me know.

Please ensure this information is disseminated to all the families as soon as possible. We have notified PMO and they will assist with directing traffic at the gates as well.

CE Marines should not be arriving before 1000, so we ask that families not arrive before then. Also, due to safety concerns, we request all families and friends to wait for their Marine at the 13th MEU CP/Parade Deck. There is a significant number of vehicles and equipment being offloaded at the Del Mar Boat Basin and we cannot have people down there. Thanks for all your help.

S/F

Captain Kirk S. Thacker
Asst. Communications Officer/S-6A
13th Marine Expeditionary Unit (SOC)
DSN: 312.555.0777
Comm: 760.555.0777
From I-5 N or I-5 S, Exit Oceanside Harbor (head West) (If coming from I-5 N, do not take Camp Pendleton Exit, use the next exit).

TURN RIGHT at T-intersection and proceed to Del Mar Gate (once on base, road is Sante Fe Ave).

Follow Santa Fe Ave to first stop sign (Fire Station is on the right) TURN RIGHT.

Within 50 yards of that turn, you will be at another stop sign at A St. It is a T-intersection, however you will only be able to TURN LEFT due to road construction.

Follow A St. north (parallel to I-5) to the north end of Del Mar. The road will make a 90-degree turn to the LEFT. Continue on this road.

The second building (first is a barracks) is the 13th MEU Command Post (2-story tan/brown building). The Parade Deck is just after the CP and is the location of the Homecoming Event.
Duty Phone: 760-763-0880
February 18, 2006 –
      Belay my last. I am sending you to completely the wrong place. Sorry... – Charleston
February 18, 2006 –
      Both sets of directions are the same. Is that were I am supposed to go? – Talle
February 18, 2006 –
      No you need to go to Camp Horno. Come in the gate at San Onofre and follow Basilone Rd. You'll see signs for 2/1. I'll call you when we hit the beach. Just keep your cell phone nearby. I love you. Can't wait to see you.
      Don't reply to this e-mail anymore.
      I'm coming home…
      Love, Charleston

Attachments

Article 1 – Sexist article
Letter 1 – Letter distributed for our return from deployment
Photo 1 – My platoon as we were pulling into port in Hawaii
Photo 2 – Charleston + Talle
Photo 3 – Charleston + Talle at Dining Out
Photo 4 – Talle walking into work
Photo 5 – Our last dinner out.
Photo 6 – Talle in apartment
Photo 7 – Training area on fire just south of Darwin, Australia
Photo 8 – Wog day, Triton and the men you have to worship
Photo 9 – Marines porting in Hawaii
Photo 10 – Talle with sister in Cabo
Photo 11 – Charleston + Talle at the beach.
Photo 12 – Our three rifle company commanders, Maj Ray Mendoza on right died 3 days later. He will forever be remembered as 'Achilles.'
Photo 13 – Delivering warning order to platoon
Photo 14 – Snipers set in position
Photo 15 – Singapore
Photo 16 – Hong Kong
Photo 17 – Charleston + Talle in Hong Kong
Photo 18 – Charleston on ship
Photo 19 – I painted her portrait for our 1st Anniversary.

- Gather up schoolbooks, toys, paper etc and then run a dustcloth over the tables.

- Over the cooler months of the year you should prepare and light a fire for him to unwind by. Your husband will feel he has reached a haven of rest and order, and it will give you a lift too. After all, catering for his comfort will provide you with immense personal satisfaction.

- Prepare the children. Take a few minutes to wash the children's hands and faces (if they are small), comb their hair and, if necessary, change their clothes. They are little treasures and he would like to see them playing the part. Minimise all noise. At the time of his arrival, eliminate all noise of the washer, dryer or vacuum. Try to encourage the children to be quiet.

- Be happy to see him.

- Greet him with a warm smile and show sincerity in your desire to please him.

- Listen to him. You may have a dozen important things to tell him, but the moment of his arrival is not the time. Let him talk first – remember, his topics of conversation are more important than yours.

- Make the evening his. Never complain if he comes home late or goes out to dinner, or other places of entertainment without you. Instead, try to understand his world of strain and pressure and his very real need to be at home and relax.

- Your goal: Try to make sure your home is a place of peace, order and tranquillity where your husband can renew himself in body and spirit.

- Don't greet him with complaints and problems.

- Don't complain if he's late home for dinner or even if he stays out all night. Count this as minor compared to what he might have gone through that day.

- Make him comfortable. Have him lean back in a comfortable chair or have him lie down in the bedroom. Have a cool or warm drink ready for him.

- Arrange his pillow and offer to take off his shoes. Speak in a low, soothing and pleasant voice.

- Don't ask him questions about his actions or question his judgment or integrity. Remember, he is the master of the house and as such will always exercise his will with fairness and truthfulness. You have no right to question him.

- A good wife always knows her place.

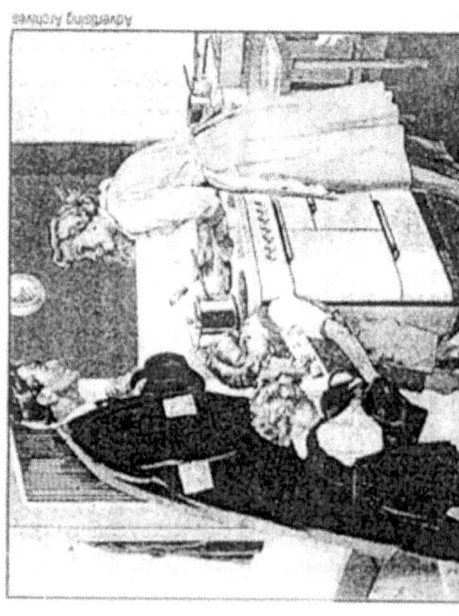

Advertising Archives

The good wife's guide

- Have dinner ready. Plan ahead, even the night before, to have a delicious meal ready, on time for his return. This is a way of letting him know that you have been thinking about him and are concerned about his needs. Most men are hungry when they come home and the prospect of a good meal (especially his favourite dish) is part of the warm welcome needed.

- Prepare yourself. Take 15 minutes to rest so you'll be refreshed when he arrives. Touch up your make-up, put a ribbon in your hair and be fresh-looking. He has just been with a lot of work-weary peopl

- Be a little gay and a little more interesting for him. His boring day may need a lift and one of your duties is to provide it.

- Clear away the clutter. Make one last trip through the main part of the house just before your husband arrives.

Article 1

UNITED STATES MARINE CORPS
Battalion Landing Team 2/1
13th Marine Expeditionary Unit
Box 555442
Camp Pendleton, California 92055-5442

1500

From: Commanding Officer, Battalion Landing Team 2/1

Subj: BLT 2/1 RETURN AND REUNION INFORMATION

The following information is provided to assist families in planning their travel arrangements to meet the return of BLT 2/1 from its current Western Pacific Deployment.

Ships will be offloaded at Del Mar Beach Camp Pendleton starting **the morning of 19 February**. This is expected to be a long and time consuming process. The initial focus of the off load will be the Marines and Sailors themselves. Even though they are the focus, the off load will take several hours. For your safety and to help expedite the movement of personnel and gear from the beach to their respective camps, families are discouraged from going to Del Mar to view the off load. All personnel will be taken to their camp. Please refer to the information below for particular information on your specific Marine or Sailor. My number one priority is to ensure the Marines and Sailors of the BLT get released to their families as soon as possible. In order to ensure that happens please follow the guidance listed below and please be patient. Your cooperation will ensure that your Marine or Sailor gets released as early as possible. We will be just as excited to see you as you will be to see us. Please direct any questions to the BLT KVC; Katie Lark (760-555-6719) or the Command Representative SSgt O'Malley (760-444-8858)

For those of you who have Tigers returning they will leave the ships with their sponsors/Marines and move to the reunion locations listed below. You should plan on meeting your Tiger at the designated camp when you arrive for the reunion. For example, AAV families will meet their Tigers and Marines at Camp Horno when the rest of the Platoon arrives.

2nd BN 1st MAR. (H&S Co, Weapons Co, Echo Co, Fox Co, Golf Co.) Marines and Sailors will return to 53 Area, Camp Horno, 2nd BN 1st MAR parade deck. There will be special event signs posted to aid you in finding the correct location. MCCS will provide food, tents, chairs and activities for the families while they wait for the return of their loved ones. We will also open the Regimental Class Room (right next to the parade deck) to provide a waiting/changing area for families with small children. Marines and Sailors will move from Del Mar Beach by bus to Camp Horno. Upon arrival they will turn weapons and other serialized gear into the armory and then march in formation to the parade deck. Each Company will follow this same sequence. Upon arrival at the parade deck they will be allowed to visit with family and friends until the rest of the Battalion arrives. Once the entire Battalion and designated attachments are at the parade deck there will be a BLT formation for final dismissal. At this time Marines and Sailors will be free to leave the area. The formation is scheduled for **no later than 1500**. It is recommended that families arrive at the Parade Deck no earlier than 1300.

Letter 1

Photo 1

Top to Bottom & Left to Right: Photo 2 - 6

Top to Bottom

Photo 7 – 9

Top to Bottom

Photo 10 - 14

Top to Bottom & Left to Right

Photo 15 - 19